Land of Snow and Secrets

Seasons of Fae Book 1

Sonya Lawson

SauceBox Press

Contents

Note to Reader (TWs)

This book contains scenes that may depict, mention, or discuss: anxiety, arranged marriage, attempted murder, blood, chronic illness, rebellion, violence, war and military battle. Please take care of yourself as you read.

To all those out there who also believe love, in all its forms, is its own type of magic. Keep that magical bond alive, darlings.

Chapter One
Ghel

Prince Ghel's sword swept upward in a large arc, hitting his opponent's weapon in its downward descent, driving it up and back, forcing his attacker to scramble away. Sweat poured down his face but he ignored it, despite having to blink his eyes against the salty sting. His hands tightened on the hilt before his breath came out in a gust as he pounced, his large body moving with surprising speed and grace toward the now-off-kilter man in front of him. Instead of coming down in a killing blow, Ghel twisted his arm back and came up with his elbow, landing it right in his opponent's stomach.

"By the gods." Prince Jarok wheezed as he doubled over. "You could be a little gentler, brother." Wind rushed the ring, ruffling Ghel's loosened hair as it swirled around Jarok, his magic helping him find his breath easier than other Fae.

Ghel grunted, breathless from exertion. Unlike Jarok, wind not at his beck and call. He pulled from his fighting stance to stand towering over his younger brother. They were not brothers by blood, though no one would dare say such a thing out loud to the princes, or the king and queen. Ghel was tall, well over six and a half feet of full brawn packed beneath skin that appeared tan despite the lack of sun in the Winterlands. His muscles, exceptionally smooth and scar-free due to his affinity for healing magic, were on full display despite the frigid temperatures of the Ice Plains practice ring where the brothers sparred.

He wore leather pants, his chest bare and glowing with the sweat. His dark hair, often unruly in its wild length and wavy curl, stayed off his face thanks to a tight leather strip wrapped in a thick knot at the base of his neck, except the random strands that always came loose when he fought. Every good warrior knew long hair needed to be shoved away as best as possible. Like his body, his face was also broad, sometimes cold as the perpetual winter where he lived, and centered around a wide nose with often-flaring nostrils and fierce, piercing coal-black eyes. His full, bushy beard matched the wildness of his hair and left little else of his face visible besides his full, thick lips.

Jarok, having finally risen from getting the wind knocked out of him, was slighter, though his frame was deceptive. It was compact muscle, corded and strung tight. Younger and shorter than his brother, he wore his black hair short on the back and sides with a teasing floppy length at the top, which highlighted his chiseled, lean, and clean-shaven face, along with his down-turned and deeply hooded dark-brown eyes. His skin, the golden color of the Autumnlands wheat fields before harvest, barely peeked out from beneath his tight-buttoned leather overshirt and pants. He straightened his clothes as he brought himself up, breathing easy once again, and rather quickly given the blow he took from his big brother.

"How are you to learn if I am always gentle with you, Jarok?" Ghel asked.

Jarok's laugh cracked like a whip in the frozen, empty practice field. The princes had come for a change of pace from their usual sparring sessions, needing some time out in the fresh, frigid air, away from the Winterlands Palace. They were royals, but such royals required no guard beyond themselves. The two could handle any threat just fine, as Ghel well knew. His question was gruff and may have sounded condescending to an unknowing ear, but it was Ghel's usual tone. Any who knew him, such as Prince Jarok, understood the joking nature underlying the question.

"You don't know the meaning of the word gentle, you big brute," Jarok replied, walking up and shoving Ghel in the shoulder. "Something I hear from the ladies as well."

Ghel's face went red. Jarok's jab wasn't true, of course, more a tease about Ghel's gruff nature or the way many others, including ladies, assumed his harder exterior revealed something of his personality. All it denoted was he was a quiet man who liked to observe, but his muscles and aloofness often combined to make others assume a great deal about the prince.

Jarok's joke was a direct hit, in the way siblings could manage without even trying, so Ghel made a direct hit of his own, bringing his fist once again to Jarok's stomach and plowing into it in the exact same spot he'd hit previously.

Jarok let out a harsh breath and clamped his hand on his brother's shoulder to stop his heaving stomach and buckling knees from taking down his whole body. Once he yet again caught his wind, he huffed out, "Fair enough, brother. Apologies."

Jarok's extra squeeze on his shoulder and the serious glint in his eyes told Ghel he meant it, and his brother always meant it. He tended to say biting things before thinking better of it, an annoying trait mitigated by his profuse apologies afterward. If he hurt someone he loved, Jarok made amends immediately. On the other hand, Ghel had seen him both physically and emotionally beat opponents into a pulp. Jarok's sword and his tongue were sharp, and Ghel felt lucky they were always on his side.

Ghel flipped a hand in the air, a silent signal he felt unbothered by Jarok's joke. Not exactly true, but he never let his brother's words wound him for long. He was good enough at wounding himself.

Ghel took a moment to take in the space. He used the practice ring at the palace when not out here with his men, leading the Winterlands Forces as their general. Now all of it sat empty except for him and his brother, the desolate expanse of the Ice Plains uninterrupted by soldiers or extra tents or the goings-on of a military encampment. It was as the Ice Plains were supposed to be: a blank canvas surrounding the base of the mountain where the palace sat, offering a clear view and the additional protection of the environmental dangers lurking there. It was a hard, icy line of defense for the looming palace perched high above the rest of the land, casting a long shadow in Winterlands and over Ghel.

Today all was quiet and desolate and coldly beautiful for Ghel. Not because there were no threats to the palace. Threats persisted constantly. However, King Frit Borau, even in his waning health, ensured his military forces were given enough rest. The king and queen had given the bulk of their forces a week to visit their homelands before reconvening for their usual duties. A week here and there kept everyone in high spirits and let them remember who and what they were protecting when they swung swords for their king—yet another sign to Ghel of how intelligent and just his father was. A big crown he would one day wear, one he feared he could never fill half so well.

"Do you think—" Jarok cut himself short as Ghel noticed a man scurrying their way. He'd believed them alone, so Prince Ghel squinted hard, bringing his hand to the hilt of the sword at his side. There were rumblings in the Winterlands, and a warrior never knew what might come at them in the cold.

The speed with which the other Fae moved, and the bright-red color of the streak he made as he traversed the icy ground, was enough to tell Ghel who it was: Render, the king and queen's personal messenger. Having a Fae with an extraordinary speed affinity was more than helpful at times. All Fae were fast, but Render was a flash compared to others, and it took no real effort on his part as it was powered by his internal fount of magic, the spark inside every Fae giving them their specific abilities. Speed was not an unusual affinity, but Render's loyalty and fighting skill made him a formidable ally for the royal family of the Winterlands, one used to pass messages and protect when necessary.

The Fae came to a smooth stop a few feet from Ghel without a hair out of place or a whisper of hard breath leaving his lips. He began speaking immediately, as if he had simply walked up to them and had not sprinted the five-mile distance from the palace to the Ice Plains at supernatural speeds.

"Princes," he said, inclining his head in a small bow of greeting. Unlike the monarchical rulers of the Springlands, the Winterlands royals rarely sat on ceremony or pomp, although the Winter Fae offered respect to their leaders. Ghel and Jarok did not expect more from the messenger beyond what Render came to tell them. With a smirk, Jarok rolled his hand in a circular motion at the new arrival, as if he were slow to tell them something and they had to impatiently wait. Ghel snorted a laugh at his brother's antics but turned serious eyes toward Render, giving him his undivided attention.

"The king and queen request an immediate audience. In the royal chambers."

Ghel's dark brow furrowed more than a bit. His father should have been in his study, or the Royal Meeting Chamber by this time. The lingering fear for his father always churning in his stomach rose up. His health waned, and he grew weaker daily, which meant they would lose him one day far too soon. Not only would he bear the death of a father he loved dearly, but the entire kingdom would be deprived of a righteous king who had led their land well for many centuries. Ghel would also be forced to move through his own personal loss as others looked to him to take up the crown and be his father's son, be a good ruler of the land. He was unsure at times which he dreaded more: his father's death or what would come after. Which, in turn, made guilt mix with grief and fear in his mind.

Jarok's asked, "Is he unwell this morning?" in a tone far more worried than his usual, which often rode the line between jovial and snide.

Render simply stared at the brothers, unwilling or unable to reply. All knew the king was more often than not unwell. The Fae were long lived but not immortal, and one of the illnesses that could befall an older Fae had begun ravaging their father, King Frit Borau, three years ago. They all lived with the certainty of his death, the one question remaining being when his death would come. Every day it appeared to rush closer to their once-happy palace.

Ghel shook off his troubled thoughts and cleared his throat. "Very well, Render. Thank you for relaying the message. If you could, please inform the king and queen we will be along shortly. We rode here and must return with our mounts."

Render gave an official salute and sped away, a red streak in the mostly white background, winding its way up to the palace once again.

"Ghel, I fear Father gets worse every day."

He grunted in reply. What else was there to add? It was more than true, and emotion and fear and hurt made it hard for the prince to get any words out. Not that words were easy for him at the best of times.

Ghel dropped the topic and instead said, "Let's get the horses." The princes could have run to the practice ring for some brisk exercise, but they'd originally planned to ride out farther onto the Ice Plains after a short sword practice to inspect some of the magical defenses. Ghel gave himself a mental note to task a guard with the inspection, the safety of the lands outside the palace and its people always being important to the prince. Jarok commanded palace security, although Ghel often poked and prodded as many older brothers did, checking his work.

The brothers said little else as they climbed their large, woolly horses, stout and sturdy creatures bred in their lands. Winterlands horses were built not so much for speed but for survival in their climate over long distances, but even they needed extra protection from the cold and snow. The Fae of the stables with affinities for horses used their magic to spell their hooves so they didn't freeze over or get slick with compacted slush. The two horses they'd brought with them clomped heavy hooves over the road made of packed snow with more ease because of this magic, slowly but surely carrying the two princes back to their mother and father, to whatever they wished to say on this usual, gray Winterland day.

People were scattered across the small, snow-covered entrance, going about their business. Some ignored the two princes as they rode on, and some gave slight nods of acknowledgment or small bows, as Render had earlier. Guards in armor and thick woolen cloaks stood sentry at the gates and at intervals beyond, all of whom Ghel knew by name and rank—another part of his duties he took seriously. He nodded at each as they passed but did not stop for updates as he usually would have.

A narrow entry road used as a funnel for traffic and protection spread out into a small square, where permanent shops lined the streets and more transient seller tents popped up in the middle of the square at intervals. The shops housed merchants with more year-round need such as cobblers, clothiers and seamstresses, butchers, bakers, and the like. Tented stalls provided space for more seasonal or occasional goods based around weather or festivals. The square bustled in the late morning, and not many noticed the princes clomping through their midst. A few shouted for them to stop, buy their goods, but Ghel ignored the calls, giving the occasional grunt of acknowledgment at the Fae he passed.

He was struck with a memory of one snowy day preceding the Winter Festival of his ninth year. Jarok was new to the palace and the family, having been adopted less than a year before, and Ghel's mother and father wanted both princes to experience all the fun and games of the Winterlands' most celebrated festival. They traveled to the famed Winter Festival night market as a group, Ghel transfixed by the magical lights ablaze but hesitant to interact with the growing crowd surrounding the royal family. His father was jolly and cordial, the stalls ringing with his booming laugh and good cheer. His mother, usually more reserved like Ghel, mingled with others, talking birds and weaponry and clan affairs as she often did in such settings. Jarok, new but already permanently rooted in Ghel's heart, laughed along with their father, charming all he talked to with his five-year-old wit and precociousness. Ghel felt warmed by the light and love of his family, their ease helping him but also making him feel not quite right, as if he were an outsider, someone different set down in their midst. Somehow lesser. The king, queen, and prince would be devastated to hear Ghel say such a thing aloud, but it was how he'd felt then, and still sometimes felt several decades later. Their greatness often made Ghel feel middling by comparison. He often wondered how he would ever measure up in a future where he was expected to lead everyone in the Winterlands.

Swallowing down the memory and the mixture of love and pain coursing through his chest, Ghel pushed his horse on, wishing to get to the palace immediately, to find what his mother and father needed of him, to ensure he could help. Ghel always strived to be of service in the ways he was able, even as he worried his service to his land could only extend to his muscles and sword.

Jarok broke his ruminating thoughts as they turned down a twisting alley toward a set of sturdy, barred gates marking the Winterlands Palace. "Any guess what's ahead?"

"The palace?" Ghel said, deadpan.

Jarok laughed loud and long. "Oh, ho, brother. A joke? From you?"

Ghel shrugged but a ghost of a smile passed over his lips, the bulk of his beard keeping it mostly hidden from the people around him. It faded as quickly as it had appeared, and the Fae prince whispered to his brother, "My guess: the Monti Clan."

The smile so often on Jarok's face was wiped clean away, replaced by a hard line of lips and an equally hard look in his eyes. "Engad Monti is a fool."

"A power-hungry enemy to the crown, yes, but he is no fool. One of the things which make him so dangerous to the Winterlands."

Jarok didn't reply, leaving Ghel to battle the various worries crowding his head as they went through the smaller iron gates of Winterlands Palace. The pair gave their horses over to a Fae groom, and the brothers headed inside, toward the awaiting chill and uncertainty.

The royal chambers connected to their father's room, which was traditionally the residence of the king alone. However, King

Frit and Queen Alene were a love match made during a disastrous blizzard when the king had been stranded at the Aurora Outpost, the home of the queen's warrior clan. Their mother was the daughter of a warrior clan chief and not a Fae noble. It hadn't mattered to their father. He liked to say she swooped into his heart like one of her birds. Their mother's magical affinity was a connection with and command over birds of prey. That, and being a good mother and shrewd warrior-queen.

Their father commanded ice and cold with the touch of a finger, something handy for a ruler of the Winterlands. Ghel did not take after either of his parents in his magic, which was unusual. Affinities were often related to one another in immediate and direct lineage, but Ghel's ability to heal himself was not. Queen Alene told him it came down from her father's line, several generations back. Self-healing served him well, especially as a warrior and leader of soldiers, yet he couldn't help but believe it would do little for his kingdom in the future. Jarok was not blood related, so it wasn't surprising his affinity did not correspond with the rest of the family. However, Ghel felt his brother's ability to command any winds blowing even the slightest bit near him was far more universally helpful than his own self-serving power.

None of this mattered to his mother and father. They loved both of their children with a fierceness rarely seen in Fae nobility, which made the frailty of the king more tragic. In the Royal Chamber, meant for sole habitation but made a family place, surrounded by rich pine and lushly covered furniture, Ghel found his once tall and broad-shouldered father wrapped tightly in furs, shivering in front of the fire. He looked far frailer than he had even a year before, his body fading each day before Ghel's eyes. Healers from across Fae had been called to examine the king, but all had come to the same conclusion:

his affinity was turning inward, attacking his own body. He could no longer project his freeze outward, so it was eating him slowly from the inside out. There was no cure for reversed affinity, and eventually, it would overtake King Frit as it had all other centuries-old Fae who'd somehow lost control of their inner fount of magic.

Queen Alene stood at the king's side, holding his chilly hand, staring down at her husband with what another might call a harsh frown but one Ghel recognized as worry over her love. A worry she bore with the same warrior spirit she brought to every aspect of her life. She did look at her sons when they entered, giving them a slight nod in greeting.

King Frit's body was frail, but his mind was not yet frozen. "My boys. Come, come. We have serious matters to discuss."

Ghel and Jarok took seats on the intricately carved chairs situated on their father's right side. He turned slightly so he could look both princes up and down before he began.

"All well along the Ice Plains?"

"We didn't have time to investigate fully," Ghel answered, "but I will send a group of guards to check our wards later today."

The king hummed in agreement before letting out a sigh so deep and sad, Ghel's heart stopped for a few beats. "The Monti Clan attacks on the warrior clans increase, encroaching on others' lands, decimating their forces, killing captives if they do not swear fealty to Engad Monti. It is more than a small problem, sons. We must present a united front with all in our lands: the remaining warrior clans, the merchants and artisans, and the lords. If we cannot, I fear the Monti Clan will amass enough power to challenge the crown. I believe it may well be their intention."

Queen Alene cursed about the Monti Clan leader under her breath, which made Jarok chuckle at Ghel's side, but Ghel was intent on their father, who was also staring at his eldest son. Something new was happening, as this information was not wholly unknown to the princes, and Ghel was becoming more apprehensive by the minute.

"We specifically need support from the merchant classes and the Winterlands nobles to help call more men to arms, confront the ever-growing forces of the Monti Clan alongside the few remaining warrior clans who can withstand such a threat, like the Auroras and Windins."

"Agreed," Ghel said.

"In order to do this," Queen Alene interjected, "your father believes a royal marriage may be in order. A match which would cement certain alliances."

Ghel froze. His heart stopped for another, entirely different reason. This could not be. His father would surely not ask this of him.

King Frit waved a scroll in the air, one Ghel had not noticed in the folds of his furs until then. "I received a proposal from Lord Mikka Hollythorn."

Jarok growled at Ghel's side, but he hushed his brother with a swift flick of his hand. No one in the room liked Lord Hollythorn, and for good reason, but he needed to hear what was next. Because surely what he suspected could not be.

"He proposes a marriage, between my eldest son and his daughter. Ghel, I think such an alliance could be beneficial to us all in these trying times. Allow us to keep certain enemies close while showing allies we are willing to sacrifice as we serve our lands."

Ghel's mouth hung open in shock. Queen Alene turned softened eyes so much like his own onto her oldest son. "Ghel, we have discussed the matter amongst ourselves for weeks now. We both are in agreement, not only because of the Monti Clan's actions but because of Lord Hollythorn's connections across the Winterlands and his recent activities." She moved to her boy and laid a hand on his shoulder, giving it a hard, affectionate squeeze.

Ghel looked up into her face.

"I knew Lady Strella's late mother. She was kind, caring... a good Fae noblewoman. All I have heard of Lady Strella Hollythorn bears the same markings, though we will need to ensure certain things before we actually proceed with a wedding. Please know, we did not make this suggestion lightly."

"Suggestion?" Ghel asked, his voice strangled and hoarse.

"Of course it is a suggestion, son. We would never force you to marry someone," King Frit said, sadness marking his voice.

Ghel sat back in his chair with a thump. Marriage. To a lady he did not know. A Fae lady of noble birth he did not know, who likely had very specific expectations of marriage. A Fae lady who also happened to be the daughter of arguably one of the most powerful Fae lords of the land, a man the royals had many reasons to dislike and distrust. Ghel was speechless for a long stretch even as his head nodded. He'd think more on it, discuss it with his family, but he trusted his mother and father and always wished to help his land. In all likelihood, by the end of their meeting, he would agree to marry a stranger.

Chapter Two
Strella

A particularly harsh jolt of the carriage brought Lady Strella Hollythorn out of her window-gazing stupor. She'd been staring out of the rectangle cutout in the small carriage door for gods knew how long, her mind blankly taking in the scenery as she absently twirled a strand of wavy blonde hair around her index finger, a habit she could never drop no matter how much her father chastised her for it. The scenery wasn't much to take in, as they'd been slowly plodding over the Ice Plains road for hours at this point. White, white, and more white as far as her own icy-blue eyes could see.

She was a Fae of the Winterlands and was intimately familiar with ice. However, Hollythorn Manor was surrounded by a grove of lush but prickly holly trees and maintained a diverse winter garden on their grounds. Even Lady Piris's home, Volesion Peak, while not as large as her home, was situated in a vast forest of evergreens alongside a cliff overlooking the Great River, which ran the entire length of the Faelands. This looked blank. Nothing for as far as the Fae eye could see, which was very far indeed.

"Exceedingly dull, yes?" Lady Piris said as she lounged across from her, also staring out at the nothingness in their view, her cleft chin firmly in hand and her nose—which Piris called big but Strella insisted was regal—wrinkled at the view. Strella smiled at her best friend, who thought much like her but was still so different. She was about to nod when her father looked up from the book he'd been reading to pin each woman in place with his most lordly look. The one he gave Strella so often. The one which made her heart sink a little every time, even if it happened daily.

"The Ice Plains serve an important purpose for the safety of the Winterlands Palace and the Winterlands overall. Please do consider such before you go dismissing them in this manner." Lord Hollythorn gave a small scoff at the end and resumed reading, bending his head so his long, straight pale-blond hair, the same shade as Strella's, effectively became a curtain between himself and the women in the carriage with him. Not surprising, as her father often ignored her as best he could unless he had a point to make about something he perceived as wrong or beneath her. Still, it was more than a little awkward to do so now when they were in such tight quarters.

Strella's smile faded and she gave a silent sigh, something she'd mastered after twenty-nine years of life with her father. She loved him. He was all the family she had in this world, and she owed him. She was all he had as well, but her debt had started early. Her mother, his love, died giving birth to her. So, she kept her thoughts and worries to herself. Tried her best to be gentle and good and appeasing in all ways, which was why she was in the blasted carriage to begin with, traipsing across the Ice Plains right toward Winterlands Palace and a marriage she didn't want. He'd convinced her it would help the family, give them access to more power and social status than they'd ever had before. She didn't care for such things, but her father did, and she always wished to be helpful, give him what she could while she still could.

She had nothing against Prince Ghel, per se, although she'd heard stories from other ladies who, unlike her, had visited Winterlands Palace and interacted with the royal family. Stories of his coldness.

Stories characterizing him as a brute focused on fighting, too much of the warrior and not enough of the Fae prince for their liking. She rarely took stock in such idle gossip, but it made her nervous. More than nervous, actually. She'd never wanted to marry at all, for her own reasons. Wanted to live her life peacefully, keeping her world and loves small. Now, she was tasked with uniting all the Winterlands—clans, merchants, and nobles alike—because of an uprising of the Montis.

She'd heard talk of the Monti Clan's rise. Their fearless leader and his determination to overtake all other warrior clans. She thought it an impossible task. Warrior clans were born fighters, fierce and most often possessing some form of inner magic helpful in battle, and were trained from birth to defend their people and territory, and all of Winterlands if called upon to do so. They were not political as the lords were, not economically shrewd as the merchants' class. Strella spent much time with both, as her father held lofty positions in each. She had little experience with warriors, as her years wound away in her home. She'd never traveled to the Winterlands Palace because she did not wish to be presented to wider society or the marriage market. Her father had not pushed, but only because he had loftier plans for his child; he wished her to marry a prince. The prince who would become king, and the one direct descendant from the fierce Aurora Clan. All these facts melded together to make her nervous about her future, or what future she had ahead of herself.

She looked over at Lady Piris, whose thick auburn eyebrows waggled back at her. Strella's smile returned in an instant. Piris was her best friend. Her one true friend. She knew many ladies. Her father loved to host others at Hollythorn Manor, so she'd encountered most of the Fae nobility of the Winterlands, and even a few from other Fae lands, at her home. As hostess, she smiled and chatted and entertained. She welcomed. She engaged. She, however, never let them into her heart, as they did not need to let her into their own. Piris was the only Fae noblewoman to wiggle her way in, and although Strella sometimes worried what it might mean for Piris in the near future, she was forever thankful for her friendship. It sustained her in trying times such as these.

"Oh, look!" Piris shouted, pointing out the window they'd been looking out of for hours. The carriage rounded a curve in the road where the view was momentarily interrupted by a small cluster of evergreens, then when the green and white broke through, Strella saw a much closer view of the Winterlands Palace. It rose, pristine and shining, out of a mountain, carved from the very rock and anchored securely in the land. Strella had always considered Hollythorn Manor massive, a three-story house with two dozen rooms, far bigger than any other home she'd ever visited. This structure dwarfed her home. At least a dozen spires reached impossibly high into the sky, the tips painted a frosty blue that glittered even in the clouded light of the Winterland sun. The number of windows alone dizzied her. A massive wall hid some of the palace from sight. There were likely more than the five stories she counted. She couldn't imagine why any place would need so much space.

Below the wall was another section, a little town gathered around the might of the Winterlands, built to serve the palace and the troop of people required to run it. She understood what it took to effectively manage a large manor. She'd done it at Hollythorn since she'd turned fifteen. It consumed most of her days, and a new worry about what her duties as future princess would entail, and whether she could meet such a challenge, wormed into her head.

She hadn't noticed her father leaning into her space, so she jumped when his voice sounded close to her head. "The Winterlands Palace is a fortress built many millennia ago. It stood long before King Frit and will remain long after."

Strella did not know the king. She'd never met the man. She did, however, know of his troubles. It had dominated the talk amongst the lords and ladies and merchants over the past few years. King Frit had ruled relatively peacefully, for nearly five centuries. Most liked him, and those who did not nevertheless respected him and his rule. His illness, a tragedy among older Fae who suffered from the calamity, had remained a topic of constant discussion over the last few years. As was what would happen after his inevitable death. Which brought Strella's mind back to her intended, her soon-to-be officially betrothed: Prince Ghel. The also soon-to-be King Ghel, given the usual course of King Frit's disease. Not for the first time, she thought of how she did not wish to be Queen Strella, for many reasons, soon-to-be or otherwise.

"Imagine the games of hide-and-seek we could play in there," Piris said with a laugh. It had been a favorite game of theirs as young girls. When they were bored, they still occasionally played. The memory eased Strella's worries, which she suspected was the point of Piris saying it. Her best friend knew her well, both in her worry and how to best pull her from it.

"Nonsense. You two will do no such thing while in Winterlands Palace." Lord Hollythorn huffed at Piris. Not looking at Strella but obviously addressing her, he said, "I still do not understand why you had to bring Lady Piris along with you instead of one of your maids."

"The palace has designated maids for the future princess," Piris said. She paused, a sly smile at Strella. "Also, they are not ladies. I do believe you know the basic requirements for being a lady-in-waiting, Lord Hollythorn?"

Her father's eyes squinted at Piris's snide remark, but he said nothing in reply, choosing instead to look back down at the book in his lap.

Anyone else he would eviscerate, and he often chided Piris in the same dismissive and condescending way he had with his daughter, but he let her get away with far more than he did others who were not family. Lady Strella never quite understood why, but it made her thankful.

Piris ignored Lord Hollythorn, reaching over to grasp Strella's small hand in her larger one, which she noticed was a little shaky when her friend stopped the trembling. "You'll fit in marvelously," she whispered with a squeeze.

Her place in the palace was a worry, true. One worry among a legion of them, constantly marching around in her head. She looked back out the window, back at the palace, and tried to shake off the rest for a time. She thought it best to enjoy the view, the new experiences in her rather sheltered life and not the certain and uncertain future ahead. For the time being at least. Strella knew herself. Worry would come again soon enough.

The fanfare as the carriage pulled into the two separate gates of the Winterlands Palace had been a little daunting for Strella. Used to a quiet life marked with the occasional party and hostess duties or informal trips to Volesion Peak, her fanfare on arrival felt a bit too much. The king and queen had met them at the top of the steps leading into the palace, and both appeared gracious and happy to meet Strella. The queen was a little aloof, maybe cold, but she offered a small smile her way. The brown-speckled hawk perched on her shoulder, eyeing all in attendance with scrutiny, and the half-sword strapped to the side of her gown intimidated the lady. She imagined the queen's look shifted for a moment into something harder the second it landed on her father, but Strella knew she had to be mistaken when a small smile popped on her lips as the lord bent a knee to his queen with his usual flourish. King Frit looked sickly but was in good spirits, kissing her on the cheek and calling her daughter. Strella blushed under the attention from the king and queen and was happy to let her father take over the niceties as she stepped close into her friend, who had laid a hand on her back to help steady her.

She stood still, allowing all gathered to look at her. She imagined what they saw: a miniature version of her father with more of a wave to the same platinum hair and the uptilted nose from her mother. She shared the same lean form as her father, the same lithe shape, but was at least a head shorter than him, or even Piris, who both stood at warrior height and boasted the same muscular structure. Piris's compact muscles stayed hidden by her expertly cut dress. She was supposed to be a lady, after all. A quick look between the queen's short sword on full display and a glance down at Piris's thigh, where she knew her friend hid at least one wickedly sharp weapon, made her wonder about the privilege of royalty, or more aptly the privilege of never having to hide who you were.

Strella's mind had wandered, but she focused back on what was happening around her, which was not much. There was little said outside the palace outside basic niceties. The king and queen informed her Princes Ghel and Jarok were off fulfilling royal duties but would return long before their scheduled tea service the next day. Said tea service would be Strella's first meeting with Prince Ghel, where the official marriage proposal would occur, as tradition mandated it happened in front of at least one representative of each family and one outside observer. King Frit and Lord Hollythorn then broke away to discuss terms of the marriage, which Prince Ghel and she would agree to after tea. Soon after, the official luncheons and dinners and announcements would commence, along with the other tiny parties and events and scheduled functions that marked a Fae noble wedding. Strella wasn't certain, but she assumed even more would be expected because she was marrying a royal.

She was ushered to a gorgeously settled suite of rooms, where she spent the rest of the day and night barely eating and occasionally talking to her friend. At least, until Piris disappeared late in the night with talk of finding out more about the palace. Strella passed a fretful night, tossing and turning in a soft bed. Dawn broke, then maids came in with a midmorning meal, and all the while she moved back and forth from general anxiety to specific worries about what she'd agreed to do to give the Hollythorn name more status.

Because of all this, Strella stood in the middle of the massive changing room in her even more massive guest suite an hour before the scheduled tea, slightly paralyzed, her mind whirling over things expected and to come. Worst of all, in the immediate moment, she was unable to decide what to wear to the important tea where she'd magically bind herself to a prince she'd never even met. What was someone supposed to wear to an arrangement like this?

"How did I know I'd find you here, just like this?" Piris asked as she breezed into the room situated between Strella's bedchamber and her own. The lady-in-waiting was to help the lady in question with changing and preparations and such, so it made sense for this to be the connecting portion. Still, Strella startled at her entrance.

"Come on, Star. You already know what to do," Piris said, using the nickname only she used, the one connected to the starlight created through Strella's magic. It was beautiful magic to behold, sparkling light cascading out of her. However, unlike her father's piercing light magic, or Piris's more secret and serious magic, it was a mere parlor trick. Pretty but useless to Strella or anyone else.

Strella shook out the maudlin thoughts crowding her this day and looked around the space. Her clothes hung from cedarwood hangers on long rods positioned across the room, which were interrupted by corners filled with intricately carved shelves for her non-hangable clothes. The palace maids were efficient; Strella would give them that. They'd hung her five trunks' worth of clothes, a requirement from her father so she would never be seen in the same dress twice, in record time, each beautifully placed and on display.

Piris went to the sky-blue day dress they had picked for the tea service, which Strella had forgotten all about in her anxiety. It was ordered by her father, as all the clothes here were, so they'd been forced to pick from a limited selection instead of making choices with the seamstress. "No real fun picking these out, but your father does have excellent taste." Piris rubbed the silk sleeve between her fingers before twirling around and clapping her hands together. "All right. We have one hour to turn you into a princess."

Strella stepped back, bumping into a small, tufted stool in the middle of the room, and plopped down hard on the soft surface. She hung her head and her shoulders drooped as she whispered, "I thought I could, I don't know, at least pretend. Hold off as long as necessary." She looked up at Piris. "The king and queen were so nice. If Prince Ghel is also, I don't know if I can do it, Peep."

Piris walked over and crouched so she was face-to-face with her friend. Strella knew she did not believe the prophecy, so she was un-surprised by her reply. "Star, you lovely woman. How about we go day by day? See where each day leads and not worry about something which may never come to pass?"

Piris wished to help, sometimes even at her own expense. She was here, in fact, in the middle of Winterlands Palace, a place a Fae like her should not be. Strella grasped her friend's shoulders and pleaded with her for the hundredth time. "You can leave, Peep. There is no need for you to be here, to be so close to danger."

Piris shook off her worry and her hands, giving a bright smile. "As you just said, the king and queen were kind, so I have nothing to worry about."

"But if any of the royals discover your magic—"

"What magic?" she asked with a wink. "Every noble knows I'm a null, remember?"

It was what every noble Fae thought, that the only child of Lord and Lady Volesion was born without her own fount of magic, making her one of the few nulls among all the Fae, and a near outcast among the snobby noble set. People shunned her for it, acted better than her. It was one of the things sure to bring out Strella's temper, which was hard to raise but burned bright when necessary. Only the Volesions and Lady Strella knew the truth of Piris's power because the truth could make her a target if anyone in the palace or beyond ever guessed. It was dangerous and foolish for her to be there, let alone stay for an extended period. She hid her magic well, had done so for most of her life effectively, yet this was a risk she did not need to take. Her parents had begged her not to come, but she'd defied them. Lady Strella had done the same as the Volesions, claiming she did not need her friend, despite her wishing in her heart Piris could be with her. Once again, her friend knew her true self, and she'd shown up at the carriage with her own trunks packed and ready to leave, saying something about Strella needing protection and a true lady-in-waiting. Piris was a fighter, also secretly, but she was more. Strella couldn't argue too much in front of her father, who she'd kept this secret from, as it was not her secret to reveal. Somewhere in her heart, the daughter understood the shrewdness of the father, and although she'd never admit it out loud, she could admit to herself he was a calculating Fae who might use such information to his advantage one day if forced to do so. Strella kept few secrets in her sheltered life, except, of course, from the woman in front of her now.

So there they both were, in the middle of a huge dressing chamber in the center of the Winterlands Palace, each hiding their secrets from all but each other. "I love you, Peep" was all Strella could say.

"Love you too, Star. Now let's get you dressed." She pulled Strella up to standing, and they prepared for tea and Strella's first meeting with her prince.

Chapter Three
Ghel

Prince Ghel had fought with three guards in the palace practice rings midmorning on the day of his betrothal, to relieve some of the nervous tension making his shoulders bunch and his stomach knot. It did little to help, leaving him panting and sweaty before the meeting with Lady Strella Hollythorn. Which, of course, made him panic. Luckily, Jarok called him away for another task.

"Shouldn't I be getting ready for my meeting with Lady Hollythorn?"

Jarok eyed his brother and his fighting leathers. His disheveled and sweaty form. His hand stuck to the hilt of the huge broadsword at his side. Prince Ghel knew then he had made a grave mistake, and his shoulders slumped in defeat. All was bound to fail, but he did not have to encourage the failure.

Stopping him mid-stride, Jarok turned him by his shoulders and looked his brother square in the eye. "All will be fine, brother. Yes? Father and Mother handled the initial welcome to the palace, and there is time for you to prepare for the betrothal. Hours, even. Now, there are things we must attend to immediately."

These words made Ghel's ears perk and eyes narrow. There really was too much happening in their usually quiet corner of Fae, and he needed no more surprises. However, when Jarok opened the small oak door leading to his own study and Ghel saw who sat inside, a rare, broad smile popped onto his face.

"Cylian Padalist," he boomed, taking two massive strides over to his friend and giving him a hearty pat on his shoulder.

"Do watch yourself, Prince Ghel," the Fae noble said, teasing him as he stood. "Those massive paws of yours do damage."

Ghel ignored the rebuff and wrapped those paws around him, lifting his slightly shorter and less-muscular friend off the ground in a bear hug. Jarok chuckled behind him before Ghel set the lord down to let him speak.

The fire-haired Fae in front of him straightened his impeccable courtly attire, all golds and forest greens and muddy browns, as befitted the formal wear of the Autumnlands lord and ambassador. He smiled, the scar running down his face from forehead to cheek on his left side crinkling as he clasped Ghel on the shoulder. "It is good to see you too, friend, and on such an auspicious occasion. I hear congratulations are in order."

The sly glint in Cylian's golden eye and the tease in his voice made Ghel bristle and mumble incoherently as he plopped down on one of Jarok's wide leather chairs.

"My brother is worried, as you can clearly see," Jarok said.

"For good reason, I suppose. I would not wish to be forced into a marriage."

"I'm not exactly forced. I agreed."

"Still," Cylian said. "Do you know Lady Hollythorn?"

The way Cylian asked made Ghel wonder. "Do you?"

"Yes. I have met her on a few occasions, at her father's estate."

Jarok straightened from his lean on his desk and squinted at his friend. "Why, exactly, were you at Hollythorn Manor?"

Cylian rolled his eyes. "As the ruling lord of the Autumnlands, my father has varied interests I must attend throughout Fae, as you well know. At one time, this included a trade deal with Hollythorn. However, my dealings with him ended five years ago, so it has been some time."

Cylian's face drew down in thought. "Lady Strella is petite and lovely. A perfect Fae noblewoman, always attentive to her guests and duties. But..." Here he paused, his sharp eyes distant but focused as he thought hard on something. "She remained aloof often. Kind, yes. Helpful, always. Yet never fully a part of any festivities or immersed in any gatherings."

"Is she cold?" Jarok asked, worry bleeding into his dark eyes and usually smooth voice.

"Not cold, exactly. More standoffish? Civil and gracious and never fully invested in the parties or festivities where she served as hostess. As if she wanted to help her father but never really wanted to fully connect with others. Which, by the way, is her prerogative. Might even be best, considering her father and his associates."

"What do you know of Lord Hollythorn's associates? And why are you here, now?" Ghel asked, narrowing in on what Cylian implied.

He gave a mocking bow and spoke. "Dear Princes, as always I come in the interests of my father, who wished to have a representative in Winterlands Palace during your upcoming nuptials, if it is agreeable with the royal family."

"Yes, yes, Cylian. You're welcome here always, as you well know. Now tell us what you know and stop your diplomatic games."

"I know there is unrest among the warrior clans, and you wish an alliance within your own kingdom, hence the marriage to Lady Strella."

"Anything else?" Jarok pushed.

"I have my suspicions, but nothing I can confirm at this time." Cylian's mismatched eyes narrowed, the right, golden eye flaring with an inner fire as the left, silvery eye interrupting his scar showed nothing. "I do believe your suspicions align with my own, given current events."

Ghel gave a curt nod. Cylian did not need to say more. Ghel knew him well enough, from their years together in various courts and the brief but memorable time they spent while Ghel apprenticed in the Autumnlands holdings, to know his friend was smart enough to see the outline of the problem they faced. "You come as ambassador and friend, and are most welcome."

Jarok snorted. "Especially now. Prince Ghel is set to meet his future princess in a short amount of time, and this is what we have to work with." Jarok's tease riled Ghel, but he had no room to complain. He was sweaty, half-dressed, wild-haired, and unused to what would be expected of him in such a situation. His parents indulged his quiet nature, allowing him to pick and choose what he would participate in and how he would participate as a royal, yet now he worried. Maybe they'd indulged him too much. A great deal, for his family and the Winterlands as a whole, now relied on him doing what he'd avoided for most of his life: acting like a royal prince instead of a hardened warrior.

Cylian rubbed his smooth chin, looking Ghel up and down as he squirmed in front of him. "Yes. I see. You do have a lot of work to do, Jarok. Possibly too much work."

Jarok laughed and clapped their friend on the back as Ghel growled menacingly. Cylian leaned over and said, "None of that, Ghel. We don't need you growling at the lovely lady and scaring her off."

The joke, meant in good fun by his good friend, hit true. It was Ghel's main concern. He worried he would be too rough, too unlike what she was used to, too much for Lady Strella. His being too much for her—her backing out of the wedding—was not an option. He needed to marry Strella for their defensive plans to unfold just as they wished. He'd take all the help he could get to do it too.

Straightening his slumped shoulders, Ghel muttered, "I could use your help, friend."

Cylian's voice softened at the admission. "I am always at your service, Ghel, but I believe you may be more worried than you need to be."

"As is always the case," Jarok quipped as he stepped into their close circle. "Now, however, you must change. Wait, no. Bathe, then change."

Ghel smacked his brother on the side of the head, listening to his curses as he turned to leave the room. He stopped before exiting, looking over his shoulder at Jarok and Cylian. This was a trying time, for him and his kingdom, in so many ways. It was heartening to know he would continue to have help along the way. "Thank you," he said, gruff but forceful. Both acknowledged the thanks with tilts of their head, but Ghel did not see them. He was already out the door, headed to his chambers, ready to take a quick bath and prepare for a different type of battle.

Ghel tugged at the tight collar of his formal tunic. He acknowledged it looked good, with intricately embroidered patterns in gold thread over soft, light-blue satin. He just thought the damn thing was too tight around his big neck, nearly choking him. Or maybe it was his nerves. The pants also felt both restricting and not enough, thin gold satin breeches he could rip at a moment's notice, especially where they stretched tight around his thick thighs as he twisted and bent his knees to try to feel more comfortable.

He received an elbow to the gut for the movements. "Stop fidgeting," Jarok hissed.

Ghel stilled, took a deep breath, and focused. He drew on his battle practice, the meditation he did as a fighter. The fight ahead differed greatly from what he was used to, but it was still a fight. One he had to win.

Cylian drew up on his other side and touched his arm. "All will be well, Ghel. I have a feeling."

"Oh, then by all means, let's no longer worry. Cylian has a feeling," Ghel muttered, his joke bringing a surprised bark of laughter from his brother.

"There's the Prince Ghel wit and charm. You'll be just fine," Jarok said as he waved a hand at the large, closed doors in front of them. The tearoom. Where his soon-to-be betrothed was waiting for him. Ghel swallowed hard, past the constricting neckline of his tunic and the sudden lump forming in his throat, but did what any good soldier would do. He braved into battle.

He might have braved the battle a little too hard, however, because his stomping steps echoed in the silent room where two Fae women sat in chairs side by side, their heads bent as if they had just been whispering to each other. The one closest to the door was tall, Ghel could see as much even from her sitting position. Her eyes were sharp, narrowing as she immediately evaluated the group entering her space. Her thick auburn eyebrows creased, then smoothed, and she leaned back in her chair, giving herself the appearance of ease, although the clench of her jaw and the rigid tension of her back told Ghel she was ready for anything.

His eyes understood this opponent in a moment, as well as the fact she was not his focus, so he moved to the other woman. And his heart stopped for two or three beats before it barreled ahead like a white bear chasing a fox. This woman was obviously Strella Hollythorn, as she looked very much like her father. They shared the same thin shape, facial structure, frosty-blonde hair, and piercing blue eyes. Lady Strella's eyes, however, looked kind but curious, whereas Lord Hollythorn's always had a calculating glint in his. Her nose was small and upturned, a perfect little thing sitting right in the middle of her face, and her mouth, slightly ajar for some reason, was a gorgeous pink bow. She was also small. Tiny, really, from her blue-heel-clad feet to her tilted head. Hands fluttered like little birds in her lap for a moment, but she eventually clasped them together as she squared her shoulders and locked eyes with Ghel.

Cylian stepped up to fill the momentary silence. Ghel could not find his voice for some reason. Although being abysmal with words was a normal occurrence for him, this felt different. Like a blast of ice and flame somehow intertwined and made him completely immobile. Immobile except for the thundering heart in his chest.

"Lady Strella Hollythorn and Lady Piris Volesion, a pleasure as always."

The auburn-haired woman smiled at Cylian. "Lord Padalist. A pleasant surprise to see you here."

"I go where I am needed, Lady," he said with a wink of his golden eye. "I do believe I may be needed for introductions currently." He turned to the brothers as the ladies rose gracefully out of their seats. "First, allow me to introduce Prince Jarok Borau, Lord of the Winding Forest, Guardian of the Winterlands Palace, and Second of the Winterlands Forces."

Ghel inwardly groaned. He'd forgotten about formal introductions and dreaded what would come next: all the pretentious mess that came along with his name and titles spilling out into the room.

Jarok, however, was bending over Lady Strella's small hand, giving it a quick kiss, which made heat stir in Ghel's gut for some reason. "A pleasure to meet you, my lady."

Pink streaked across Lady Strella's pale cheeks as she dipped into a proper curtsy for his brother. "The pleasure is mine, Prince Jarok. I thank you for welcoming me into your home."

Jarok hummed and turned to Lady Volesion. "Lady Piris. You do look familiar. Have we met before?"

Lady Piris hit Ghel's brother with a hard look and a sneer. "I do not believe so, Prince."

He smirked and bent over her hand, maybe lingering too long there as he said, "Quite right. I do believe a meeting with you, Lady, would be a memorable experience."

Lady Piris snatched her hand away, and Lady Strella whipped her head to her friend, studying her reaction to Jarok. Seemed the lady also realized something was off between these two, for whatever reason. Ghel had no time to investigate further. He was too busy gritting his teeth against what was next.

"Finally, I am pleased to introduce you to Prince Ghel Borau, Lord of the Ice Plains, Captain of the Aurora Outpost, General of all Winterlands Forces, and future king of the Winterlands."

Cylian bowed to his friend, but when Ghel stayed frozen in place, he ticked his head toward the ladies, urging him to say or do something. Anything.

Shaking his head to get himself in line, Ghel stepped up first to Lady Strella. Her small frame was dwarfed by his, and he felt like a bumbling oaf as he took her hand in his. His eyes widened when their skin connected, sending a zing of sensation down his spine. He watched, fascinated, as Lady Strella's eyes dilated, and a soft glow, like distant starlight, appeared there before she shuttered her gaze.

Despite the leaked magic, she kept her composure much better than him, dipping into a deep curtsy and staying down as she said, "An honor to meet you, Prince Ghel. Please accept my humble thanks at your warm welcome into your home."

Ghel couldn't tell if her words were a formality or a dig because he'd been too occupied with his own worries to welcome her to his home as he should have, and now he regretted the fact more than ever. All he could do was grunt in response. However, he tugged gently on her arm, telling her without words to rise. As she did, he brought her hand to his lips, leaving a ghost of a kiss there, yet it was enough to make his lips crackle with awareness.

He was decidedly unused to such reactions to women, so he took a huge step back, dropping Lady Strella's hand as if it burned him, before turning to face her friend. Lady Piris looked between the two and gave the prince a much warmer smile than she'd given his brother. "Prince Ghel, a pleasure to meet you."

Ghel said nothing but did the usual small bow and quick hand kiss expected in these introductions before stepping well out of reach of both ladies—stepping back enough to bump clumsily into his brother, who hovered close behind him. He looked back at him, his lip curving in a grimace while Jarok simply smirked. The grimace didn't leave his face when he turned back and saw Lady Strella startle at him for a moment before she went back to the perfect picture of a Fae noblewoman.

Cylian, thankfully, moved into the breach with his smooth diplomatic demeanor. "Please, ladies. Do sit."

Ghel watched, somehow transfixed, as Lady Strella bent back into her seat with a practiced ease he'd never conquered, her back remaining straight and her hands daintily clasped the entire time. He thought her the image of grace, which made his gut twist once again. He was anything but graceful, and if she expected such sweet manners and decorum from him, she would be disappointed.

He didn't know what to do with himself... his hands, his eyes, his words. Not as if he did in social situations often, but this was different. Important. Yet the more he screamed at himself internally to do what needed to be done, to charm like Jarok or be as smooth as Cylian, the more rigid and frozen he stayed.

Lady Piris looked between her friend and Ghel. Lady Strella's eyes were downcast, avoiding his gaze. She reached up to twine a piece of hair in her finger, and Ghel was mesmerized by the movement of her slim hand in her wavy blonde tresses, until Lady Strella yanked her hand down quickly and stiffened as if she'd done something wrong. She offered a sweet smile that looked wrinkled around the edges, too brittle for Ghel's liking, and nodded toward the men.

Her sweet, bell voice was soft but sure when she gracefully swept her hand toward the chairs across from her and Piris. "Please, do have your seats. My father will be along shortly."

Finally, she'd offered something Ghel could do, even if he did it jerkily, forcing himself into every step toward the trio of chairs across from the ladies. He plopped down a little too hard, his chair making a harsh scraping noise across the wooden floor when it shifted back several inches at his force and weight. Again, he grimaced. Jarok and Cylian sat without incident, because of course they did, Jarok easing back with a little too much insolence, staring hard at Lady Piris for some reason. Cylian was perfectly straight, perfectly in control. Damn him. Ghel thought in the moment if he could choose any form of magic to be his, he'd wish for the ability of a mimic, though it was, more often than not, a terrible burden. At least then he could also be perfect on the outside when it was required of him.

Again, Cylian eyed him, tilted his head, and attempted to get Ghel to engage in a meaningful way. He scratched his head, then muttered, with his own eyes looking everywhere but at his soon-to-be betrothed, "I hope your journey was pleasant."

"It was, Prince. Long, but pleasant. I have never ventured far from Hollythorn Manor, so it was fascinating to see more of my land." Lady Strella's voice was soft but sure, with a lift and lilt Ghel thought sounded much like the whistle of songbirds.

No one spoke again for an awkward minute, then Jarok cleared his throat and offered a follow-up question. "Did you travel by carriage or sled, my lady?"

"Oh, carriage. Sled would have been faster, but—" Lady Strella stopped mid-thought and bit her lip. Ghel stared at her too-white teeth sinking into her pink lip. He felt an odd sadness when she refocused, because her teeth disappeared behind her lip, and he suspected she shifted the direction of her initial response for some reason. "We needed to travel with many things, so carriages were best."

Jarok inclined his head and smiled at her, so at ease in this type of interaction. Ghel simply sat back, silent, crossing his too-big arms over his too-big chest and leaning back to watch their interactions.

"Sledding across the Ice Plains is a truly marvelous experience, Lady Strella. If you wish, I could show you."

A snort escaped Lady Piris, decidedly unladylike but something Ghel appreciated because he felt the same way about his brother's offer. "If she is to sled the Ice Plains, Prince Jarok, I do not think it will be with you."

Ghel blinked at the bite in her voice. It'd been a long while since anyone other than a battle-hardened enemy had taken on his brother. Jarok had the face of a man smacked by words, and in his bewilderment, he turned questioning eyes at his brother. Maybe he realized what he offered was inappropriate after Lady Piris's chastisement. Ghel hated the look on his face, so he gave a silent nod, his own language Jarok knew well, and his brother's stiff posture loosened once again.

Jarok then turned to Lady Piris, and with more venom than was necessary, said, "I do not believe you are the judge of what Lady Strella would or could do."

Lady Piris's eyes narrowed. "I am her lady-in-waiting, Prince. If I remember correctly, it is a basic function of the job."

Ghel couldn't help it. He let out a snicker. The banter between them was heated, but he found it amusing someone was taking his sharp-tongued brother to task, giving him a dose of his own medicine, as it were. His laughter did not come full and deep, however, because he then looked at Lady Strella and saw the distress on her face. Heat rising in his own, he clipped out a harsh "enough" at the two sniping Fae, and both stopped whatever it was they were doing.

He had opened his mouth to apologize to Lady Strella for his brother's behavior when the door to the tearoom opened and Lord Hollythorn strolled in without a care or any sign of concern, as if he weren't late for this important event. Lady Strella immediately jumped to her feet and gave her own father a deep curtsy, muttering a soft, "Greetings, Father." It was an odd response, and one Ghel did not like. He had plenty of reasons to dislike Lord Hollythorn, it was true, but this rose to the top of the list.

He remained seated, arms crossed, eyes narrowed on the tall Fae in front of him. Standing side by side, he and Lady Strella looked even more alike, though the differences piled in his mind. Most he'd already noticed, but now he also saw the different way they took up space, the difference in the way they interacted with the world around them. Lady Strella may have been aloof, but she was not acting as if she were above the situation or her surroundings. Attitude and arrogance dripped off her father and grated right across Ghel.

The two Fae stared at each other, until Lord Hollythorn broke first. He gave a halfhearted bow to Ghel and said, "Prince Ghel, a pleasure to see you once again. I do hope you find my daughter to your liking?"

He grunted at the man, unable to say what he wanted to say, which was it was strange he'd said something like that right in front of his daughter. It made him feel like he was buying Lady Strella. He wanted to bark at this man to be a decent father, to see the shock fleeting across his daughter's face at his words and correct them. He couldn't. Words too often escaped him. He did, however, manage a menacing growl, which Jarok attempted to cut off with a tight grip on Ghel's knee.

"Lord Hollythorn. I do believe you are late," Prince Jarok said as he sneered at the lord, using his more imperious voice, the one Ghel usually hated but loved in the moment. It looked like Lady Piris even appreciated it, given the smirk dancing across her lips at the moment. "Sit."

Lord Hollythorn was unhappy about the command but obeyed it nonetheless, taking the empty seat by his daughter. Ghel's teeth ground seeing how he ignored her, offering her no comfort or even basic pleasantries. The lord sat stiff-backed with his face a blank mask of indifference, waiting for someone else to speak.

"I believe all who are required are now in attendance," Cylian called into the empty room. "Lady Piris and I will serve as outside witnesses. Prince Jarok and Lord Hollythorn will be the family witnesses. We may begin."

Ghel swallowed hard but forced himself to stand. His body did what it was told even if his brain was running wild. His nerves jangled in his head, but he stepped up to Lady Strella, pulled her to standing by her hand, and clasped both hers in his. It was a ridiculous sight to him, seeing her small hands disappear in his massive paws. So many reasons why he shouldn't do this, including the slight tremble he felt as he held her hands tightly. However, there were more pressing reasons why he had to, and he hoped one day Lady Strella would forgive him for it. She seemed gracious enough he had hope. With a deep sigh, he muttered, "Lady Strella Hollythorn of Hollythorn Manor, daughter of Lord Mikka Hollythorn, do you agree to be my betrothed?"

Lady Strella blinked up into his face, searching for a few seconds, before giving a sad smile in return. "Yes, Prince Ghel Borau. I agree to be your betrothed."

Ghel hadn't noticed the scroll Lord Hollythorn had produced from somewhere until the flare of light sealed their fate. Embossed on the vellum was their promise, the simple magic set up so long ago by noble Fae to create a betrothal bond. It felt like a small string, fragile and barely noticeable, now linked him to the scroll, as he knew it also must for Lady Strella. She shivered in his hands, and he ached to comfort her in some way.

"Excellent," Jarok said, clapping his brother on the back a little hard. "The magic is now set, your bond settled until the marriage bond is created." He plucked the scroll from Lord Hollythorn's pale hand, and for a moment it appeared as if the lord might fight for it, but he acquiesced in a stiff bow. "Of course I, as Prince Ghel's brother and fellow Prince of the Winterlands, shall keep the bond safe until the wedding." Betrothal bonds could be broken for many reasons in Fae, but they could also be severed with malice, which had its own set of consequences the longer the bond held. It was fitting for Jarok to protect it for his brother.

"Quiet," Ghel muttered, unable to muster happiness despite the tingles of sensation he felt at Lady Strella's touch. He wanted to rub at the spot in his chest where he felt the tug of the bond, the tiny slice of magic reinforcing the promise. He wondered how it felt to Lady Strella, whether she chafed at the feeling. He couldn't pretend she was completely happy with these events. Not after the look on her face and the steel threaded through her voice at her confirmation of the bond. It made his stomach sick to think he'd somehow trapped her, forced her into this as her father had likely forced her. He couldn't feel good about any of this right then, especially after meeting her. Now, more than ever, he was determined to get this done so he could save his kingdom and the people in it, including saving Lady Strella from whatever worries she might have about their union. Accustomed to doing what needed to be done for his people, fighting battles on his behalf, he hurt for Lady Strella being forced to do so when it was never her lot in life. All he could do was swear to himself he'd make it right for her. Somehow. In the future. When all was safe and well again.

Chapter Four
Strella

I t was two days after her introduction and binding betrothal to Prince Ghel, and she had yet to see him again. Which, to be fair, was not something she was actively attempting. It may have been a little cowardly, but she was fine with avoiding the prince for now, until they were forced to attend to some official duty or another. Strella thought back to her introduction to the prince: his dark eyes assessing and shrewd, his face impassive and slightly cold. Except when he looked at her father at one point with a curled lip. A small movement revealing so much. His hand and his lips had been warm, enough to heat her belly, but his look, his aloofness, and his clipped but strong voice told her he'd found something wanting in the match. Not a good start for a union she herself hesitated over, albeit for different reasons. Yet she was a lady and would fulfill her duties as long as she was able. All she saw and heard of him informed her Prince Ghel would do the same, for his family and the land he would one day rule, so she vowed to herself she would be kind, formal, and as unobtrusive as possible so the prince's sacrifice was honored. Their relationship would be one of show, she knew, and she planned to reflect well on him and her family at all engagements, even if the relationship was a mere shadow of an illusion.

Strella was nervously anticipating an event this day, but Prince Ghel would not be in attendance. With this event, however, she was unsure if his absence was a good or bad thing. She was to have a lunch, alone, with the queen. Her stomach rumbled thinking of it. Queen Alene, also known as the warrior queen of the Winterlands, was intimidating for a host of reasons. First, her magic was formidable. Strong and sure, it called birds of prey to her. Everyone knew a bird stayed with her, always, and would not hesitate to do her bidding with the slightest indication from their mistress. Added to this was that she was the daughter of a famous clan leader, raised as a trained warrior from the Aurora Outpost who wielded a sword in a way many said appeared as instinctive to her as her magic. She also looked like a warrior, acted like a warrior, and discussed warrior things with warriors like her king and her sons and her family.

Some amongst the lords and ladies grumbled, claiming the queen was no true lady and therefore no rightful queen. Lady Strella was not one such lady, but many she'd hosted over the years were. They talked out of the sides of their mouths of the uncouth warrior queen and the shame she brought to King Frit. Strella saw nothing to be ashamed of in her valor and skill. Unlike herself, she had firm place in this land and could be counted on to continue to protect it as she had for centuries past. Remembering how King Frit had gazed at his wife when they'd first arrived, she also had no doubt the king saw nothing shameful about her either.

Wife. Thinking the word brought a sigh to her lips as Strella perused the library shelves. She and Piris had discovered the library yesterday while wandering the halls of the palace aimlessly. She was not used to idle time, as running a manor the size of Hollythorn was a tremendous amount of work, so finding the library space was a blessing for her. Strella loved books. All tales, really, but there was comfort in the solitary world of reading she very much appreciated. Hollythorn Manor's library was filled to the brim with all forms of stories, some true and some not, and Strella had managed to read through most of them in her life. She'd always wished to read them all, had made it a personal goal. Now, however, with time and events not on her side, it was no longer an option.

However, the Winterlands Palace library eased the ache of a goal unattained. Situated in the western part of the palace a few hallways over from her guest chambers, it was a cavernous room taking up three stories. Ladders and stairs allowed access to all the shelves, and Lady Strella thought nothing could be as joyous as days spent roaming the space, learning all its nooks and crannies and finding its secret treasures. She thought a library this vast would hold many treasures, and she wished to be the hunter to find them.

Piris had wanted to train this morning, so Strella had left her to it, telling her friend to find her in the library when she was done with her daily routine. She was wandering the bottom floor, running her hands along the spines of a section of what looked to be Winterlands law tomes, when she was startled by the clearing of a throat behind her.

Spinning to see who was about, she saw Prince Ghel hovering close to a study table, his dark, wild-haired head looking down at his own hand planted firmly on the sturdy wood. Strella swallowed, fascinated by the play of ridges and veins and muscles along the prince's large, exposed hand and forearm. He'd taken her breath when he'd entered the tearoom two days ago: the epitome of a warrior Fae—all height and force and weight, hard muscle, and keen eyes. When his eyes had looked displeased throughout the rather awkward event, she'd tempered her initial rush of reaction to his proximity, immediately reminded it was to be a marriage of political convenience. They were betrothed, tethered by magic, but he had not appeared overly happy about it. He did not appear overly happy now, which made Strella wonder why he was coming to her.

"Your Highness," Strella said, dipping into a low curtsy and bowing her head.

"Lady Strella," he grumbled back, his voice a deep tone ringing in her chest, causing her heart to beat faster.

Strella waited for him to say something. Anything. To comment on the weather or some other inane topic as any other lord would do. He did not. Instead, he stared, his eyes assessing. She couldn't see them, as she was still casting her own downward, bowed as she was. She somehow felt them, however, a prickling sensation trailing over her where he must be looking.

"Do rise, Lady Strella," he growled, his voice a breath away from a curse for some reason. She worried she'd offended him somehow, so she did as he asked, though she looked at the shelves, the tables, and the lamps flickering. Looked at anything but Prince Ghel and his hard, unhappy gaze.

After a solid minute of no talk, Lady Strella's training forced her to speak. "I do hope it is no bother for me to be in the library?"

The question hung between them, Prince Ghel's shoulder lifting slightly in an informal shrug as if dismissing whatever she had to say.

Lady Strella deflated more, her hand moving up to her hair on instinct, twining it around a finger before she could stop herself. Prince Ghel's eyes snapped to her hand in her hair, and she instantly shoved it back down, internally cursing her nervous habit. The prince took a step toward her, his look still trained on a curling lock of her white-blonde hair falling against her shoulder, but he froze before he moved in farther, his formidable frame locking in a rigid stance.

Once again the prince cleared his throat and in a gruff timber, low and gentle to Strella's ears, said, "You are to be my wife, Lady Strella. You have free rein throughout the palace."

Strella nodded, gave another slight bow, and to do something with her hands other than mess with her hair, she moved to the shelf and pulled a law book down, eyeing the cover. "Do you visit the library often, Prince Ghel?" She thought this may be something they could bond over, a love of books or reading or stories.

"No." Short. Clipped. No elaboration.

She turned back and placed the book on the beautifully shined desk situated between them. "I spent much time in the Hollythorn Manor libraries," she confessed, offering something of herself up, hoping he would latch onto it.

"You enjoy reading?"

A question. An olive branch. Something Strella could cling to in the awkwardness between them. "Oh, yes. Whenever not attending duties or spending time with Lady Piris, I read. Any and everything I can."

Prince Ghel snorted, a harsh sound echoing through the room, as if dismissing whatever she might enjoy or considering her love of reading frivolous.

An unfamiliar heat rose in her chest, forcing her to step closer to Prince Ghel, stare up in his face, grit her teeth and add more than a little bite to her next words. "Apologies, Your Highness, if my reading offends." She had no idea where such snark came from. Likely Piris, who was a master at it. Lady Strella had never been. She'd endeavored to be unobtrusive, demure, acquiescent. She locked her jaw and stared down at the beautiful rug beneath her feet, willing her heart to stop thumping and her body to calm.

"Shit," Prince Ghel muttered, almost like he was talking to himself, and the curse, from a prince and in her presence, made a laugh bubble and spill out of her mouth. Her hand moved to cover her mouth, the thing she'd always been able to control and which was, at this most inopportune time, going completely wild on her.

She refused to look up at him but saw as he stepped closer—felt his bulk and heat and stare on her. Then she felt a whisper of a touch, not along her skin but on her hair, as if the prince stroked the tendril of hair she'd been nervously teasing moments before. Her head flung upward in alarm, not at the touch or his nearness but at the tingle both caused across her body. Their eyes locked, Prince Ghel's gaze softened a touch, and he tugged the bit of hair he held between his large, calloused fingers, a tease causing her to let loose a breathy gasp.

A low growl left the prince and he moved closer, his body searing her front, the hand still clinging to her lock of hair coming to rest against her upper arm, his hand moving to not skim against her chest. It still felt like a brand through the shimmering mint green of her formal day dress. She stopped breathing, going as still as a hare sensing a predator, even though Strella felt no fear growing in her gut. What she felt was uncertain, complex, and warm, but definitely not fear.

"Strella," Prince Ghel whispered, his own eyes fixed on the bit of her hair he rubbed between his fingers. He did not continue, and Strella thought her chest might burst from his lack of words, his cold face turning to fascination, the ache in his voice. The sizzle she felt along her skin.

"There you are!" a man shouted from the library doorway.

Strella started, stepping back from the prince so quickly her hair pulled, and she winced. Instantly, the prince dropped their connection, spinning around to snarl like a bear at Prince Jarok, who she now saw leaned against the doorway of the library, though he was mostly hidden behind Prince Ghel's large, hovering back positioned squarely in front of her, as if to shield her.

"Surprised to see you here, brother," the newcomer said, completely ignoring the bristling energy radiating off Prince Ghel. "You usually ignore the library."

She stepped to the side and gave a small bow to Prince Jarok in greeting. "Ah, Lady Strella. This explains it." Prince Jarok gave her a warm smile, which turned into a smirk as he looked over his brother. "I do hate to break up whatever it was you two were doing alone in here, but you're needed in the royal chambers, Ghel."

Ghel muttered a name under his breath, Monti, and it sounded like a curse. She knew there were issues with the Monti Clan. It was the main reason she was here and to be married. The prince's tone made her want to learn more, so she could somehow help. Except, how could she ever help, besides giving her hand to form alliances, which she was already doing? Ghel let out a harsh breath and without a word stalked toward his brother and the door. Prince Jarok gave a flourishing, courtly bow Strella's way, and Ghel stopped at the entrance once he harshly shoved his brother through the frame and into the hallway. He did not look back at her as he gave soft words to her: "A pleasure, Lady Strella."

She said nothing in reply. Did not move. Barely breathed. Simply stood in silence, surrounded by books and wondering why, exactly, she felt as if her knees would give out at any moment.

S trella swallowed hard as she looked on the small table centered in the vast, sunny room. She'd been directed here, the queen's aviary. Had expected the roosts and trees and such. She had not expected the small, intimate seating arrangement in the middle of the space, where she found the queen sitting alone, save for the powerful snow hawk perched on her shoulder.

She hesitated a touch too long, and the clear, strong voice of the queen echoed in the room, calling her forward. "Come, Lady Strella." No niceties, only command. Not royal command either, but a no-nonsense type of gruffness Strella somehow found both refreshing and disconcerting. Without hesitation, she moved to the small, round table piled high with Winterland delicacies. A dainty, winter-rose-patterned plate and cup rested at her empty seat, a pretty picture for a royal luncheon. She managed to fold into her seat with the practiced grace drilled into her head over her lifetime, even as she kept a deep curtsy and her head bowed low.

"Forgive me, my queen."

Queen Alene waved a hand dismissively. "No need for apologies, Lady Strella. Women of Fae are far too apt to apologize for every little thing, even when it is unwarranted."

Another hard swallow for Strella, who worried she'd offended the queen. She caught back the automatic apology before it flew from her lips. Instead, she looked at her queen, clasped her hands together to stop her fidgeting, and nodded. What else could she say? One didn't argue with a queen, especially when her queen's words were just proven right by her own impulses.

Queen Alene appeared unfazed and unconcerned to Strella. She sat straight and tall, her back not in proper posture through years of etiquette training but rather years of training as a fighter. Strella even noticed she was positioned to see all around her as best she could, and what she could not see, strategically placed owls and eagles off to Strella's side could surely track.

Nodding toward the trays piled of food between them, the queen said, "Please, Lady. Do help yourself." Strella waited, allowing the royal to take the first piece in order to appease years of social drilling from her father. After the queen filled her own small plate with smoked meats and winter fruits and small, steaming pastries stuffed with sweet and savory delights, Strella followed suit, avoiding things the queen picked to make sure she did not take the pieces she might want later in the meal.

With her own dark, hawk-like eyes, mirrored by the constant look of the silent, brilliantly white hawk on her shoulder, Strella knew she did not miss a single movement made at the table. When she finished, having placed a few small pieces on her plate and sitting straight, hands in her lap once again, Queen Arlene let out a loud, long sigh. A wild curl of dark hair escaped her tight bun as she shook her head. "Not nearly enough, girl. You need more to keep your strength up in this place."

Before she could protest, the queen scooped up Strella's plate and piled it high with food, passing it back before lifting a jug of cool water to fill both their cups. "Would you like something else to drink, Lady?"

"Oh, no, my queen. You honor me by serving me with your own hand."

"You would honor me by eating," she countered, a dark brow quirked up in a hard arch.

Strella gave no argument and began to eat. The queen did as well, occasionally pausing in her own meal to feed certain meaty morsels to the bird at her shoulder. When she turned to it, offered it food from her fingers, it pecked delicately, its feathers ruffling as it made soft noises in its bird throat. When it wasn't eating, however, it stared right at Strella, assessing her. Just as the queen did. Just as Prince Ghel had. The similarities between the three struck her in the moment, but she had little time to contemplate it before the queen opened conversation.

"How are you enjoying the palace so far?"

"Marvelously, Your Grace. My rooms are lovely, as are all the rooms I have visited thus far. I feel particularly fond of the library."

"A reader, then?"

"Yes, my queen."

"Hm," she said, turning her attention to feed the bird at her shoulder once again. "Can't say my son is much for reading."

"I gather not, Your Grace."

Two shrewd sets of eyes locked onto hers. "You would know this how?"

Strella's palms sweated at the question, and possibly at the memory of whatever it was that had happened in the library earlier in the morning. "Your son came upon me in the library this morning and hinted he was not one to enjoy books."

"Ghel was always better in a practice ring than in a library."

"A noble endeavor in service of his kingdom, I'm sure." It was said quietly, almost whispered, but Strella surprised herself with the force behind the words, at the prickle along her scalp at what she thought could possibly be a small dig from Prince Ghel's mother.

A whip-sharp laugh echoed in the room, causing the birds all around to squawk and adjust their wings. "I see you did not appreciate my tone."

"Oh, no, my queen. Please—"

Hand raised toward Strella, Queen Alene silenced her before continuing. "Again, do not apologize. I appreciate it, as it was on behalf of my son. And do not confuse me. It was not a statement of judgment, merely of fact. Prince Ghel is a true warrior, equal parts strength, skill, and intelligence. Traits all true warriors must possess."

"Agreed, Your Grace."

"You know, owls are assumed wise and noble. Are often discussed as if somehow more civil or couth or intelligent than other birds. Seen as more controlled. Yet they are also birds of prey, becoming violent when the need arises."

Strella, unsure why the queen spouted such a fact, simply nodded and took a small bite of a buttery cookie as the queen continued her bird lecture.

"Hawks, however, are feared by all. Because of their strength, their talons, their beaks, their speed. They are seen as killers. Maybe because they are solitary creatures. Yet those who know of them know they are not completely solitary. There are exceptions, such as with breeding pairs and their young. Hawks also fiercely protect their territory, seeing it as their sole responsibility."

Queen Arlene did not flinch when the huge hawk on her shoulder flapped its giant wings and rose in the air, managing to knock over a good bit of food with the wind it generated as it took flight. Strella flinched, but she studied it as it rose, watching the power of its wings and the focus in its gaze, the purpose and poise. She'd never considered those things before when looking up at hawks flying high above her in the distance.

She thought of the queen's meaning before she spoke, hoping she was picking up her proper meaning. "Noble creatures, fierce and true. Creatures to be respected."

"And loved," the queen said off-handedly, as if it did not matter to her one way or another, even if the words sounded like a wish to Strella's ears. She watched as the huge bird floated above them, circling before it moved to a large nest where another snow-white hawk waited for it. They greeted each other as it landed, nestled up and picked at feathers as they roosted together high above.

"I knew your mother," the queen said, and Strella jolted. Queen Arlene had a way of swiftly changing course in conversation, much like the flight of the birds she commanded, but this was not a direction Strella would have expected. She said nothing, choosing to look down at her plate and study the half-eaten cookie resting there.

"I liked her, your mother. A kind lady, kinder than many I have met as queen of the Winterlands. A strong lady as well. Strong enough to stand toe-to-toe with your father on several occasions. Some even I witnessed, which, I must admit, were entertaining moments." The queen reached for another pastry and took a bite, a small smile dancing across her lips as if the memory of Strella's mother amused her.

That was startling information. She never imagined such from her mother, who by her father's accounts was the perfect picture of a lady. "Truly?"

"Yes, Lady Strella. Lady Kirah was a real lady, which like a real warrior, takes a vast number of skills not many truly possess. Any woman can be born a noble Fae, just as anyone can become a fighter. It takes something else, something in the mix of the head and the heart, to make one great at either. I can't say I'm a lady, but I am a warrior, and I recognized the spark of it in your mother. I'm happy to see the same spark in you."

Strella involuntarily rubbed her chest, the spot where her own starlight seeped through when she let her magic unfurl. "Thank you, Your Grace."

"No need for thanks either, Lady. Now, would you like to hear embarrassing stories of Prince Ghel as a boy? I do believe beyond our initial assessment of each other, it is the purpose of this little luncheon."

Strella chuckled, and the stiffness in her spine melted slightly at the ease of the queen. "Yes, Queen Alene. I would very much enjoy hearing your stories."

Chapter Five
Ghel

Ghel once again pulled on the collar of a formal tunic. He thought it was absurd to have to wear another in such a short time span. A hard thud hit his back, and Jarok popped around his side.

"Do stop fidgeting with the thing, Ghel. You look like you're going to rip it right off your body."

"I might," he growled back, but he forced his hands down to his sides, flexing his fingers as he did.

"You look good, Ghel," Cylian said from his chair across the room.

Ghel gave a short, curt nod in reply and turned to look at himself in the mirror. He thought he looked like an impostor, a fighter who should be in leathers but was stuffed into a silky, white tunic with winter ivy embroiled along the cuffs, collar, and bottom with golden thread. Gold satin breeches, so impractical to Ghel's mind, hugged his massive legs.

"Why are these damn things always so tight?" he asked no one in particular as he moved in his unfamiliar clothes.

"To keep Fae from battling on the dance floor, I suppose. Fights can't break out often if the men believe they may split their pants when they start to tussle."

Ghel laughed at the image of snotty lords ripping holes in their pants but stopped when he thought of those same men on the battlefield. Surely they had fought before, but he was not used to seeing such. It was almost as foreign to him as the clothes and the betrothal ball he would soon be attending.

Thoughts of the ball sent his mind down other corridors, toward worry over his betrothed. Fear she did not wish to marry him but felt the same pressure and duty as he did. He couldn't deny the lust coursing through his veins when he thought of her pink-bow mouth and the way she nervously twirled her white hair around a finger. The feel of her hair, softer than the silk of his tunic. The small gasp she'd made when he'd moved toward her... touched her. The heat rising in him as he thought of the other sounds he could coax from those beautiful lips.

Ghel shook the thoughts from his head and refocused. He did not need to lust after her like the brute so many thought him. He needed to respect her and her sacrifice for their kingdom.

"I see your wheels turning, brother," Jarok said from behind him. "Do not fret too much over tonight. It is a simple thing; you and Lady Strella lead the opening dance and then move around the room, greeting all the guests as a couple. Nothing to fear."

Nothing for Jarok to fear, Ghel thought. He felt plenty of fear and nervousness and pressure. The worst of it was he worried about how Lady Strella must feel in the moment. How she must dread being with a stupid oaf of a warrior when the smooth tongue of someone like Cylian would be such a better match for her.

He turned from the mirror, the deep scowl he saw when thinking of Strella and Cylian together still firmly planted on his face.

"Gods, man. Wipe the look from your face." Cylian chuckled. "You'll have the whole ballroom thinking you're about to attack."

It took a moment, but Ghel felt his face smooth, and he let out a deep sigh. "I don't think I can do this."

"What, exactly?" Jarok asked, moving closer to his brother.

"All of this. The clothes and the parties and the royal obligations. I'm no charmer like you, brother. I am a fighter. That's all."

"You are a warrior." Cylian corrected him from his seat, hard-flame eyes on his friend. "Act as one. I have been the Autumnlands' diplomat for nearly a century and know a thing or two about the moves Fae make in such settings. These court rituals are battles of a different kind. You have one of the best strategic minds in Fae. I've seen it on the field. You can use it here as well."

By gods, Ghel realized he'd never considered it as such. He knew Winterlands maps and military positions and battle plans like the back of his hand. Possibly, just possibly, if he came at it from his own experience, he could get through these official events and not make a fool of himself or his family. Or Lady Strella.

"Okay. Right," he clipped out as he moved to a desk scattered with blank parchment in the corner of his sitting room where he liked to map out his ideas. He grabbed a charcoal stick and sketched the outline of the palace ballroom from memory. "You two come here. We need information if I'm to form a battle strategy."

Ghel was announced with ridiculous fanfare, at least to his mind, and waited at the bottom of the stairs outside of the ballroom to take Lady Strella inside once she was announced. A slew of lords and ladies hovered, though luckily his family and Cylian remained closest to him, giving him silent strength and courage. "It's a battle and one I will win," he whispered to himself as he fought the urge to straighten his tunic or pull on the collar.

"Introducing Lady Strella Hollythorn, daughter of Lord Mikka Hollythorn and the late Lady Kirah Hollythorn, bearer of starlight, heir to Hollythorn Manor, and bonded betrothed to Prince Ghel Borau of the Winterlands."

Ghel's eyes landed on Strella, and all else faded away. She looked like a goddess come down to Fae. Her dress was as white as his tunic and had similar decorations. They matched, likely purposefully, except her golden decorations were holly leaves instead of winter ivy. The dress itself was tight across the bodice and hips and flared out around the knees, a pool of silk cascading down to her feet. It looked so tight, Ghel wondered how she could walk, and he instantly knew he should stop complaining about his clothes.

Her hair was piled in high curls on top of her head in an intricate pattern, encircled and held tight by a ring of gold-plated holly leaves on her head. Her face, smooth as the silk of her gown, glittered in spots that made her cheeks, her lips, and her petite, upturned nose glisten and shimmer in a most enticing way.

In a word, she was breathtaking to Ghel. He struggled to breathe looking at the glow and grace of her, this woman who was to be his wife. Forced to be his wife, he reminded himself. His teeth gritted and he straightened his stance, finding he'd leaned forward, toward her, without consciously being aware of doing so. He locked down his body, wiped his face, and stepped to the center of the stairway as he'd been instructed by Jarok and Cylian earlier.

When she reached him, he noticed she stood taller, though she was still several inches shorter than him. He looked at her feet and saw gold sandals with high spikes in the back, her delicate toes peeking out for all to see. He couldn't help but stare at her toes, the perfect picture of them searing itself into his brain, when a throat softly cleared behind him. His father, damnit. He'd just begun but had already messed up.

Pulling his gaze from her feet, he held out a hand to her. Strella took it and he felt the zap he'd felt every time they touched. He thought he saw her shiver as he did, but he was uncertain, so he shoved the enticing thought aside and proceeded as he'd been told to do. He bent, placing a whisper-soft kiss on her hand before pulling her down to his side and tucking her delicate arm in his. Turning to face his family, he boomed loudly for all to hear, "King Frit Borau and Queen Alene Borau, I present my bound betrothed, Lady Strella Hollythorn."

His father and mother stepped forward, each kissing Lady Strella's cheek as a sign of approval before his father spoke to the crowd. "We are overjoyed to welcome our son's bound betrothed into the royal family. May their union be swift and blessed, for themselves and their land."

Applause rose in the tight entry space, and Ghel skimmed the crowd, looking for the men and women he'd discussed with Jarok and Cylian earlier in his sitting room. He had a plan, and part of the plan was to direct attention to certain friendly and useful lords and ladies in attendance. He caught the eye of Lord Hollythorn, hovering close to the royal family with a smug, satisfied look on his cold face. Ghel thought some warmth was there when he looked at his daughter but couldn't be certain, especially with all he knew of the Fae. His lip started to curl but he pulled it back into his neutral mask. No growls or barks or curling lips this evening.

He looked down at his formally and magically betrothed and saw her looking at her father with a sad smile. Leaning down close to her ear, he whispered, "Are you ready, Lady Strella?" wanting to make sure she was indeed prepared for their dance. He didn't miss the hard quiver of her muscles this time, and a thrill of excitement racked through his own body at the feel of her, so close and so affected. She visibly swallowed and gave a small nod before looking toward the tall ballroom doors.

Ghel led them, from the foyer into the ballroom, positioning Strella in the very center of the massive dance floor before easily turning her in his strong arms. His hold was intentionally gentle, soft, as he placed his hands at her waist and shoulder, getting them into position. Luckily, dancing was no issue for the prince. It was one of the few formal activities he enjoyed because it was physical. Here and now, however, the physicality of it and his proximity to this partner who had such a pull for him, one he needed to tread lightly around, made his body feel more clumsy than usual. Still, he righted his body and mind, and as soon as the strings sounded, he stepped lightly toward his betrothed. She countered, stepping back and leaning away, and a part of Ghel wanted to stalk her, hold her tighter in both arms, and make sure she never stepped away from him again. The sudden urge was startling, and for the first time, Ghel suspected where dancing came from, the push and pull of need from which it originally grew. He grinned. It was all part of the battle, after all, and he was very good at pursuit in battle.

Lady Strella stared up at him, missing a step as she looked hard into his face, but he moved her pliable body easily with his own, never missing a beat as they moved together across the dance floor. "Lady?" he asked, worried something was amiss.

Lady Strella blinked her eyes, and he watched her refocus, her face and body becoming more controlled, more measured. "Forgive me, my prince," she said, looking over his shoulder as she spoke. "I was momentarily distracted."

A not-so-small part of him hoped she was distracted for the same reasons he was, but he dared not voice the thought. "No need for apologies, Lady Strella. Apologies are only required when offense is given."

"Your mother told me something similar days ago," she said, still not looking at him. He ached for her blue eyes to land on his, but he did not push for it.

"It is a sentiment she often rails against," he said, fondness leaking into his voice. He loved his mother, her fierceness, her strength, and her love for his father and his brother and himself.

"A true sentiment indeed." There was quiet for several beats, a fleeting glimpse of startling blue before her eyes caught on something in the distance, and she went forward with conversation. "You dance beautifully."

Ghel almost missed a step of his own at the way the compliment hit his chest, but he forged ahead. "Thank you, Lady Strella."

Her eyes locked on his, his breath whooshing from his body at the second impact to his chest in seconds, and she whispered, "You called me Strella the other day. In the library. After..." Her cheeks turned a lovely shade of pink, and she looked away.

"Do you wish for me to call you Strella?" Even to his own ears, his question sounded strained.

"Yes," she said, becoming firm in her look and her words.

"Very well. You shall also call me Ghel." It was a declaration, a decree, and the tether connecting them twanged somehow, became tighter. As did Ghel's arms. He pulled her closer, her soft chest meeting his hard bulk, and another delicious gasp he'd later savor left her lips. He smiled, big and true and broad. She matched his smile with her own, and they twirled through the last few seconds of strings before coming to a stop in the center of the floor, breath a touch too deep, eyes locked, and arms tight. Somehow, they were unable to let go until other couples filtered into their space, crowding the floor for the next dance.

P rince Ghel made several rounds, and he thanked the stars he'd formed a battle plan with Cylian and Jarok beforehand. The two other Fae men's knowledge of who was there and what their behavioral tics were gave Ghel the confidence to navigate every situation. He successfully avoided unknowns and found his partner, Strella, to be more than prepared for the social scrimmages they faced.

In fact, he was awed by her. She was graceful and kind, remembered small bits about Fae she knew in passing, asked questions of those she'd never encountered, listened attentively whenever someone was talking, and added her own voice to the conversation in a way that did not overshadow but did allow her personality to shine. She was a wonder to behold, flitting with him from group to group, a general in her own way. Ghel found himself mesmerized by her, not just her looks but her wit and thoughtfulness and sincerity in a sea of Fae he often considered the most insincere in his kingdom. It made him question himself and his assumptions, though time for self-examination was not currently at hand. The couple had at least one more hour of small talk to navigate before the ball was to end.

Ghel, lost for a moment as he strode with Strella on his arm, was jolted back when she stopped in place. He followed her stare, noting the strain of concern on her face, and saw Lady Piris and his brother talking in a darkened, empty corner. Not simply talking, no, as Ghel recognized the hard, angry stance of his brother.

Without hesitation, he stalked toward the duo no one else seemed to notice, maybe stalking a little too hard as Strella trailed behind him. Lady Piris, facing the crowd, saw their approach first and straightened from the lean she'd held, a lean putting her own scowl right in Jarok's face. "My prince, Lady Strella," she muttered as they came within hearing distance and dropped a quick curtsy and bow.

Jarok did not turn. Hands clenched at his sides in hard fists, he gritted out, "Brother. Lady Strella."

"What have you done, brother?" Ghel was certain Jarok's flippant attitude had ruffled Lady Piris's feathers. He didn't need that, with the way Strella looked at her lady-in-waiting with such deep concern and care. They were close, maybe as close as he and his brother.

"It's nothing, Prince Ghel," Lady Piris said dismissively while eyeing his soon-to-be bride. He suspected a whole conversation passed between them, with Strella looking none-too-pleased with her friend.

Jarok's cold laugh, the cutting one he reserved for harsh moments in environments such as this, whipped around the quartet. "Nothing on my end, I assure you, brother."

"Doubtful," Ghel growled, command leaking into his voice, Jarok becoming an errant soldier he wished to reprimand for jeopardizing the mission.

"Of course, my oh-so-wise prince," he said, turning his heat on his brother and giving a mocking bow. "How could I forget? I am always the one at fault."

Ghel loved Jarok, but when he was determined to fight, with words or weapons, he would fight. There was no talking him down, no sidestepping. "Brother—"

"Prince Jarok. My apologies," Strella said, wading into the crackle of energy now passing between the royal brothers. "I know you were in conversation, but I have need of my lady-in-waiting." She placed a delicate hand against his chest, looking on him with those icy eyes, and part of Ghel wondered what she saw there, what she might appreciate more than when she looked on his usually harsher face. "May I take her away with me?"

Jarok, swinging eyes around the three people, hurt and anger and something else flaring for Ghel to read, said nothing. Shocking, indeed. He nodded and stepped back, sweeping his arm in a grand gesture toward Lady Piris, who was half snarling at the Fae as he did so. Strella moved with surprising speed, locking her arm with the other lady's and muttering, "We'll return in a few moments," before moving Lady Piris toward the doors of the ballroom with a firm grip on her arm.

"What is wrong with you?" Ghel hissed when they were out of hearing. "We all need this night to go well. All of us, Jarok." They'd discussed this fact earlier in the day, and their continued need for alliances given the looming Monti threat, which meant good behavior amongst the crowd gathered. Cylian was helping behind the scenes, as was Jarok, smoothing the way for more formal talks of support and alliances. Ghel needed to maintain appearances, do the best he could, and marry as he was sworn to do. Still, all needed to remain vigilant and true to their end goal: a fortified front against the encroaching clan wars.

Jarok shook, his hands unusually glittery as they unclenched and came to rub down his face. "Brother, I apologize. Lady Piris is not what you think."

This made Ghel freeze, inside and out. Was Strella hiding something from him with her lady-in-waiting? He had his own secrets, secrets she surely would not appreciate, but they were all in service of his family and kingdom. Ghel couldn't imagine Strella intentionally doing something devious or harmful. But could she?

"Explain. Now."

"She's a warrior" was all Jarok said.

Ghel stared at his brother for a beat then asked, "How in the gods did you not realize that the first time you met her?" It had been obvious to Ghel, a warrior himself, by her bearing and focus. He didn't understand what his brother was going on about.

"I did, actually, as I met her skulking around the palace in fighting leathers the first night they arrived, even before we met them at tea."

This was more news, and somewhat disconcerting. "Do you think her a spy?"

Jarok considered it for a moment. "I do not know. I know she hides things. Her intention behind it is unknown. She could simply be a guard for Lady Strella, which I would not begrudge her for having. If she is more, for Lady Strella or Lord Hollythorn, I can't yet say."

"Why are you just now telling me this?" Ghel asked, his voice a low grumble.

"Because you have enough to worry on, especially if she is simply a secret guard for your lady. I will handle this, brother. Do not concern yourself with it."

"Very well, but handle it more discreetly. Your near argument might not have gone unnoticed."

Jarok looked around then, as if remembering where he was and what they were about. "Damnit, Ghel, I'm sorry. I will restrain myself better in the future."

Ghel knew he would but didn't say as much. He gave his brother a small smile as he bumped his shoulder with his own, maybe a little too hard, as Jarok nearly fell over. The brothers laughed. Jarok slung an arm across Ghel's shoulder and whispered, "Let us forget drama for a moment until your betrothed returns. Have a decent chat with father, mother, and Cylian, who've somehow managed to sequester themselves over by the food tables."

Chapter Six
Strella

"What have you done, Peep?" Strella whispered in her best friend's ear as they exited the ballroom and headed down a less crowded hallway. They bypassed the ladies' waiting room and continued, Piris eventually taking the lead and ushering them into an empty room much farther from the dancing and noise.

"I've done nothing," Piris said, her voice and her cross-armed stance full of exasperation. "It is that infuriatingly nosy prince. He follows me. Corners me. Asks too-pointed questions. Gets too close."

Strella's hand went to her hair, and she twirled it mindlessly. "But why, Piris? What makes him suspect you?"

Piris let out a deep sigh and sat on a small sheet-covered chaise in the middle of the odd, unused sitting room. Dust ruffled up around them, tickling Strella's nose as she sat there and lowered her head in her hands.

She muttered something to Strella, who couldn't hear it, so she moved closer to her friend, poking her playfully in the ribs so the woman peeked back at her from her hands. "Say it, Peep."

"Okay. Okay. I really didn't want to worry you. It is not an issue, I swear. Prince Jarok did catch me out on the first night we were here, while I was doing a perimeter sweep. In my fighting leathers."

"Why didn't you tell me?" Strella cried, rising from the dusty seat and pacing. "Did he see you do anything? Oh gods, did he hear you do anything?"

Piris blocked her friend's pacing with firm hands to her shoulders. "No, Star. He suspects I'm secret security. Likely also suspects I'm a spy. He doesn't know anything else."

Strella sagged against her friend. "If something happened to you because of me—"

"First, I made the choice to come here. You actively discouraged it. If anything were to happen here, which I highly doubt, it would not be on you. Second, I can handle myself against the prince." Piris spit out the last word as if it tasted rotten in her mouth.

"I trust you and your abilities. I worry."

"Because you love me," Piris said with a smile.

"Exactly," Strella said, hugging her dear friend to herself tight, not wanting to let go but knowing they had to return to the ball before anyone, including the princes, came looking for them and became more suspicious.

Strella sighed. "Come. We must return." She sneezed and wiped at a few stray tears falling from her eyes thanks to the dust in the air. Waving at her face, she said, "Maybe we can use this mess to end our time at the ball a little early."

"You don't wish to dance more with your prince?"

"I think it will be better for us all if I do not."

"Why? You looked happy to be in his arms." Piris took Strella's hand and held it tight before she continued. "You know, I worry for you as well. Not because of the warrior prince, who I think will be a good match for you after meeting him. I worry you will not let yourself have this match. Not truly."

Strella pulled her hand free. "You know I cannot."

"I know you believe that you cannot. Whether you can or not is up for debate."

Strella moved toward the door, wanting this conversation and the feelings it raised to end quickly. She knew she could come to care for the prince. After their dance, she felt he might be able to find something pleasing in her as well. She could not allow it to happen, for his sake. "I think few would argue with the words of Seer Willow, Peep. She was clear in her prediction. I will die the same age as my mother. This very year. All I need to do is hold out a while longer, then everyone else can move on without me."

"Star..." Piris's tone was tight and unyielding, but Strella wasn't in the mood to argue once again with her friend about this. Piris was the only one who knew her secret. The one Fae who knew years ago the famous Seer Willow found her in the holly grove in her home to give her a special prophesy: she would not die like her mother but would die the same age as her mother. Whether or not a famous Fae seer should have told a lone eight-year-old such a thing may have been debatable, but the accuracy of her other predictions were not. It had become Strella's duty to make her impact small, to ensure she affected as few people as possible so her death would not cause the same hurt as her mother's. The hurt she still saw lurking in her father's eyes. Hurt she herself had caused going into this world in the first place.

She'd leave behind no children. Had wished to leave behind no husband. The last part of her plan had become thwarted, but she hoped Ghel's honor and duty would see him through, and to another woman he chose to be his wife.

The secret she kept, even from her best friend, was the shudder of her body whenever the prince neared. And the way her heart was beginning to tell her mind a little harmless physical affection might be okay as long as she minimized the prince's expectations and shielded his heart.

When the two returned to the ballroom, not much had changed. They spied the royal family together across the room, Lord Cylian Padalist with them, and headed toward the group.

"What do you think Lord Padalist is about here?" Piris whispered.

Strella shrugged. "He's a diplomat, so I assume he has official business."

"For Autumnlands or in service of the Winterlands?"

"Why not both?" Strella asked.

Piris snorted as if it were absurd, and Strella thought it might well be. Everyone in Fae knew the Autumnlands' Lord Padalist was no true friend to any other court, nor to his own people. Lord Cylian's charm gained him friends and entry, though his welcome often ran out when he was pressed into actual business for his father. He looked comfortable here, as if he were truly welcomed and enjoyed. He appeared to be friends with the princes, and Strella hoped so. Lord Cylian had always been kind to her, funny and thoughtful and articulate in their meetings, and she hoped he had true friends in a life that seemed rather dire from her view. Then again, she had little room to talk, given her constant thoughts of death and how it would find her.

They reached the five Fae chatting amongst themselves as her father also swooped in from behind them, coming to grab Strella's unoccupied arm and tugging it in a harsh but silent move, forcing her to move in step with him the last few feet.

"My King, Queen, Princes, and Lord Cylian," her father greeted, bowing low. "The ball has been a grand tribute to our alliance."

King Frit nodded, a half smile on his face, but said nothing. Neither did anyone else, though harder looks passed between her father and Queen Alene, who had a small, reddish-brown kestrel perched on her left shoulder. The bird ruffled its feathers and flapped its wings, but the royals gave it no mind.

The thread of magic tying Strella to Ghel twanged in her chest, and she looked at her betrothed, his brows in a deep V as he stared at the place where her father's arm looped in hers. He stepped forward, and with harsh grit in his voice, said, "I will take Lady Strella, Lord Hollythorn. She is now my responsibility."

Her father's eyes narrowed at the words, and she heard the sizzle of light dancing in her father's grasp. Surely, he wouldn't fling magic at the prince for stating how things have changed... Her father had bound her to him; he knew the rules and etiquette. Why pull against it when it was too late?

A tense moment passed, but it passed. Piris had long stepped aside to watch from behind, and her father took his arm from hers. Before he left, he bent to kiss her cheek, a fatherly sign of affection she was as used to as the birds of prey in the royal family, but one rarely bestowed in public. Her father was distant, always had been, but there were glittering moments she cherished when he showed he cared, such as this one.

Then he turned on his heels and, without leave, walked away from the royal family. The rudeness and incivility of the act made her stare after him. He'd drilled etiquette into her head from a young age, so to see him not adhere to it was startling. Strella pulled on the training herself, placed a soft smile on her face, and turned toward the royal family. "Please forgive my father, Your Graces. He seems to not be himself."

"I would not say such," Queen Alene grumbled.

King Frit took Strella's hand and patted it before handing her to his son. "Nothing for you to fret on, dear."

Ghel's face was a harsh mask, but it cleared somewhat when he looked down at her. Oddly, he took her cheek in one of his large hands, sending a zap of feeling racing from her face right down her spine. "Have you been crying?" he asked, tilting her face up to look deeply into her eyes, so deeply she feared he could see right to her soul and her secrets.

"Oh, no, my prince. I encountered some dust earlier in a corner of the ladies' waiting room, which often makes my eyes water."

He hmphed at her and turned to his family to declare, "The ball will end early."

Prince Jarok laughed but turned it into a cough when his mother and her bird both pointed dark, fixed eyes in his direction. "As you wish, son," King Frit said, and the king and queen moved toward the dais at the edge of the room, to end the festivities a little earlier than planned.

"You did not need to end the ball itself. I could—"

Ghel waved one hand while he gave Strella's a light squeeze with his other. "I am more than ready to end the ball. If you do not feel well, more reason to do so."

Strella stared at his profile as the prince watched his father and mother thank the guests and officially close the evening, battling how she should feel about this strong and apparently thoughtful Fae. She knew what she was beginning to feel, but she was unsure if she should allow herself to feel it, for his own sake.

S trella was woken early by Piris the next morning, much earlier than she would be expected to wake after a late ball night. "Get up, Star," her friend called from the closet doorway, ripping her from sleep. "The royal messenger just informed me we were supposed to be in the throne room ten minutes ago."

Strella jolted upright in bed, suddenly wide awake. "What? Why?"

She rolled from her bed and moved to the window, noting the hazy tendrils of light reaching across the horizon. It was barely sunup, and she knew no reason why the king and queen would need her in the throne room so urgently at such an early hour, or why no one would tell her of it. Running her fingers through her messy hair, she asked Piris, "What do you think this is about?"

Piris looked angry and unsure all at once. "No idea, and I don't like it, but get dressed. Quick. We can't leave the king and queen waiting."

S he received questioning looks from King Frit and Queen Alene when she entered the throne room and made her way to the central dais where they sat. The princes stood behind them, tall and proud, giving away nothing. Yet another surprise was the presence of her father at the bottom of the steps leading up to the throne, smiling widely at her.

She and Piris hurried forward, dipped low in front of the royals, and waited for instruction as they should.

"Please, Ladies Strella and Piris. Rise," King Frit said, his voice calm and soothing, if a little weak.

The queen, and the snowy owl on her shoulder, looked between the two women and Lord Hollythorn, her face bleeding into a deep scowl. "She does not know," she declared, further confusing Strella.

Her father smirked at the queen and said, "I did not feel it relevant nor necessary as there are many quite valid reasons for her to never need to know."

Ghel growled and his powerful body flexed as if preparing to strike. He was beyond angry about something, her father had hidden something from her, and all the royals were confused. She needed answers and to defuse whatever situation she'd been thrust into this morning.

"Forgive me, my queen. If someone could inform me why I am here so early, I would greatly appreciate it."

"Dear girl, we thought you were told of the ceremony and knew it would be today. We do apologize for what now appears to be a sudden call," the king replied.

"There is a particular ceremony among my people," the queen said. "A betrothal ceremony separate from the magical binding. I promised my father, long ago, all children I bore would adhere to a few of our traditions from the Aurora Clan, and this is one of them."

"I would be honored to help you fulfill your promise," Strella said with quickness and true sincerity.

The queen smiled warmly at her. "I suspect you will, but it is not an easy task, and I do wish you would have been given forewarning. Alas, there is no time."

"Whatever is required of me, I will do."

"You must travel to Aurora Outpost with Ghel for the ceremony, which is to occur at some point within the three-night span of the waning moon, new moon, and waxing moon. Meaning, my dear, you must travel there today to ensure you make the deadline. Ghel can explain more particulars of the ceremony along the way."

All seemed fine to Lady Strella, and she was unsure why everyone was angry about her lack of knowledge. "Piris and I will be ready to leave immediately, Your Graces."

"No, Lady Strella," the queen said. "You and Ghel are to go. Alone. Prince Jarok and I can't travel with you because of our current obligations here." She looked at her husband, worrying clouding her face for a second, and Strella understood why they needed to remain close.

Strella's heart thudded at the idea of being alone so long with the prince. Piris seemed equally worried, but for her own reasons. "Your Graces, may I request—"

Prince Jarok's voice was hard when he interrupted her. "No, Lady Piris. You may not. You are to stay here, at the Winterlands Palace, as only those connected with the Aurora Clan can attend a fasting. Prince Ghel and Lady Strella should be gone one evening. I believe my brother, your prince, is warrior enough to care for her without you."

Piris bit her lip and hung her head, which gave Strella some relief. She knew all too well Piris could be snarky with Prince Jarok when she wanted, but not in the throne room in front of the king and queen.

Her father, distant until then, moved to her side. "Are you truly fine with the arrangement? I can demand you stay. Postpone the ceremony until the next new moon. Given current circumstances, such a trip is not necessarily safe. I only wish to keep you safe, daughter."

The queen gave a sharp laugh. "Your gambit then, Lord Hollythorn? Relying on your daughter's fear? Your daughter seems made of sterner stuff. As you well know, there are other issues to discuss business with the Aurora Clan as soon as possible. Prince Ghel and Lady Strella must leave this day."

Lord Hollythorn's eyes crackled for a fraction of a second, and Strella knew the queen's words to be true. Her father had set them up for failure, be it for true concern for her safety, overprotectiveness, or something else. She centered herself, quieted the voice in her mind saying she shouldn't be alone with the prince, and stood tall in the face of her father. "I am fine, Father. I will help the queen keep her word and honor the traditions of the family of my betrothed."

His jaw flexed, the flutter in his cheek one she might only notice because she was so familiar with the hidden signs of his icy anger when it came. He dipped his chin before stepping away and leaving without a word when the king and queen dismissed him, the hard clips of his steps echoing in the nearly empty chamber. He behaved oddly with the royals, same as last evening, and Strella had no idea why he would act in such a manner. When he'd explained the marriage contract to her, he spoke of connection and power, elevating the family in the Winterlands to royals. Why then was he hovering so close to rudeness with the family he wished to align himself with by marrying his daughter to Ghel? Strella originally thought simply being in the palace, in close contact with the royals, would allow her father into their good graces with his cool and pleasant manners so even if she put off actual marriage until the prophecy was fulfilled, he could have what he seemed to desire from all this: a close relationship with the Boraus. Now, however, his behavior, stretching closer to insolence by the day, would ensure their dislike of the lord. Why then was he doing all of this? Why be so determined to see his daughter married into this family?

It was something to think on later, however. Now was a time to plan. Looking up at her queen, she said, "How long do I have to prepare, and what do I need?"

"First, you need much warmer clothes. You'll be traveling by sled," the queen said. At least there was that. She'd finally get to ride in a dog sled.

Chapter Seven
Ghel

The magical string connecting Ghel to Strella thumped hard in his chest, and a glow radiated through his body at the sight in front of him. Strella knelt, clad in a thick white bear-fur coat, a practical woolen dress and breeches, solid leather gloves, and sturdy boots, letting a group of highly trained and sometimes vicious dogs lick her face and jump excitedly around her. Beaut, the female leader of his sled dog pack, did not often take to strangers. Today, however, she was so enamored with Strella, she didn't seem able to control herself, bumping hard into her side as if she had no training whatsoever and toppling the crouching Fae lady to the dirty stable ground.

Ghel immediately whistled harshly at his dog pack, who instantly stopped their excited yelps and jumps, dropping low to lie on the floor, though they still surrounded Strella. Inconvenient, that, when he was trying to step over them to help her to her feet.

He faintly smelled the barn, dusty and dirty and filled with various unpleasant animal odors. Somehow, Strella's fresh scent, a smell reminiscent of oranges and winter evergreens locked in frost, overpowered the barn smell. Ghel couldn't help himself. He moved closer, breathed deep, and tried to mask his need to feel her hair once again by gently plucking a stray bit of straw from the strands at her temple. "Lady Strella, are you hurt?"

A gorgeous pink stained her cheeks, and a lovely light filled her ice-blue eyes. Now righted, she laughed, the sound of bells calling a Fae to worship, then replied, "I am well, Ghel. I should have been more careful. I simply couldn't help myself. They're so sweet."

"They do seem to like you, Lady," he said, "but they are highly trained dogs who can attack when called upon to do so or if they are provoked. It is best to be careful in their presence."

"These adorable things?" Strella said with disbelief. "Surely not," she whispered as she ran a hand lovingly over Beaut's head, which nearly hit the shorter Fae's chest. The dog gave a soft whimper and leaned into the touch, asking for more. The lady gladly complied, digging in to scratch the giant dog's ears, making her tongue loll out of her head and her eyes close in happiness. Ghel never imagined he'd have reason to be jealous of a dog, but there he was, wishing Strella would so freely and happily touch him.

"What's your name, beautiful girl?"

"You are close, actually," Ghel said, finally stepping up to Strella and placing a hand gently on her back. "This girl here, all white with blue eyes, is Beaut, and she is the pack leader. The similarly white two beside her, with the blue and brown eyes, are her sons: Obie and Eron. The black-and-whites on your left are a mated pair, Rowan and Yew. These are my sled dogs, all selected and carefully trained by my hand."

"Impressive," she said, the single, off-handedly given word burrowing deep into his gut. "And where is your sled?"

Ghel ushered her down a few stalls to the section where their dog sleds were placed. His was made of sturdy black wood, sleek and small for a faster ride. He walked around it, checking all the parts to make sure it was safe and prepared for their journey as she asked questions about the structure and features. As Strella came around the back, she pointed down at the small bundles of reeds tied to the bottom of the sled's feet. "What are those?"

Ghel felt embarrassment creep up his face, but he explained, "They act as brooms of a sort, obscuring the tracks of the sled."

Strella studied them, fascinated by the simple design. "Are they usually included on sleds?"

Clearing his throat and shifting his feet, Ghel stared down at the dirty floor as he said, "No. It is something I added to the standard design."

Strella's head turned toward him, and her smile hit him with the force of a blow. "Clever," she said as she went back to looking over their mode of transport. Ghel couldn't speak for long beats, fascinated by her look and the word she'd given him, and idea no one had ever said about him before. Not in his memory at least. Thinking on her, how sweet and good and kind she was, Ghel couldn't stop himself from giving her an opportunity to end their trip before it began.

"Strella, it is admirable you agreed to our task so quickly without thought to yourself, but you must know more before we leave."

"Tell me," she said, pulling herself straighter at his words.

"With my team, using this sled, the ride to Aurora Outpost is much quicker but by no means quick. It will take at least five hours' time. You will be seated in the front, without much room to move and little protection from the cold." It was a simple sled, after all: a place for the driver to stand at the back with the ends of the long reins to steer the whole and a smallish, tapered flat bed for transporting goods. Or, in this case, an extra person along with two small rucksacks.

Strella looked at the sled. Studied it as if learning every nook and cranny. Then she shrugged, apparently unbothered. "Can I have a blanket?"

"Of course," Ghel answered, moving to a supply cabinet to retrieve a downy white bear fur, which perfectly matched her coat.

"Very well. I shall be fine." She moved to twirl her hair in the way which fascinated Ghel, but her blonde locks were pulled back in a tight bun. Instead, she nervously adjusted, then pulled up her hood before she added a caveat with some hesitation. "It is my first time on a sled, so I may need a break during our journey."

Ghel realized she was afraid to say as much, to cause what she might perceive as trouble or inconvenience. Ghel ached to tell her she could never be a trouble to him but held himself back from such an admission. "There are designated outcroppings, Strella, where sled travelers can stop for rest and to regroup if need be. We will stop a few times along the way, for both our sakes and the dogs'."

Ghel pulled two clean white headscarves from a stack in the supply closet along with shades for eye protection. "You will need these as well."

She efficiently pulled each on without hesitation and adjusted herself accordingly. "Okay. I'm ready," she said, although her words were slightly muffled by the fabric covering her face.

Ghel gave a nod and pulled her to the sled. He sat her down and strapped her into the seat, his hands attempting to be as respectful as possible as he tied her down across her lap. He shook his head out to clear away images forming in his mind of him being this close to her in a very different context. Such thoughts were not for him. Not with her. She need not be bothered with his lustful intrusions.

He gently laid the additional furs on her body, wrapping her as tightly as he could and using both their packs as added protection from the cold to come. "There. You're now as tight as a snow hare in its burrow." Ghel thought he heard a soft chuckle from her, so he gave a small, true smile in return before patting her legs and rising to prep himself.

Swift and practiced, he tied off his dogs and readied himself. "Ready, snow hare?" he asked, the playfulness in his voice surprising him. He was rarely playful, and usually only with his family. Seemed Strella had burrowed her way into him.

She waved a hand in a sign to proceed, and he gave a different, sharper whistle to his team. Beaut, leading the way with her children paired directly behind her and Rowan and Yew in the rear, pulled slowly at first, navigating them out of the barn and the surrounding area, weaving them deftly away from the populated areas until she hit the open road. Then she ran, her team keeping pace, and Ghel was thrilled to hear a clear, loud peel of laughter come from Strella as they took off toward one of his homes in the wilds of the Winterlands.

It was their third and final stop, this pull-off being about ten miles from Aurora Outpost. Good thing for Ghel, because his hands were already freezing from the cold despite his thick gloves. He hoped Strella had fared better.

Once he'd pulled his mask down, he asked, "Strella, are you well?"

"I surely am, Ghel. Just as I was at the previous two stops," she replied as she untied her own restraints and pulled her mask from her face. Her words could have come off as harsh if her dazzling smile and laughing eyes weren't now visible.

"I worry," Ghel grumbled. "You—"

"Are a sheltered lady unused to such rough rides."

"I'd never say such a thing."

"But you would think it?"

Ghel couldn't rightly answer. It was not a harsh judgment on his part, but a judgment he'd made nonetheless. He was worried because of who she was when she'd given him no real reason to do so. "I apologize, my lady," he said with true feeling.

"I accept," she answered. "However, I can't blame you. I admitted I'd never ridden on a dog sled. You have a right to some worry over my experience."

"How has your experience been thus far?"

Strella turned in a circle, taking in their surroundings. The turnoffs for sleds were marked with parallel dark-wooden posts about ten feet apart. In small snow-covered chests made from the same dark wood and warmed by magic, containers of water for riders and their dogs were provided for any in need. They were sparse, open places, used mostly to mark distance and rest momentarily along shorter journeys. Those taking longer journeys generally mapped out caves and such to use overnight, which Ghel himself had done a number of times in his life with his brother and cousins. The land around the Aurora Outpost might look bleak and barren to some, but Ghel knew the land well, could distinguish hill and valley in the white blindness of the snow-covered plane. Knew where every small shelter of trees and deep cave was located so close to his mother's home. Could see the telltale indentations where snow fox dens likely rested and even noted a set of white bear tracks off in the distance, thanks to his honed Fae sight.

However, Ghel knew any Fae unused to the area, or discerning the minute details of winter landscapes so far from towns or villages or manor houses, could not see as much. To someone unused to the vastness of the Winterlands, it was a sea of indiscernible white, so there was little for her to evaluate. So Ghel was surprised when she whispered, "It's gorgeous."

He stared at her, the soft smile on her slightly chapped lips and her eyes closed and her chest rising and falling with deep, purposeful breaths.

When she was finished taking it all in, she elaborated. "It's so vast. So peaceful. It smells like a clean world made fresh and new with ice and snow. I can see so far and see nothing but peace and quiet and home. And us, of course. It's humbling, experiencing a piece of my homeland and understanding how I may never know it fully but can still enjoy it for what I can know."

There was a bit of sadness in her voice, from nowhere Ghel could tell, but she was smiling when she moved closer to him, coming to stand toe-to-toe in order to look up in his eyes. "Thank you."

"For what?"

"For showing me a bit of this world I would have never seen without you," she said.

An ache echoed down their connection. Ghel didn't understand it, but he wanted to erase it permanently from Strella, whatever it was. It strangled him, the need to not only touch but to soothe, even if he had no idea what he was actually soothing. Feeling choked him, making words impossible. All he could give in the moment was action, like the fighter he was.

Really, he couldn't stop himself if he'd tried. He was driven to take away her aches. Also, she'd said such beautiful words about a land he loved so fiercely, and he knew she meant them. Her body, so warm and inviting, wind-tossed from their travels but still gorgeous despite the elements assailing her along the ride, called to him. Her spirit, most of all, drew him in. Before he could think of the many reasons not to do so, he gave in to his growing impulses, taking her in his arms and bending her back across his strong hold as he leaned forward. He hesitated as he looked into her face, asking without words if they could pretend. She was breathless, the look on her face echoing his uncertainty. Still, he was once again surprised when she closed the scant distance between them, putting her lips oh so gently against his.

It was a jolt of lightning straight to his groin. The taste of her was frost and snow and starlight, power and softness mixed on her lips. He swallowed the gasp she released and pressed more firmly to her lips, needing to be closer to her. She moved tighter into his chest, and he let out a sound of his own, a growl that was a plea for this to never end, for the fire painfully running riot through his system to keep raging all of his long life.

He coaxed her mouth open with quick nips of his teeth and slipped his tongue inside, reveling in the deeper taste of her. His hands clenched around her, his frame nearly engulfing her in his hold. He wanted to wrap himself around her fully and never let go. This was not his first kiss, but the moment his lips touched hers, he knew no other would ever compare. It was what a kiss was supposed to be, and every part of his being screamed for him to keep it going, to never stop. Especially the string connecting their chests, which vibrated so much, it made its own soft music in his mind.

Pain seared through his back shoulder, mere inches above his heart, and for a split second he thought it was from the passion released with their kiss. When Strella let out a yelp and pulled away to look down at her own chest he thought more on it, felt the sear more fully. Then he saw the arrow protruding out of his chest. Small red dots of blood marred the pristine white of Strella's furs, and his world turned from lust to violence in a stuttered heartbeat.

Chapter Eight
Strella

S trella's mind reeled from the kiss. It was not her first, though she admittedly had little experience. Stolen kisses and soft touches here and there with younger lords at various functions at Hollythorn Manor. She'd never done more. Not because she didn't enjoy the kisses or thought herself pure. The Fae did not believe pleasure should be curtailed in many regards. However, she'd spent her life walling herself off from others, protecting them from her eventual and inevitable demise. She didn't wish to create more connection, more feeling, or more opportunities for others to be devastated by her loss in the way her father was forever devastated by her mother's death. She owed the world that much.

However, all the caution and distance and reason she so easily employed with most other Fae evaporated as soon as Ghel's lips gently touched hers. She'd reached for him. Breached the tiny distance he'd left between them as a question. Strella had done so on instinct, or maybe the tug of their magical connection. Whatever it was, as soon as her mouth touched Ghel's, all thoughts of what should be done fled. All that remained was feeling, deep and warm and inviting. The type of feeling someone could fall into forever and never wish to leave. Her magic agreed, pushing forward and pounding in her chest to the frantic beat of her heart, likely shining through the layers of clothes between the two of them, though she would never pause to check.

What did force her to pause was the sudden jolt to her chest. A tiny prick of pain scared a yelp from her. She was in her body, fully feeling all the delicious things Ghel pulled from her, when an impact drove Ghel into her and a twinge hit her shoulder where Ghel's massive chest bent forward over her much shorter frame. She moved back, confused, and saw it: a huge arrow sticking out of Ghel's chest, right above his heart.

Strella screamed. She couldn't help it. She'd never seen someone shot with an arrow, and it was jarring to say the least.

Ghel's eyes, clouded with lust seconds before, snapped into a cold focus, reminding her of the queen and her birds of prey once again. "Down!" he yelled, shoving her none too gently down to her knees as he spun around to find the source of the arrow.

Blood dripped down his back, and the quiver of the arrow rippled with every breath and movement. Strella stomped down the rising bile in her throat and surveyed the scene for any sign of attackers.

It didn't take long for her to see them. Arrows were flying in a high arc above them, and the wind carried with it faint sounds of Fae. Their small forms dotted the landscape now, a group of ten Fae standing along the horizon in an arch, positioned between her, Ghel, and the direction of the Aurora Outpost, according to their past navigation, all with bows trained right on her and the prince.

Ghel cursed and threw himself on top of Strella, then rolled them away so the arrows thudded into the hard packed snow, where Ghel had stood, rather than right into him. The dogs growled and whined to be released from their ties, ready to defend.

"What is happening?" Strella asked. It was clear they were under attack from a group of archers. Who the archers were and why they were attacking them were the real questions swirling in Strella's mind, but she had little wherewithal to express them.

Ghel grunted, staying planted on top of her and rising enough to lift his chest from her. He ignored her question and instead gave her clear instructions. "Strella, I need you to reach behind my back and grasp the shaft of the arrow. Hold it firm and tight for me."

She did as he said, gripping the arrow's rigid wood in her hand, holding it as tightly as she could, as Ghel moved his own hand up to his chest. He snapped the head off the arrow, the force causing Strella's hand to jerk, but she kept it closed around the shaft without jostling it too much.

"Now, I need you to pull the arrow out from my back."

"Won't that cause you to bleed out?" The arrow went so close to his heart. There were any number of ways the wood and metal could have done damage they could not see from the outside. To her, it seemed far more logical to keep it in until they could get to a healer.

"My magic is already healing me. If I don't do this, my body will knit itself around the arrow."

Ah, yes. She'd forgotten. When she'd first heard about her intended betrothal to the prince, Piris had given her all the information she knew regarding Ghel, including the fact his magic manifested as self-healing. A handy trait for a warrior. An especially handy trait in this moment, Strella thought, because there was little she could do to help the much-larger Fae if he passed out from blood loss or the like.

She didn't waste any more time. Breathing deep, she pulled the wood from his flesh, dislodging it with a swift, straight pull. Once she felt it free, she threw the offending thing from her hand. She couldn't help but watch it fall off to their right, watch the blood litter the snowy ground as it landed softly. It was such a small thing compared to Ghel, but able to do such damage.

Suddenly she was rolled again, to the left, then the right before another volley of arrows landed with a hard thud in the snow where they'd been seconds before.

Ghel cursed. Loudly. Then said, "We need cover." Without more explanation, he jumped to his feet in one graceful, powerful motion and scooped Strella tight into his arms. Luckily, they'd yet to untie the dogs for their rest, and Ghel sprinted right for the sled, flinging the white cover around Strella before setting her on her feet in front of his standing position. "Brace yourself. We need to do this quickly."

She had no time to confirm and little time to comply. She'd planted her feet on the small sliver of wood in front of Ghel's and gripped the handles of the sled tight when Ghel gave a harsh whistle and the dogs took off, bounding toward the open snow and away from where the arc of archers were scrambling to follow. They didn't appear to have dogs of their own, so they soon trailed far behind, though not far enough behind for Strella's liking.

Luckily for them, Ghel knew this land like he knew the palace. Strella marveled at his command of the dogs, his deft maneuvering at such speeds, and the way they glided over hills and dips and lost the other Fae in minutes. Her mind reeled at what had happened: the kiss, so raw and real and warming to her soul, followed by chaos, blood, and violence. The first several minutes of their frantic ride away, she barely breathed, afraid the sky would once again erupt with arrows at any second, until Ghel leaned down and said, "I think they have fallen too far behind to detect us now."

She hadn't seen sleds or dogs or even horses, though she knew horses did not fare nearly as well in these more untamed parts of the Winterlands. She'd seen little, true, but she thought she would surely have recognized dog sleds at an archer's distance, which was not exceedingly far for the average Fae's keen eyes.

Ghel's words calmed her, allowed her to think through what happened and the implications. If she saw no sleds, there were two possibilities: the archers had trekked out to the wilds of the Winterlands on foot and sat waiting gods knew how long, or they had steeds or dogs at a distance to not give away their position. The second option seemed far more likely, which also meant the Fae had to return to their transport and then follow whatever tracks had been left by her and Ghel. However, given Ghel's ingenious and unique sled design, they'd left no tracks, or at least none the average Fae could detect. Whether these archers were average Fae was the real issue.

As they slowed slightly, traversing a series of small hills and dips Strella hadn't noticed in the distance, she wondered why she wasn't more concerned. She didn't need to worry for Ghel; his healing would work well now that he was free from the arrow. She'd have thought she'd be more worried for herself, actually, but she wasn't. She worried about who attacked them and why, worried about how they would get to the Aurora Outpost in time to complete the ceremony, and worried about the stamina and needs of the sled dogs who'd seen them to safety. She realized she had little worry for herself or her safety. Not when she was with Ghel.

The dogs, steered by flicks of Ghel's wrists, eventually led them to a small valley where a five-foot hole was etched into ice and rock. The dogs ran directly inside as Ghel bent forward so he and Strella comfortably fit within the small opening. When he pulled up, she saw they'd entered a large ice cave, about ten feet high and filled with icicles as wide as her dangling from the ceiling. Ghel lifted her easily, setting her aside and stalking to the opening to stare into the distance a few beats. He reached into an inner pocket of his fur coat and handed Strella a kindle stick. "Can you light this?" he asked.

Strella, offended by the question momentarily before she remembered the prince had never actually seen her use magic, answered by snapping a spark over the dried stick, causing a flame to catch and dance between them. Ghel untethered his dogs before moving to the edge of the opening and rolling a large, carved rock she'd just noticed over the entrance, where it fit snug so no daylight peeked around the edges.

"Come," Ghel said, moving one large hand to the small of her back as he scooped up the tiny flame lighting their way in his other. He gave a soft, low whistle, and the dogs followed as well, their small pants the only noise outside the crunch of boots. Ghel steered them around a corner in the depths of the cave, a hard right turn that opened up into a hallway of sorts, or at least a far more enclosed space. It was straight and narrow and several dozen feet long. He took another hard turn, this time left, and a steep downward slope led them down into the depths of the cavern. Strella felt wetness on her skin and a warmth from ahead before the walls contracted, then expanded into an entryway of sorts.

Ghel stooped by the entrance and touched the dying kindling to the floor, and flame sped across the perimeter of the space via some inlaid mechanism, lighting the huge room from the ground up and revealing a large, steaming pool to Strella. The floor wasn't hewn rock there but intricately laid tile, leading to the large unground tub filled to the brim with clear, clean swirling water. The arched ceiling was short, barely giving Ghel clearance to walk without stooping, which may have been why the warmth lingered so well in the space.

"What is this place?" Strella asked. She'd never seen anything like it, which wasn't too surprising given how little she had seen of her world. But she'd never read about anything like it, which was astonishing to her.

"A diverted hot spring fashioned into a bathing area of sorts. There are a few out here, created long ago by the Aurora Clan, who guard the secret well. They like their solitude and don't wish for visitors invading these sites." He chuckled to himself, as if thinking of some joke, before taking off his coat and placing it on a low bench along the side wall. "Here, Strella. Do sit while I take care of a few more things."

She planted herself on his fur and watched him stalk from the room, his dogs padding behind his heels. Strella had a great deal to think on—what had happened to them, what that kiss meant for her and her plans for distance, and what Ghel may be feeling and how it might crash down on him when she died and how unfair all of it was to him—so her time alone in the space went quickly.

Ghel returned with supplies tucked under one of his massive arms. He gingerly laid them out on the bench beside her without a word: a small cheesecloth filled with food, the additional furs and blankets they had, and her rucksack. "I didn't know if you needed anything from your sack this evening," he muttered as she rubbed a hand over her bag.

"Are we staying here tonight?"

Ghel's eyes hardened. "Yes. I think it may be safer to wait out our attackers here, for at least one night."

"Will this interfere with your clan ceremony?" Strella did not want to disappoint him or their queen or their extended family.

Ghel shook his head. "We have this evening and next, but if we cannot complete the ceremony now, there is always the next new moon. Please, don't worry too much about it. We have much larger worries."

Knowing his words were certainly true, she noticed the dogs did not follow. "Beaut and her pack?"

"Stationed at the end of the first hall as guards. They have their pad and will be content there for the evening."

With nothing else to say, she finally asked what she'd wanted to ask since the arrow had pierced his back. "Who attacked us? Why did they attack us?"

Ghel huffed out a sharp breath and sat hard on the bench beside her, close enough his knee almost grazed hers when he turned to look her in the eye. "The Monti Clan."

"An outright attack on the royal family then? Are you positive?"

"Yes. The arrow sported their usual color and design, and I have few other enemies who would dare such an open attack."

Strella was stunned. Of course she knew about the issues with the Monti Clan and its clan leader, Engad Monti. He'd been in quiet rebellion for a while now, long enough for the lords and ladies frequenting her father's parties to talk about it more and more. She'd even asked her father about it once, though he'd dismissed her concern and told her not to worry about such things.

Luckily, Piris's father did not treat his daughter the same and had told her what was what; the Monti Clan was attempting to overtake all the other warrior clans in the Winterlands, and they were winning battle after battle as they marched against each. They'd started with the smaller clans, taking each out or folding them into their own when they surrendered. Now the three most powerful clans were all that stood in their way: the Auroras, the Windins, and the McClarry Clans. However, the Montis were united, whereas the others were not, even if they were united under a would-be tyrant.

"Is—was this the first direct attack on you or your family?"

"Yes," Ghel said, "which tells me Monti grows bolder, possibly more ambitious."

Strella nodded, processing the information before an idea struck her. "Do you think it's because of our impending marriage?"

Ghel eyed her a moment, not speaking, before he leaned his head against the wall of the steamy room and said, "It is possible, though I have reason to doubt it."

She sat thinking through the information and the implications. She may be to blame for the new aggression, but Ghel didn't think so. Granted, he knew much more about the issues at hand than she did, but she still felt a direct attack on them meant they both were involved somehow, even if she didn't have all the facts a royal might have. However, she felt uncomfortable pushing him, as she often did with her father, so she tried her best to let the ideas go. The heat seeping into her clothes, warming her chilled bones, relaxed her more and more, allowing her to let more of her stress slide. There was one thing, however, she could not let go of, not until she saw it with her own eyes. "Very well. Now, let me examine your wound."

Ghel bristled. "It is fine."

"I will judge whether it is fine. Come, let me see."

She moved away a fraction, giving him space to move his arms freely. He hesitated but eventually complied, unhooking his heavy wool shirt and pulling it over his head. Strella sat frozen, staring. There was blood on his chest, smeared and dried, but no wound. "Turn," she said, her words sticky in her mouth at the sight of Ghel without his shirt. He grumbled but complied, twisting so she could see the back of his shoulder was the same as his chest, smeared with dried blood but otherwise whole. Also, very tightly muscled and heaving with quick intakes of breath.

Strella couldn't help herself, once again. She reached a trembling hand out to his shoulder. A zap of awareness rode through her body at the contact, and the twang of their connection sounded loud in her ear. Leaning farther when she felt his body shudder, she laid her palm on his back, tracing the spot where the arrow had been, then moving down his muscles to feel more of him.

Ghel whipped around fast as lightning and grabbed her hand at the wrist, holding it in the empty air between them. "Strella," he said, a crack in his voice and the shine in his dark eyes the first hint something else was happening. She felt it then, a different warmth, the one marking her magic in her chest. Looking down, she saw it, the small bit of starlight glowing in the center of her chest, pulsing there along with her heartbeat and pushing light through all her thick layers.

"Sometimes, my starlight glows when I'm, uh, affected," she explained.

Ghel's other hand came up and almost touched her chest, right over where her magic glowed, but he stopped himself. "It is beautiful. Like you."

"Useless." Something she rarely admitted to anyone but something her father had said more than once. Her magic did little but light and warm her.

"Is something beautiful ever useless?" Ghel asked.

"Compared to my father's control of light or your healing magics, I would say so."

"Trust me, Strella. Comparison does no one any good, although I know it is tell yourself that at times."

Strella swallowed hard, the truth she let shine like her magic hanging between them. Ghel had also let the truth slip there, giving them something to cling to together. It was a nod toward how two Fae, so very different from all accounts, shared certain sad thoughts. It made her hurt for him, because she recognized a pain similar to her own. She wanted to do something to take both of their aches away. She pushed up, trapping their joined hands between them, and kissed the prince.

In no time at all, the fire and flame returned, overtaking all other thoughts. Her magic pulsed, the magical connection between them thudded heavy and true, and Strella wanted to feel every part of Ghel on her. In her. She wanted everything with him, this beautifully gruff prince who had his own issues and worries.

He scooped her up in his free arm and held her tightly but gently, before he planted her on his lap, her thighs falling open so she could straddle him. He broke away from their kiss, letting out a hiss as his head hit the wall once again. Strella was too distracted by the sensations she experienced to mark it, and Ghel gave no signal he wished to stop. She rubbed herself against him, felt his arousal, and knew he felt her too, through all their layers of warmth, because of the jerk of his hips upward.

"Strella, we can't—" Whatever he was about to tell her they couldn't do was broken off by her mouth meeting his once again, her tongue dipping deep behind his lips, tasting him and reveling in every drop. She ground down more firmly on him, dragging herself along the hard length she felt in his pants, making her own core feel like needy flames. She'd never felt like this before, never imagined what she knew of sex to feel like this. So raw and driving and filled with its own special type of magic. In the moment she couldn't think about her looming death or what it might mean for Ghel after. She could only feel and need, her mind flipping to something more primal than the fear and worry normally controlling her.

Ghel must have felt the same because he finally disentangled his hand from her wrist and dipped it down to the hem of her dress, sliding it up her thigh and squeezing deliciously. He made his way to her leather breeches and untied them with ease, snaking his hand into her pants. He groaned deep and loud in her mouth when his flesh hit hers, and all she could do was echo his sound.

He continued, dipping into her wet heat, teasing her slick entrance with his large fingers. Strella ripped her mouth away, tipping her head to the ceiling and giving a loud cry at the sensation. It was more than she'd ever felt. Ghel was continually giving her more and more, and she was unsure how she could take it and stay who she was in the end.

Ghel pulled her tighter to him with his other arm, locking her in place and growled up at her, "Mouth." She obeyed, because what else could she do in the moment? She would have done anything he asked to ensure he never stopped.

His hand moved deftly, fluidly, teasing her slightly before finding her clit and giving it a hard, slick stroke. Strella whimpered into his mouth but kept kissing, moaning, and licking, as he'd asked. She'd not be the one to rip them apart. He pressed harder, pausing a moment to hone in, before he stroked in fast circles, no more teasing or coaxing.

She whimpered as pressure built higher and higher, a rope twisting more and more taut until she knew it would snap and cause havoc. He pulled his mouth away, looking up at her with pools of eyes so deep and black, she could get lost in them if she wanted. "I'm going to watch you come, Strella. See your light spill out for me."

She dropped her head to his, leaning forehead to forehead, and let the rope break, felt the release and warmth of it as she yelled her pleasure in Ghel's face. Her magic met the moment, filling the space between them with warm light, engulfing both Fae as Strella's body shook with the amount of pleasure and magic coursing through her veins. When she came down, she noticed Ghel giving soft kisses to her cheeks and chin, whispering barely audible words in a language she didn't know.

"What are you saying?" she asked, her voice hoarse from her yells of passion.

"Never mind, Strella. For another time," he said as he eased his hand free from her pants. He took her head in his large hands and asked, "Are you okay?"

Strella barked out a laugh. "More than okay, Ghel." She wanted more, though, and knew he did as well, if the hard length in his pants indicated anything. She smiled and ground her hips down again, letting herself slide oh so deliciously across his lap.

He stopped her, however. "No, Strella. No need."

"But—" She began to argue, but Ghel cut her off by raising her up and off his lap, setting her down with gentle care on the bench.

"I'll make a pallet for us on the floor," he said, not even looking at her as he moved around the supplies. "Then we need food and sleep. There may be much to do tomorrow."

Strella swallowed her words and her worry, a bit of trepidation coiling in her gut. She wondered if he was unhappy with her, how she'd been. If she'd displeased him somehow. There was something distant in his stance, but he took care of their space. Made a pallet for the two of them before saying, "We'll have to sleep together—for warmth," which didn't make Strella feel better.

He laid out food for them and forced Strella to pick what she wanted first. They then ate in silence before he asked her to prepare for bed. There was little to prepare for, though thankfully there was a small place to relieve themselves hidden behind one of the walls. Ghel told her they were well maintained and cleaned regularly, and he had not lied. She'd still gone quickly. He'd taken a little longer and was noticeably less stiff in certain areas when he returned.

Strella sat on the pallet of furs, twirling her hair between her fingers nervously and not caring a bit about it when he returned. She stretched out as he lay down, letting empty space linger between them.

Throwing the large fur blanket over them both, he scooted forward, sighed, and pulled her against himself, situating her tight against his body as she faced away from him. He gave her a gentle kiss on the crown of her head and whispered, "Sweet dreams to you, Strella."

Strella, however, didn't dream. Not for a while. Instead, she worried and fretted and wondered why Ghel was so cold and so very warm all at once.

Chapter Nine
Ghel

Waking to a small, lush, warm body wrapped around him was a new experience for Ghel. He'd had lovers in his time, usually warriors from other clans or artisans or merchants he met in travels. He steered clear from ladies for a wide variety of reasons. Feeling Strella clinging to him beneath the warm layers of furs, cushioned by more pads and blankets, he felt cozier than he'd ever had in his large, comfortable bed in the palace. The smell of her, like clean water and crystal-clear skies in the snow, was all around him. As was the warmth her small body exuded, a surprising amount of heat and comfort from someone so small.

He shifted his head to look down at Strella, whose face was burrowed deep, her cheek smashed to his broad chest. She looked like the hare he'd called her yesterday, small and delicate and cute in the most heart-melting of ways. He let out a deep sigh and closed his eyes again, bringing his one free hand up to rub his face. Which was a mistake because it still smelled like Strella's slick, wet body. He stilled, taking in the fading smell lingering on his fingers, wanting to savor it. He'd surely savor the memory of it, the delicious little sounds she'd made, the look in her icy eyes as she came... the way her inner walls clenched around him, driving him insane, almost making him lose control and plow into her.

The last bit was why he couldn't allow her to touch him after what they'd done. He'd been barely in control of himself, a chain pulled tight and ready to break at any moment. Strella, ever the graceful lady, deserved so much more than a wild rutting in a dank cave. If he were honest, he thought she deserved so much more than him, a brute who could never be gentlemanly or even gentle with her. Not with the way lust rode his mind and body so hard when she was around.

He thunked his large head back on the ground, a soft thud muted by the pads under them echoing in the space. He feared he'd done a great disservice to Lady Strella the previous night and vowed he would have tighter control over himself, his body, and his emotions, in the future. She may have wanted him physically, but their relationship started as a strategic move by both of their parents, and he needed to remember there was more at stake for each of them, that desire didn't need to always be sated when emotions might be disconnected. He swore, as he held her tight, to protect her from any harm that could come her way. Including harm his bumbling and wild lust might cause her mentally, physically, or emotionally.

"Ghel," Strella mumbled, her head twisting on his chest before she looked up at his hovering face.

He stroked a few loose strands of silky hair from her face, cupped her cheek, and said, "Good morning, Strella."

She smiled shyly up at him, taking a moment to bury her face in his chest. He thought he heard her take a deep breath there, as if scenting him, but he couldn't be certain. Still in his chest, she said something soft and muffled.

"What, Starlight?" he asked, unable to stop himself from the new name, thinking about the delicate light her magic cast and the beauty and warmth and comfort of both it and her.

Strella raised herself up and planted her elbows in his chest to look steadily at him. They bit slightly, but he'd never tell her to move them. There was no way he could force his mouth to say anything that might cause her to put space between them, no matter the vows he made to protect her from himself. With her head cocked, she said, "Piris calls me Star."

"A fitting name, Strella. May I call you Star also? At least sometimes."

Her eyes twinkled with magic and inner light as she whispered, "I'd like that very much, Ghel."

She focused on his lips, licking her own, her tongue darting over the plump pink bow of her mouth enough to almost drag a moan from Ghel. He knew one thing for certain; they couldn't kiss here again. He'd never be able to control himself.

Instead of taking her up on her thoughts, Ghel easily maneuvered them both to sitting, then turned toward the entry and gave a sharp, high whistle. His dogs came bounding in, rested and relaxed after no nighttime attacks. They pounced on Strella, circling her, so Ghel had to let her warm body go or get several paws in the face. She laughed, high and happy, as the ridiculous pack hovered and huffed and barked for her attention. His arms felt emptier than they ever had in his life after letting her go, but the sight of her laughing with his dogs filled him in a different but no less sustaining way.

He took the dogs' distraction to rise from their makeshift bed, quickly and discreetly adjust the erection straining the ties on his leather pants, and move to wash his hands and face in the warm spring. Her steps were light behind him, but the dogs still circled her, and they were not quiet at all, their yips filling the cave.

"Enough, you," he growled at them, clicking his tongue in chastisement. Beaut stopped in an instant to sit at attention. The rest followed suit, giving Strella enough room to move toward the warm pool without Ghel fearing they might trip her up in their excitement. She knelt beside him, her side brushing his, and he couldn't take it, so he shot up like an arrow and moved toward their packs. "Breakfast?" he asked, searching for anything to get his mind off her. He found it as he shuffled through his pack. There was enough food for two meals for each of them, which meant they needed to leave their hiding spot today.

He frowned in thought as he turned and found Strella sitting cross-legged on their pallet, waiting for him to serve her. A lump formed in his throat, thinking about feeding her with his own hand. Or better yet, hunting for their food and then serving it to her. Some sort of primal need welled in him at the idea, but he smashed it down as quickly as it had risen. He had no time for such nonsense, and Lady Strella wouldn't likely appreciate it either way.

He handed her a packet of hard cheese and crusty bread, a simple but fair enough breakfast, as he took a seat as far away from her on the pallet as he could. He couldn't trust himself close to her, yet he couldn't make himself sit too far away. To his rational mind, his reactions seemed ridiculous, but they were what they were, and he had larger worries to focus on, like how to get Strella and himself inside the safe walls of the Aurora Outpost. He saw only one way to do so with any certainty.

"Strella, we need to get to Aurora lands today. After breakfast, I'll take two dogs and the sled, seal the entrance closed behind me with you and the remaining three dogs staying behind as guards, and make my way to the Aurora Outpost. Once there, I'll return with a contingent of Aurora warriors so you can travel in safety."

She broke off a large chunk of bread, topped it with cheese, and popped the whole thing in her mouth. She chewed, looking down at the pallet, though Ghel noticed her brows were knitted together in concentration. "How far are we now from the Aurora Outpost?"

"No more than fifteen miles. However, Aurora guards will be placed at least five miles from the outpost. There may even be a scout searching for us now. It is likely I will find help at a shorter distance. Still, according to weather predictions, more snow is likely to fall today, which could extend the trek."

"Then why must I stay behind? Alone." She looked scared, and it pierced Ghel's guts to see it.

"You'll be safe here. Only the Aurora Clan knows where these baths are located. With the entrance covered, no outsider will know anything rests here. If, however, someone does enter without me, Beaut and her twins will guard you with their lives."

As if on cue, Beaut gave a deep growl and moved up to nudge Strella's cheek with her wet nose. The lady chuckled and patted Beaut's head. "I have no doubts of your bravery or prowess in battle, girl. You are a fierce and true warrior, just like your prince."

Ghel's chest puffed out more at her words, at the idea she thought of him in such a way. Maybe she wanted a more gentlemanly husband, but at least she knew and respected who he was. It was a good start for an arranged marriage.

"I don't worry simply for myself, you know. I also worry for you, Ghel. What if you are attacked before reaching any Aurora guards or scouts?"

"Precisely why you should stay behind. Safe and secure in this hidden cave."

"No, I'm sorry. I cannot and will not do it. There has to be a better way."

"The way forward is to get help from the Aurora Clan as quickly as possible."

"Then we travel there. Together."

Ghel shook his head hard and he felt his face fall in a deep scowl. "It is open snow plains between here and there, Strella. There is no cover, no way to not be a perfect target for more archers."

Strella rubbed her dimpled chin and concentrated. A new light hit her eyes, and Ghel was struck by all the ways her magic shone in her gaze, telling anyone who paid attention what she was thinking or feeling at any given moment. "If we had cover, would you consider taking me with you?"

"I suppose," he admitted, though he knew of no way to get cover, so it seemed a useless point to him.

She jumped up without another word and rushed out the door. Ghel followed close on her heels, though he let her lead with a kindle stick, down the halls and to the sled. Strella stooped to study the structure, testing it with her hands in various points before a sly smile passed her lips. "The dogs do well with ice, yes?"

"They are sled dogs, so, yes. They tolerate ice well."

"Excellent!" she exclaimed, clapping her hands together as she spun around. "First, we undo the standing structure of the sled from the flat pack section. Then we prep the harnesses and reins."

"Why?"

"For cover. If we tie ourselves down to the flat pack, we can use the various white bear covers as camouflage in the snow. Then, we freeze the harnesses and reins, making them more obscured. Finally, we tie off Beaut, Obie, and Eron, allowing the white dogs to lead us. We'd be nearly invisible then, especially if it is to snow today. You and your dogs know this land well. You can lead us to the Aurora Clan, even with cover and snow."

Ghel stood dumbfounded. She'd concocted cover in her mind, right on the spot. He was in awe of her once again, her strategic mind on full display. Gods, it made him want to take her even more. He shook the idea loose from his head, bent to examine the sled and reins more closely, and pulled back to his full height. "I do believe it will work."

Strella did an adorable shuffle of her feet, then stopped cold. "Will it be okay to leave Rowan and Yew behind?"

He hugged her to him, though he used one arm, so they were touching side to side rather than chest to chest. He doubted himself with the latter, but he also wanted to hold her a moment, assure her and let her feel his wonder at her—her intelligence, her care and concern, her everything really.

"We will secure them in the cave as I said we would secure you. They'll be safe here until I and a group of warriors return later in the day to retrieve them."

She twirled her hair and muttered, "Good. Good."

As lovely as she looked, and as much as he wanted her, he pushed himself to do what needed to be done. "It is settled. We will prepare and be on our way."

Surrounded by a contingent of five Aurora scouts they'd encountered about eight miles from the outpost, Ghel and Strella arrived through the massive wooden gates of the structure two hours after they'd left the cave. Strella had not complained at any point, the cold mitigated by the close proximity of Ghel as they moved over the ice and snow. Once the gates shut behind them with a loud creak, Ghel unstrapped himself and Strella, then jumped up with speed and agility so he could give Strella a hand. She started to get up on her own, however, and instead of appearing uncomfortable or tired, her cheeks were rosy and her face was sparkling with wonder.

"It's massive," she whispered, turning in a circle to get a full view of the Aurora Outpost.

It was massive, but Ghel was so used to the place, much like Winterlands Palace, he rarely noticed it. He was happy to tell her all about it. In the future. There were other tasks to complete first.

A crowd milled, but he saw his giant of an uncle making his way toward them with sure strides, his aunt and cousins in step beside him. Uncle Alo was the leader of the clan, not because of his heritage but because his warrior prowess meant he won the championship over clan leadership when his father had died, which was the way most warrior clans chose their leaders. His Aunt Sky was ferocious as well, although her small frame didn't bring such ideas to mind, much to the detriment of any new opponent she fought. Their children, twins Stone and Gem, flanked each, with son Stone to his father's right and daughter Gem to her mother's left. Each commanded respect, but all together they were a formidable quartet. To Ghel, however, they were family, and he treated them as such.

He gave a loud yell, happy to see them after long months apart. Almost a whole year, in fact. His uncle and aunt gave a similar whoop as the twins took off in a sprint right for him and tackled him to the ground. The trio landed with a hard thump and wrestled a moment on the ground, until Ghel remembered Strella standing there at their side. He thought she must be horrified at their antics, but when he rose to dust himself of snow and apologize, she had a bright, open smile for the three of them.

"Your family?" she asked.

"Was it that obvious?" he muttered, still trying to clean himself up a bit for her.

"There is a resemblance," she said as his uncle and aunt reached them, "but it is more your behavior. You treat those you love a certain way." The last part sounded wistful to him, wanting maybe, but he didn't want to read into her words, so he ignored the pinch it gave his heart and the twinge it caused in the magic connection between them.

"Lady Strella Hollythorn," his uncle boomed, thrusting a large hand—even larger than Ghel's—at her. "Welcome to our clan, for your first time and soon as family yourself."

Ghel didn't know if she'd ever shook hands with a man, but Strella didn't miss a beat. She clasped his uncle's hand in hers and pumped it several times. "A pleasure, Leader Alo. It's an honor to be welcomed to your home and as a future member of your family."

His Aunt Sky wasn't as formal. She engulfed Strella in a large bear hug, taking her off the ground two inches as she did. "Welcome, welcome," she said.

"Where's Jarok?" Stone asked, stepping up and shoving his way beside Ghel. "And why were you a day late, cousin?"

"Jarok had to stay behind to handle Winterland business, but he told me to smack you for him," Ghel joked. He turned serious as he looked at his uncle. "Yesterday, as we hit the last pullout before the outpost, we were attacked by a group of archers who'd been lying in wait for us."

Alo cursed, loud and low, and growled, "Monti?"

"Most definitely, from the arrow that pierced me."

It was his aunt and cousin's turn to curse then, but none of them fussed. They knew his healing would work wonders.

"We fled, hid in one of the bathing caves overnight. Left two of my dogs behind, which means I now need to retrieve them before the ceremony tonight. And I also need my sled fixed before we return to the palace tomorrow."

Gem knelt by the sled, looking at what they'd done to the structure to make it more stealthy. "Clever, cousin."

"All Lady Strella's idea," he said, giving a slight squeeze to her shoulder as she blushed and dipped her head at the attention.

"Then you've chosen a woman with both beauty and intelligence. Good for you, Ghel," Stone said, a wide smile on his face.

Strella, still in his grasp, stiffened at the words, and Ghel cursed himself. He hadn't chosen. Neither had she. And he didn't like her reaction to the reminder, though he also could not blame her.

His voice gruffer than earlier, he turned Strella toward his aunt. "Aunt Sky, will you take Lady Strella to her quarters and help her prepare for the ceremony? We must leave for the bathing cave now to make it on time."

"Of course, nephew," she said, grabbing Strella by her hand before she could protest.

"You will be safe here, Strella. Go with my aunt."

"Yes, my prince," she muttered, looking down at the snow-packed ground and their dirty boots.

Ghel didn't reply or assure her again. He simply turned with his cousins toward the stables, trying not to look back at Strella. He failed. When he glanced over his shoulder, he saw her doing the same, her teeth worrying her lip, the usual light in her eye absent. He hated to leave her here without him, but there was much to do before the ceremony. Miles of snows to cross before their fasting occurred. He'd assure Strella more then, about the Auroras and their arrangement.

Chapter Ten
Strella

S trella was ushered into the depths of the Aurora Outpost by Ghel's aunt and cousin. Both women were nice, though not overly talkative. Strella worried over Ghel, the dogs stuck in the cave, and what would happen at the ceremony that night, so she wasn't exceedingly talkative either.

She did soak in the outpost around her. Unlike the palace and Hollythorn Manor, which were built from mountain stone, the Aurora Outpost was constructed primarily of wood. In fact, it was the largest wooden structure Strella had ever seen, in real life or sketched in books. Situated in a deep valley at the bottom of sheer cliff walls, there was one narrow entrance into the place, but the buildings themselves climbed up the cliff edges like winter ivy, clinging to the rock at dizzying heights. At first she thought there were multiple buildings, each about four stories, lining the valley, but in actuality each was connected by intricate rope and board walkways, which swayed with the winds and allowed snow to drift off easily.

Each building had high, steep-angled roofs and low-slung windows. When she studied one closely as they passed on a wooden boardwalk, Gem Aurora leaned into her and said, "Designed to help the snow fall instead of accumulate."

"Here, too much snow on a roof can cause a cave-in quickly," Sky Aurora said. Strella, looking from roof to sheer cliff to open, gray sky, shuddered at the idea of a wood-and-snow avalanche crashing down on them.

"Don't worry," Gem said, knocking into her shoulder hard and causing her to stumble a step. "Aurora Outpost has stood for millennia now and is well maintained. Your death won't come from snow here."

It didn't sound exactly comforting to Strella. She knew death would come barreling toward her like a runaway carriage. She had six months or less before she would die, according to Seer Willow. Now she was in this place, in the wild heart of the Winterlands, about to complete a ceremony binding Prince Ghel to her once again. Guilt niggled at her brain, wormed into her heart. After what she and Ghel had experienced on their trek here, the attack and all that had come after, she felt she should talk to him about what would happen soon, especially before he tied himself to her in another way. Thinking about telling him her secret, a secret she'd told one other person in her life, made her mouth cold and dry. Strella knew she had to do it, at some point, to help him adjust to the inevitable, but she didn't like the idea. Just as she no longer liked the idea of thinking of Ghel as someone who could help her father gain power rather than a noble, worthy Fae man who deserved love in his own right, a love not tied to death—not that she believed he fully loved her yet. Still, the way he held her, spoke to her, and cared for her told her he might be destined for pain soon if she wasn't more honest and forthcoming.

As she pondered her secret problem, she was ushered into a low-slung doorway by Ghel's family and walked down a narrow hallway of wood beams and rough-hewn floors, until they turned into a side room. The place was a wooden cave, with low ceilings arched into a tall point along the center. There was a massive stone fireplace off to one side, blazing so it added both heat and light to the small space. A wood frame bed, large enough for a giant, was situated against the opposite wall, piled high with furs and blankets and topped with a bundle of clothes and a large box. The Auroras steered her toward a space off to the right of the fireplace wall, where a few wood and leather chairs sat in an arch around a large mirror leaning in the corner of the room.

Ghel's aunt sat her down firmly in a seat before she and her daughter took their own. Sky Aurora had similar coloring as Ghel and Queen Alene, though she knew the leader was the queen's true blood kin. Her dark hair was wild and curled, pulled half up to be off her strong, sharp face. Her eyes, a light brown almost golden, assessed in the way warriors did, taking in all of Strella as she sat there, hands clasped firmly in her lap and back ramrod straight so she wouldn't fidget.

The cousin, Gem, leaned back against her chair, powerfully muscled but lean arms crossed, nodding her head at some thought she had. She looked like a taller version of her mother, though her eyes were as dark as Ghel's and the queen's, so they were likely the eyes of her father.

She was also the first to speak. "Doesn't look like you fight much." Her tone lacked judgment; she seemed to be simply stating fact as she saw it, but it made Strella shrink internally nonetheless.

"Gem," her mother snapped. "She is a lady of the Winterlands court. No reason for her to fight."

A bit of her ruffled at the idea no lady would fight. She thought of Piris and her skill, which she'd seen in the practice ring a few times before they'd come to the palace. "Not always the case, I assure you," she replied, her voice firm and unyielding in tone. "However, it is true for me."

Gem smiled wide at her, her teeth dazzling and oddly sharp for a Fae. Strella wondered if she was a shifter of sorts, which usually showed in the teeth, but she didn't ask. It was rude to make inquiries about another's magical affinity because they may be a null, even if nulls were rare. "You fight in other ways. Use your head well too, if you devised the sled cover."

"I did."

Ghel's aunt and cousin both nodded in approval. "You will work wonders for our Ghel then," his aunt said before clapping her hands hard on her knees, startling Strella a bit. "Okay then. We need to ready you for the ceremony."

She turned to say something to her daughter, but Strella stopped whatever it was, raising her hand between them and saying, "I'm so sorry to have to ask, Madam Aurora—"

"Please, do call me Sky."

"Sky it is. I am sorry to ask, but I'm still not sure what the ceremony is tonight. Could you explain it?"

Gem's mouth hung open. "You traveled all the way here and have no idea what you're going to do?"

Squirming in her seat, she said, "For... various reasons... I was not informed of the ceremony until the morning we left, and there was little time for explanations. I knew it was important to the queen, your clan, and by extension, my betrothed, so I agreed."

Sky's eyes narrowed, as if studying Strella once again and finding something new and interesting there, but she didn't give voice to whatever she might have seen. She did, however, give a brief explanation. "The ceremony is a formal hand-fasting. From what I hear, it is like a combination of the betrothal binding and marriage performed in the wider Winterlands."

Strella was shocked by this. "It is an actual marriage?"

"For us, as close as. For you and your court, no. There is no legal or contractual component as with your unions among the Fae nobles. No lord or lady would consider you truly married. Here, however, you would be seen as bound and united, without needing any other ceremonies or signings."

Gem said, "We are a tad less formal around here," with a snort.

Strella blinked as her mind whirled. Was this why her father had tried to stop her from coming, because he didn't want her to engage in a marriage ceremony he did not attend or approve of in practice? Possibly. Still, the idea of the fasting being a form of marriage, albeit outside her original concept of marriage, made her stiffen. Ghel may well see them as good and married from this night on, as he was part Aurora. "Will I see Ghel again before the ceremony?" She needed to talk to him, tell him her secret, before he was bound in a way he could not easily break. To dissolve a betrothal binding was one thing, to dissolve a cultural marriage was a whole other. Kind, brave, honorable Ghel needed all the information before he completed the ceremony.

"Unlikely," Sky answered. "It will take hours for him to return with the dogs, and then he'll have little time to ready himself."

Tears welled in her eyes at her blunder. She'd done this, lied by omission, which in turn had opened the possibility she'd do more damage to the prince. It was what she'd always feared doing, leaving behind yet another person who might mourn her too much, be too affected by her loss. She held guilt over how her father and Piris would react. Now Ghel was added to the list, all because her father wanted more power in the Winterlands when he already had enough. She'd gone along with it, as she always had, but the consequences shamed her even as a hidden but growing part of her wanted to marry this good, caring man.

"Don't fear, Lady Strella," Sky said, leaning forward to place a strong hand on her knee. "It is a simple ceremony with small magic involved. For you, it will mean little. For us and the queen, it means more."

And for Ghel, Strella thought. It likely meant a great deal to the prince as it did to the queen. Also, she'd already agreed, and it was too late to stop Ghel from leaving so they could have an in-depth discussion of future consequences. She hoped she'd at least have a moment alone with him beforehand, to say something, anything to make him understand there were things he didn't know, options still open to him, before the ceremony started. That hope was what she needed to cling to now.

She wiped the welling tears with a discreet hand and shook her head clear. "Very well. And, please, do call me Strella." She gave a weak grin and said, "Now, tell me more of the actual ceremony and what my role is in it."

She'd been cleaned, primped, and dressed in a lovely gown of heavy, dark, luscious black fur skimming the floor and fastened and pinned with decorative metal buckles and a matching pair of black lace-up boots, which hit right below her knee. It was a stark contrast, given her pale coloring, but from the silver Strella thought it arresting. Right before she left the rooms at full dark, after all her prep and talk and whatnot, Sky had brought in a small chest. Opening it, Strella found layers of snow on the bottom, and a sparkling ice crown, the frozen, intricately woven pieces somehow carved, so light played on its surface. She gasped at the delicate beauty of it but dared not touch it.

"For you, Strella," Sky said.

"Is this tradition?"

"It might be a little more fancy than normal," Gem admitted. "We wanted to impress the lady."

Strella looked between the women, who she'd become more and more comfortable with as the hours ticked by, and her gut tugged at the idea they might have also been nervous to meet her, a stranger coming into their home who could possibly judge them harshly. "It's exquisite. Truly."

Gem gave a sharp-toothed grin and said, "Put it on then. We need to go."

As quickly as possible, she put it on her head, afraid her hands, sweaty from nerves and an odd anticipation, would cause it to melt faster.

Soon after, they led Strella out of the building and up a hidden set of stone stairs. They climbed for long minutes, and she was nearly breathless when they reached a plateau. Warriors guarded the entrance and ringed the space but stepped aside to allow the women through. Gem disappeared, presumably to take a spot in the crowd. Sky walked her to Ghel, who stood in the middle of the ring waiting for her, before moving to stand beside her husband, positioned at the top of the circle with no one else crowding around him, which made sense as Strella now knew the clan leader performed the ceremony.

She looked Ghel up and down, and her heart raced at what she saw. His clothes were much like hers, black sable fur with intricate silver metal details. He also wore a ring of ice around his head, though his was less intricate than hers. He looked strong and powerful and wild all at once, his curly hair down instead of tied back as it usually was. It was mixing with his beard, making him look like an old Fae fable character, someone from the age of heroes and monsters who was ready to swing a righteous sword to protect any and all.

Strella licked her lips, both at the heat his closeness caused and her nervousness at what she needed to do. She'd planned what to say as best she could, knowing they would only have moments to have a quick, whispered conversation before the ceremony began. She had to at least try to free him of his obligation, give him some idea she would not be his wife for long, before he could rightly agree to move forward with the ceremony. She'd deal with the consequences for her family later, and the likely consequences to her own heart.

"Ghel," she croaked out from her mouth, dry as the desert because of her nerves. "Before we do this, there are things about me you do not know."

He calmly said, "I could say the same."

"No, but, you see, I have reason to believe..." She couldn't say it. She didn't know why. She couldn't get out the words "I will die soon." Not to him, in this place, surrounded by his family and clan. She swallowed hard and tried a different tactic. "Are you sure you wish to marry me?"

Ghel's face melted into a mask of concern. "Do you wish to not continue, Strella? I would understand if you did not want to perform the ceremony with me. It's not usual for ladies to do and is something you were never told to expect. You are free to say no. Always."

He squeezed her hand gently, and her heart thudded for him. The glint in his eye, their squint, showed a vulnerability that made her gut clench. He doubted her desire for him, his own value to her, and she couldn't take that from this Fae man. She'd tried to keep herself apart but could no longer claim she won that battle. She was tied to Ghel in ways she couldn't explain, and possibly didn't want to explain. Not just the betrothal magic but by who he was and how he treated her. How he focused on her like no one in her life had before. Like no one else in her short life ever would again.

His face fell, and a shadow of expectation crossed his eyes. As bad as it was to keep her secret from him now, to let him go ahead with the ceremony without being fully informed... Her heart cracked at the idea Ghel may be hurt. May think she rejected him because of who or what he was, when he was more than she could've ever imagined for herself.

"No, Ghel. I want you. I do. I just... I just need you to know there are things we should discuss—"

Ghel cut her off, hugging her hard to him as he whispered in her ear, "We have time for more discussion. More discovery. If you don't object."

She swallowed the secret down, as she had always done, and nodded against his chest, then placed a small kiss there before pulling back to look into his face. "I don't object."

The relief in his eyes was a punch to Strella's emotions, but she shook it free and stepped away even as she grabbed his hand. "Let's begin."

He gripped her tight and moved them up to his uncle, who studied them a beat before beginning. "Aurora Clan warriors?"

A loud clang of metal and claps and shouts echoed through the space, and for the first time, Strella noticed the ring upon ring upon ring of people crowded higher up the sides of the mountain. Seemed every Aurora Clan member was there as witness to the ceremony.

"Here today we present clan member Ghel, first of his name, come to fast with Lady Strella Hollythorn, first of her name. Do any here challenge the fasting?"

Silence dripped through the mountain before Leader Alo continued. "As it should be. Ghel, take your fast-mate's hand in your own."

Ghel grabbed her hand, locking their fingers together and shifting them so they stood as if shaking hands in an intermingled manner.

"May your hands be ever strong, yet stronger together. May your hands never waver but extend in times of need and victory in equal measure. May your hands soothe and protect you both and any family you create together. May your hands and hearts become one. May both be bound by ice and sky, fasted from now unto death."

A zing of power encased their hands, and Strella stared, fascinated, as a mix of ice and color, bright green and vivid pink and deep purple, twined over their joined hands. It filled her with a cold peace she'd never known, and although she still had guilt over not revealing her secret to Ghel, in this moment she knew she had not made a mistake by completing the ceremony. Whatever was to come would come, regardless of her knowledge of it, and in this little life she had, she'd be able to know emotions she never imagined she'd experience.

Her eyes were teary for the second time that day, and she looked up at Ghel, whose hard, keen eyes bore into her with so much heat, it took her breath for a few beats. Then, she felt the cold release on their hands and Ghel looked toward the sky, so her eyes followed up, and the same colors dancing across their skin floated up there, hovering in the sky underneath the waxing moon.

All around cheered, a sea of noise crashing down on them. Ghel smiled, huge and so full of happiness, it made Strella's happiness double. It bubbled up into a joyful laugh and a yelp of sweet surprise when Ghel scooped her up into his arms, gripped her tight, and planted a soft, chaste kiss to her lips before spinning her around to more yells and clangs and noisy celebration. It almost drowned out the worry and guilt burrowed in Strella's head and heart. Almost.

Chapter Eleven
Ghel

Fastings had always seemed quick to Ghel when he'd witnessed them prior to his own. Even his hadn't taken a great deal of time, but every second lingered for him, as if his mind took pains to freeze each moment so it would be permanently stuck in his memory. The words his uncle spoke over them, the warmth of Strella's hand in his, the tingle of the Aurora fasting magic binding them tighter... It had made their betrothal magic wrap more firmly around them, creating more solid bonds than he'd even expected and made the few minutes of time seem like an eternity and seconds all at once. Ghel was certain of few things: his life as a warrior, his love for his family, and his loyalty to his kingdom. Now he was also certain of his affection for Strella and how the colors of the Aurora magic bouncing off her pale skin and hair in the darkness would forever flash in his mind when he closed his eyes.

Afterward, he held Strella's hand a touch too tightly, the need to not let go of her forcing his muscles to tense instinctively. She smiled up at him, her face as beautiful and familiar now as the snow on the Winterlands mountains, and he swallowed hard, unable to say anything, as usual. Luckily, before he could curse himself for his continual loss of words when it came to Strella, his uncle clapped him on the back. "Come, nephew. Let's move to the dining hall."

Ghel finally noticed most every other Aurora Clan member had moved down the mountain, making their way toward the traditional fasting feast awaiting them. They'd held back, of course, because the family and fasted couple entered the hall last, usually to loud, happy cheers. His uncle and cousin Stone held themselves back for a different reason as his aunt and cousin Gem looped arms around Strella and pulled her ahead.

When they were far enough to counter their Fae hearing, his uncle muttered under his breath, "Tell me what you found today."

Ghel and Stone, along with an elite group clan warrior under Stone's command called The Storm, had returned to the Aurora Outpost with just enough time to change and make the fasting. At least Ghel and Stone had made their way to the ceremony. The warriors of The Storm stayed behind to secure their find: one of the Monti archers.

"We don't know much. We found one archer on horseback, his mount hobbled by the snow."

"You would think the Monti Clan would be smart enough to not ride horses so hard and far without proper magic at hand," Stone said with a snort.

It was an obvious mistake. Sled dogs were used for distance over snowy ground because horses' hooves, even the sturdy horses originating in their lands, would pack tight with snow, causing them pain and making them dangerous for any rider. This was combated with magical protection, but the magic wore off over time and needed to be applied early and often by a Fae with an affinity toward horses and animal magics. It was why horses were used for few things. The average Winterlands Fae used them only for pleasure rides, if at all, while Fae with the appropriate affinity were employed as coachmen, leaders of large transport that dogs could not pull, and the very limited

Winterlands calvary riders. An archer out in the vast snows of the Aurora territory stood no chance at keeping a horse in good condition, as most archers had enhanced sight as their affinity. The state of the horse when they'd tracked the Monti Fae made Ghel nearly as angry as the idea of this archer being the one who'd shot him with an arrow. His anger rose to unbearable heights, however, when he thought of how the archer had threatened Strella's life, and Stone had needed to pull him off the Fae after he'd started pummeling him into the snow with his bare hands.

Not a strategic move on his part, as the Fae had then been unable to answer questions with his jaw broken and face swollen. He'd heal. Not as quickly as Ghel, however, so they'd needed to transport him back to the outpost and store him away for a talk with his uncle the next day. Or the day after. Ghel had done a great deal of damage to the Fae in a short amount of time.

Because they'd gotten back just in time, his uncle knew the basic outline of events, and the fact they had a Monti archer rotting in his cells, but little else. None of them knew much else because of Ghel's actions. Lucky for him, his split knuckles had healed on the journey back, so he'd avoided questions from Strella after she'd taken his hands during the fasting.

His uncle interrupted his thoughts. "Your aunt and cousin say they like the lady."

Ghel smiled at his family's assessment of Strella. He'd had no doubt Strella, with her kind and thoughtful nature, would win over his clan family if given time. He was happy it had happened so soon.

"She acts far different from her father," Stone added with a hard bite to his words.

There was no love lost between Lord Mikka Hollythorn and the current Aurora Clan leadership, as there was little love existing between him and the royal family. For reasons old and new, some to do with the lord's snide demeanor of anyone he found to be not useful and some to do with his current machinations, Leader Alo and Stone had every reason to dislike the Fae. He knew his uncle and cousin well, trusted them as family and warriors, but a need to defend Strella welled in his chest.

"She's nothing like her father and appears to have no connection to his business outside hosting his public events at Hollythorn Manor."

"You are positive of this?" his uncle asked.

"I'd stake my life on it." Ghel meant it. He did not doubt Strella in the least. They'd investigated her actions before, yes, but more than this, he'd come to see who she was, as a woman, and knew in his bones she was what she seemed to be: a good lady born into the wrong family. He worried over her hesitancy at the fasting, worried about how she may feel about the current events in her life and being forced to marry him, but he had no worries about her honor or integrity.

His family gave him firm nods of agreement. They trusted his instinct and judgment, as well as the judgments passed by Sky and Gem. "Very well, Ghel," his uncle said, landing a swift, hard pat on the back that would take many Fae men down.

Ghel stood against it, solid enough but stumbling a half step.

"Let's celebrate your good fortune."

A few hours later, they were wrapping up the feast, another fasting tradition meant to celebrate the couple, and the eating and drinking and laughter dragged on and on for Ghel, who wished to be alone with Strella, to talk about her hesitancy prior to the fasting and to make sure she was fine despite the broad smile she had on her face. He picked at his food, having eaten as much of the roast as he could, waiting for the time he knew would come, though not swiftly enough for his liking.

"Are you well, Ghel?" Strella asked, her smile no longer present as she looked from his plate to his face. He felt it then, the deep scowl he had in place. He cursed himself before intentionally smoothing his brow and making his mouth as neutral as possible.

A loud, booming laugh from Stone made his teeth grind. Gods, he loved and missed his cousin, but he grated his nerves this evening when all he should be focusing on was Strella. "I'm fine, Strella. Simply tired."

She looked as if she didn't fully believe him, which was fair enough. He was lying a little. Before he could reassure her again, however, his uncle's yell rang loud in the massive dining hall. Laughter, talk, and even the scrapes of cups and plates and silverware all stopped at the sound, a sign of respect for his uncle as leader of his clan.

"We have had a successful fasting this evening, and a fine feast afterward. Thanks to all who helped my kin today. I'm honored." He looked toward Ghel and Strella, lined front and center at the long wooden table at the top of the room so they faced the clan members in attendance. Not everyone in the clan could fit in the large space despite it being the sole room in the massive, squat building in this corner of the outpost. It was where most official meals took place and housed many, many people. Likely over five hundred, at Ghel's estimate. Still, the Aurora Clan was vast and had many who traveled or guarded or even chose not to participate, meaning possibly half the current clan was in attendance, not counting the young ones who were left out of such events. He swallowed a nervous lump in his throat as he thought there would likely be even more people at the royal wedding taking place in a few weeks. This crowd was downright intimate in comparison to the numbers who would file into the palace soon.

His thoughts were snapped back to the matter at hand when his uncle addressed him directly. "Prince Ghel, Lady Strella, I am also honored you keep our traditions."

Ghel didn't know what to say, how to express his happiness in the ceremony, the beauty of it and the connection he felt with his warrior clan even if he was still called prince. After a few beats of silence, Strella waded in, answering for them both. "We are the ones honored by the attention and kindness from your mighty clan. May your swords be swift and sharp as falling ice."

Ghel's head snapped to his... well, not exactly wife but also not exactly fiancée any longer. He thought of Strella simply as his. Her last sentence had been a traditional Aurora Clan saying, something she'd learned earlier that day or read somewhere. From her love of books, he guessed it was the latter.

He wasn't the only one pleasantly surprised by the words. His uncle nodded in approval, as did his aunt. His cousins, flanking their parents, let out loud whoops and pounded the table in response, the rest of the clan quickly following their lead, until the noise reached the thick wooden rafters, making the space tremble. Strella did not shrink or balk but remained straight-backed and proud at his side. He thought she was truly remarkable.

When the din died down, his uncle continued. "We will feast and drink in your honor all night, Prince Ghel and Lady Strella. However, you have other, more pleasant things in store this evening."

Hoots and whistles sounded. Ghel ruffled at the implication, afraid Strella would be embarrassed. A slight pink stain slashed across her cheeks, but she kept her head high. Best he got her away from the feast and in their chamber so they could speak privately and rest after what had been an exciting and trying few days. "We take our leave, Uncle. Thank you, my clan, for all you have done for us this evening."

Ghel led her from the hall with claps and shouts ringing behind them, happy at the encouragement but nervous about what would come after.

T hey reached their designated bedchamber. Ghel had a small room on his family's floor in one of the clan houses, but his aunt insisted they take one of the larger, more luxurious guest rooms for the evening. He noted Strella's coat hanging from a hook on the wall as they entered, and the small chest situated on a table in the corner sitting area. This was the space where Strella had prepared for their fasting.

She moved to the chest, open and snow filled, as she carefully removed the ice wreath from her head. Hers was far more intricate than his, stunning in its construction and magic, and still perfectly formed after hours on her head. It would remain so, frozen in form and time. Just as the snow in the chest would rest there, cocooning the piece indefinitely. He made a mental note to thank his aunt for the gift and ask her which artisan had made it, for future reference.

A future with Strella struck him. It had been a hazy concept in his mind until this evening, when the magic had bound them tighter. He felt her more solidly in his chest because of the fasting their recent experiences together. They would have a future together, and he knew it could even possibly be happy. It was something of a relief, after long weeks of worry over the arrangement.

"Strella, how are you? Truly." He needed to know. Had to know. Yet he couldn't start off asking the one big question: did you really want to bind yourself tighter to me, or am I the only one seeing the happiness we could have together?

Her chest rose as she took a deep, deliberate breath. It seeped out slowly, hissing into the room and making him more and more nervous before she spoke. "I am well, my prince. Truly."

"Tonight, before the fasting, you acted as if..." He didn't finish his statement, partially because it took so much effort to force himself to get at what he wished to know, and partially because she met him hand-to-hand in three quick strides to stop his words.

"No, Ghel. Don't think for a moment I did not want you. I just... There are things about me you don't know. Things which could hurt you, and I'd never wish to hurt you. Ever."

Her words were said with such vehemence, he instantly believed. He also didn't care in the slightest what she referenced. There were secrets each kept, and he suspected what hers might be, given who she was, but damnit all, he believed her when she said she did not want to hurt him.

Ghel brought a hand up to cup her cheek. "Your secrets are yours to tell, when you are ready. Whatever they are, they will not change my view of you. Nothing will."

Her face pinched for a moment, and her eyes welled as if tears threatened to fall. It tore at Ghel's chest to see her so affected by someone or something. It made him want to roar, to rage, to fight like a bear to save her from whoever or whatever made her cry. He had no words to soothe her or him in the moment, so he did the one thing he could think to do. He leaned in and kissed her cheek, and when her eyes closed at the contact, he took her head in his large hands and kissed them too, willing the tears away with his touch.

A breath shuddered from her, and she pulled away, opening her mouth to say more, but Ghel couldn't take anymore. Not this night. "No, Strella. Let's rest. No more words tonight."

"Rest?" she asked, a different rosy tinge hitting her cheeks, his own thoughts clawing at his memory of her falling apart on top of him, making a growl rip up his throat before he could clamp it down.

"Strella, we should wait—"

"We are married, at least according to Aurora Clan tradition, correct?"

"Yes, but you are not of the Aurora Clan."

She looked down as she clasped his hand in the same way they'd held each other during the fasting. "I believe tonight I became part of the clan."

"In theory, yes, Strella, but—"

A delicate finger tripped over his lips, silencing him. "No, Ghel. As you said, no more words for tonight."

In a flash, her luscious lips replaced her finger, and Ghel was lost in sensation.

Strella explored this time. She moved her hands up to twine in his beard, much like she twined her fingers in her own hair when she was nervous. Ghel pulled her closer to him, locking his powerful arms behind her back, notching her small form against his large one and moaning into her mouth at the contact.

She took it as encouragement, if her forceful surge upward was any indication. She nipped, sucked, and licked, and Ghel was more than happy to allow her the space to do whatever she wished. As her mouth moved, her hands also did, trailing from his beard down over his neck, his chest, and finally stopping to grip his waist firmly as she leaned harder into him.

They were locked like this for a while, minutes feeling like hours and seconds all at once, when she pulled back. He stopped immediately, loosening his hold in case she wished to fully pull away from him. Her eyes swirled with lust and light as her magic pulsed in a warm glow all around him. The glow somehow reached through his skin, deep into the darker, more broken parts of him, and healed them better than his own magic ever could.

He was choked on sensation and the dueling desire to allow Strella whatever freedom she needed versus his instinct to bury himself inside this woman and never leave, so she spoke first.

"Ghel, I want to touch you."

His head fell forward, hitting her forehead, and he breathed in her scent, the wintery orange smell of her and her spiced arousal mixing in the room, making it hard for him to think through what she'd said. "You can touch me however you want, my Star." He meant every syllable. He wanted her to touch all of him, now and forever. He couldn't imagine a time when he wouldn't want her hands on him, in any way she wished. Ghel would gladly take whatever she wished to give him, eat it up and greedily ask for seconds.

Permission granted, she snaked her hands around his waist, her nails gently scraping the skin across his hard stomach, causing his muscles to jump and flutter, before she moved down to his leather breeches. She skimmed the outline of his cock and gave it a soft, tentative squeeze, forcing Ghel to hiss out a breath. He bit back a curse and waited, letting Strella explore him as he trembled under her touch.

When she started to unhook and ease down his breeches, he stopped her hands. A moment of concern and clarity hit him. "Strella, are you certain?" He may see her as his, but she was a lady who'd lived a sheltered life, and what passed between them in the fasting may not have meant the same to her. The Fae were not a prudish people with strict social rules around sex, but consent and certainty were paramount to them.

She smiled softly at him, her glow and the thump of their magical connection both beating hard against his chest. "As I said, I want to touch you."

Strella eased back from his pants, moving to his overshirt to push it up and over his head, her fingers trailing fire in their wake. She teased his nipples, scraping against his flesh, and he stood motionless. If he moved, he knew he would move to take her, and he wanted to give her control in this. He almost lost his own control when she bent forward and licked the line in the center of his chest, from midpoint up to his neck, causing his blood to run riot. He clenched his hands into fists, digging not-too-sharp nails into his flesh as best he could to stop himself from intervening in her exploration.

A twinkle sparked in her eye and a smirk hit her lips, so Ghel was certain she knew exactly what she was doing to him. She bent her knees, slowly lowering herself as she kissed along the planes of his stomach. Before her knees hit the ground, however, he stopped her again, raised her slowly. "You want to touch me. I want to see you."

The lady had no qualms with this, as she immediately went to undoing the dark sable dress she wore. She shoved it down her arms, leaving her in dark wool tights and a nearly transparent linen undershirt. Ghel's attention was riveted to the dark peaks he could make out through the fabric, her nipples tight and straining their thin confines. He made some animalistic noise he'd never heard in his life and bent his head to take one peak into his mouth through the shirt. Strella moaned deep and loud, clasping her hands around his head and urging him on. He didn't hesitate, lathing the nipple with his tongue in quick lashes before sucking hard and deep, causing her to throw her head back. He moved to the other breast, giving it equal attention, and would have continued all night if he could, but she tugged hard on the back of his head.

As he popped her right breast from his mouth and looked up at her, she shook her head but said nothing, pulling him farther and farther away from his feast. He saw her nipples, perfect peaks displayed through the drenched material, and wanted to roar at the sight, the evidence of what he'd done to her and what more he could do. Yet he straightened, as she seemed to want him to stop.

Without any additional detours of her mouth, she dropped to her knees, unhooking his breeches and tugging them down over his hips as she licked her lips. Gods, he wanted what he knew she was after, but he had to stop her first.

"Strella, are you certain?"

She offered no words, only a hard, clipped nod.

"I will not last if you do this."

She smiled, full and bright and blinding. "I want to see you undone as you undid me last night." Then she hesitated a moment, biting her lip in thought. "Can you show me what you like?"

He groaned but agreed. First things first. He wouldn't have her giving him pleasure with nothing in return. "Use one hand. I want you to touch your sweet pussy as you do this."

She sucked in a breath, the inhale so close to his cock it twitched in response, as she moved her right hand under her own shirt, down her tights, her hips starting to rock as her arm moved. He couldn't see anything, but it was the most alluring sight he'd encountered in his entire life.

Cupping her cheek in one hand and taking his cock in the other, he said, "Open wide for me. Grab the base with a firm hand. Then do what feels right."

As soon as his head slipped past her lips, his hips bucked, driving him inches deep in less than a second. "Are you okay?" he asked, stopping his progress, though every muscle in his body and the blood pumping in his veins urged him to bury himself to the root in her sweet, warm mouth.

She gave the slightest of nods, sliding down farther on his cock, and he was lost. Truly lost. Her mouth was wet, hot satin wrapped tight around him, taking him in and pulling back with long, hard sucks. Stars sparked in his vision, from the sensation and from her magic spilling out, pulsing all around them.

Ghel lost track of time and fell into his senses. She moaned around his cock, a beautiful tone, the vibrations from her mouth and their heightened magical connection zinging through him. Her body shook as her head and one hand worked him and her other worked herself, bringing her closer to orgasm as Ghel's body ran headlong toward it. Gripping her cheeks while making sure he did not pinch or tug too hard, he stared down into her face as her eyes met his, her head falling up and down his cock as they stayed connected in so many ways. His heart beat in time to the pulse of her starry magic, becoming intertwined in a beautiful, lust-filled moment.

"I can't... I'm about to—" He tried to warn her but couldn't get out a full sentence.

She understood, however, and pulled her hands free of herself and him, anchored them on his hips, and sucked him deep as he spilled into her perfect mouth. Her head bobbed up and down a few times as he softened until she freed him from her hold and looked up at him with sweet expectation.

"Good girl," he said, and he felt her shiver at the words. She yelped when he reached down and dragged her upright, taking no time to thrust his hand in her drenched tights and tweak her clit.

"Your turn," he growled as he worked her slick flesh. Strella writhed against him, panting until she screamed through her orgasm, soaking his hand in the process. He pulled it out slowly and, eyeing her, licked his fingers. "I'll taste you next time."

He could taste her now, far more thoroughly, but her body had sagged in relief and possibly exhaustion immediately after she'd come. He was content to end their night there. She'd given him a gift, and he wished to cherish it. They could do more later, much later. After the royal wedding, if he could hold out that long. Now was time for rest before they traveled back to the palace the next day. Ghel set her firmly on a chair and cleaned them both up with cloth wetted from the water basin in the room and prepared their bed for the night.

He tucked Strella firmly to his side, and she quickly drifted off to sleep. Ghel stayed awake. He was happy but also worried, a state he was usually familiar with in terms of his family and responsibilities. However, this was different, the ache and leap in his chest, the way he wanted to shield her while guiding her, the way he wished to work her body to breaking but protect her from any hurt, emotional or physical. He knew what it was, why these things lingered, and he worried more about what was to come. How was he supposed to do what needed to be done for his family and his kingdom when he already loved Strella?

Chapter Twelve
Strella

S trella existed in a blissful state the next morning, on through their long trek back to the palace and up to when Ghel gently freed her from the sled on their return. He scooped her up in his arms, and her legs dangled in a ridiculous way. It made her laugh, and his soft, kind black eyes on her made her stomach flitter.

All that changed when she heard a stable door bang against the wall one second before a crackle of light hit the air. Her stomach roiled because she knew what was coming before her father stalked into the dog sled area, his face thunderous and his voice deathly chill. "Unhand my daughter. Now."

Strella twisted in Ghel's arms, and he hesitated just enough for her to wonder if he would have let her go if she hadn't indicated she wanted him to do so. "Father, I'm fine. I—"

"Was nearly killed because of the prince's neglect!" he screamed into the space, making her take a step back on one foot in shock. Her father was coldness and indifference punctuated with small signs of affection. Snide remarks and emotionless reprimands. He was not this furious, hot creature in front of her who looked like he'd try to tear the prince apart.

Ghel, who'd been in full scowl when her father entered, smoothed his face except for the deep V etched between his brows. "You are right, Lord Hollythorn."

"No, Ghel." Strella stepped toward him, seeing the blame wash over him and not liking how it felt.

"Strella, come with me. Now." Her father seemed ready to kill, and the light he could wield as a weapon danced openly across his fists, a clear threat. Strella understood it spoke more of Ghel's feelings on the matter of blame than anything else when he did not confront Lord Hollythorn's threat with his own.

The prince ground his teeth hard, his jaw flexing and working as he stared at her father before turning eyes back to her. "Go, Strella. I have matters to discuss with my brother and parents."

"But..." She started to say she didn't want to leave him, didn't want to strain the tie between them in any way. She wanted to ignore their duties and problems and live in a blissful little bubble for the rest of their days. Sadly, they couldn't, so there was no point in arguing.

He leaned down, planting a chaste kiss to the crown of her head, and said, "I will see you soon, Star. I promise."

Tucking his promise away like a talisman she could hold in her pocket, she nodded and turned back toward her father, guilt instantly hitting her. He trembled in his anger and fear, which he felt because of what had happened with her on her trip to the Aurora Outpost. "Come," he clipped out, the usual command in his tone shaded by something darker and more pained.

Strella bit down on her lip, stared at her feet, and followed behind her father as he stomped out of the barn.

When they were alone in the vast courtyard, out of hearing range of Ghel and the Aurora Clan members who'd accompanied them back to the palace for extra protection, she tried once again to reason with her father. Attempted to soothe his worry and stress as she usually did.

"Father, as you can see, I'm fine. The attack—"

Lord Hollythorn spun around, his face in a deep frown and his body sparking with light. He grabbed her shoulders a touch too hard, a little rough, something he had never been with her before, and pulled her to his chest, holding her tight amongst the fiery light he didn't allow to touch her. "My Strella. I could have lost you."

Tears clogged his voice, something Strella had rarely heard in her life. In fact, she only heard such emotion from her father when he had too much wine and talked of her mother, the love he'd lost. Strella's icy eyes teared up, knowing his worry was so strong, his love for her true and real, and how he would eventually be broken once again by her death in the too-near future. She twined her arms around him, hugging him tighter until she felt his body ease.

When they parted, her heart still hurting for him, she was sad to see his cold mask back in place, the lord ready to make commands. "You must tell me everything that happened on your journey."

She swallowed, knowing she couldn't tell her father everything about her time with Ghel, but she'd give him what he needed to calm himself. Strella was about to recount the events when a screamed "Star" hit her ears, and thundering footsteps pounding on cold stone sounded. She turned toward the noise in time to take the impact of a frantic Piris to her front, each letting out a "oomph" as they collided.

"Lady Volesion!" Lord Hollythorn admonished.

Piris, as usual, ignored Strella's father, choosing instead to smooth a large, thin-fingered hand over her best friend's face. "Are you okay?"

Strella once again fought back tears at the show of love, concern, and all it meant for these Fae in the future and answered her friend. "I am fine and well, Peep." She squeezed the hands at her face for good measure. Piris looked to release a deep breath, closed her eyes, and stepped back without a word, ready to play the lady-in-waiting once again.

"As I was saying, Strella, you must tell me what you endured with that barbaric prince."

Her back straightened at her father's words, and she immediately went on the defensive. "I am here today, Father, because of the prince and his skills as a warrior. You should be thanking him for all he did for me instead of disparaging him."

Piris smiled at her with a hint of pride at the first correction she'd given her father. Her father, however, looked like her words had landed a physical blow, literally forcing his body to rock back a fraction as he stared in shock. He cleared his face and gave a well-worn sneer before saying, "That may be, daughter, but you would have never been in the situation were it not for him."

She ignored him, taking a cue from Piris, and said, "Are we dining together this evening?"

Her father huffed and answered instead. "We will dine together, the three of us, in my suite tonight. I need a break from the royals."

Piris whispered, "Agreed," and Strella let her friend lead her on, into the palace and her rooms for some much-needed rest before dinner. As well as some time to think about why she'd been so harsh with her father when he'd questioned Ghel's competence. She was there, marrying him, because her father wished it for the glory and power. Or had been there for that reason. Now, knowing Ghel, things felt different.

Later that evening, after a somewhat awkward dinner where her father had questioned her about every detail of the attack, her treatment by Ghel and his clan family, and the specifics of the Aurora

Outpost and its people, Strella was sitting in her dressing room at a mirror, absentmindedly brushing out her hair before bed. Something in her ached slightly, and she thought it might be because she missed Ghel, which was absurd as they'd only been away from each other for hours at this point.

She startled when Piris sauntered into the space from her room, dressed in a long night shirt in a dusky-pink color that highlighted her auburn hair and glinting bronze eyes. The shirt was a tad short on her six-foot frame, just as so many clothes were too long for the petite Strella. She smiled to herself and called, "No patrol tonight?"

Piris stopped by Strella's small vanity and plush bench, her toes digging into the thick rug under their bare feet and laid a firm hand on her friend's shoulder. "I think I'd better stay in for the night, what with so many other warriors roaming the palace grounds now."

Strella looked up at her in question, and Piris nudged her aside so she could scoot onto the bench beside her. "The Aurora warriors who escorted you back to the palace have stayed for the evening. Will likely stay longer by my guess, as extra protection. The guards have also been increased, and the soldiers stationed along the Ice Plains have been placed on alert."

"Is it as dire as all that?"

Piris, her face hard and smooth as marble, answered with a definitive yes.

Strella sighed. The attack on her and the prince had been terrifying, but the events after—in the cave, the ceremony, the night following—somehow made her minimize it in her mind. Dredging up details of every little thing at her father's interrogation over dinner hadn't been fun, but somehow, Piris's information about the increase in protection measures around the palace made it all more real once again.

Piris, likely noting the worry all over Strella, stilled her hand in her hair, giving it an affectionate squeeze. "Nothing will happen to you. Do you hear me? Nothing."

The vehemence in her voice was clear, but Strella couldn't exactly believe her. She knew she would die soon. Maybe another attack was what would end her life.

"Besides," Piris said, a little too breezily and with a sly twinkle in her eye, "I think you now have more than one warrior closely guarding you." She bumped into her friend's shoulder playfully. "Tell me the good stuff. The details you left out at dinner when you skipped over the two nights you spent with the prince."

Strella's face heated. She wasn't exactly embarrassed. At least, she never had been before in her limited sexual experience. Gods knew Piris let her hear all her own dirty details when she had them to share. Still, something about her time with Ghel felt private, special, in a way she didn't wish to share, even with Piris. "The nights were... memorable."

Piris groaned. "Oh, come on, Star. Give me more."

She whispered, "I glowed for him. He now also calls me Star. At times."

Piris's bronze eyes melted, her heart shining through, and she gave her friend a hard, swift sideways hug. "I love that for you."

Strella nodded, because she loved the feeling and experience too, though she feared other things might be creeping toward love.

"I haven't told him yet," she confessed. "I didn't have time before the fasting ceremony. I did tell him I had secrets. He told me I was free to reveal them when I was ready. I... I don't know if I'll ever be ready to tell him, to possibly break his heart."

Piris sighed deep, still hugging Strella close, and said, "I have a feeling Prince Ghel would fight death for you." Strella snorted at her exaggeration. "Today, I saw you stand up to your very angry father for the prince—a first, I think. Says a great deal about what you're willing to fight for your prince too."

True, at least on her part. What Ghel felt, how deep he felt, was something she didn't know for certain. Part of her wished Piris to be right. The other part, so used to worry and distance from others, was terrified at the idea, for both Ghel and herself.

Strella was browsing the poetry section of the library, a rather robust collection compared to the library at Hollythorn Manor. Some royal long ago was a fan of poetry, or the Hollythorns had dismissed it. Either was a possibility, given what she knew of the history and disposition of the Hollythorn line from her father.

The ungenerous thought of her father made her feel guilty. He loved her, she knew. She saw it in the care and concern he took with her, even if he was often harsh, cold, and controlling at times. His love was simply broken because of what had happened with her mother. She'd spent a lifetime trying to mend that break, being obedient and acquiescent, caring for their manor, and helping him by being the perfect picture of a daughter and host. He'd shown appreciation at times but not often, and always mixed with enough criticism to make her feel she never measured up to the angel in their home, her father's ideal of a mother she never got to know.

Queen Alene's talk of her mother had startled her because of this. She was surprised to hear her mother ever talked back to her father. Ever behaved in any way he'd not deem as acceptable. Was her mother like the queen had said, a strong and thoughtful lady willing to stand up when she felt someone was in the wrong? Or was she as her father always implied, forever giving and never stepping outside of his lines of decorum? Likely she was some of both, as all people were. Sadly, she'd never know. Equally sad was the fact she'd spent a life trying to live up to a ghost who may have been a figment of her father's imagination.

Pushing her maudlin thoughts aside, she reached for a volume at random, pulled a slim red book off the middle of the shelf, and turned it in her hands. Its leather binding was shining, as if newly made, but the book opened with the ease often-read books had, falling flat in her upturned palms to a sonnet about love—comparing it to the winds of the Ice Plains, something natural, stark, and strong. A fitting metaphor in many ways, though one she'd not considered.

She was flipping the book closed again, to find the title page and author, when she heard Ghel call her name from the first floor. Strella smiled at the sound of his voice and moved to the outer railing opposite the bookshelves. "Up here, Ghel."

Looking down at him, she marveled again at his size, his mass of hair even when it was pulled tight away from his face as it was most days, and his gruff and alluring outside edges. It contrasted with the way his eyes softened when he saw her, and the small, sweet grin he had half-hidden in his beard.

"I'll come to you, Strella," he said, moving with his fighter's grace and strength up the side stairs, taking them two at a time without issue. He met her in moments, standing before her deliciously in his fighting leathers, which he tended to wear whenever he wasn't required to wear something else for appearance's sake. She quite preferred the leathers and the way they hugged the muscles in his chest and legs and everywhere else on him, but she didn't say as much. She didn't say anything, being too busy taking all of him in as her heart pounded in her chest and the connection between them twanged like a lute string.

"Lady Piris told me you were here," he said, grabbing her hand as if he couldn't help but touch her in some way. Strella related to the feeling.

"Did you need something?"

"Nothing in particular."

"Is everything well?" Strella knew things were not well since the archer attack on them, but she worried something else, something even worse, had happened.

"As well as can be expected, given recent events," Ghel grumbled, looking away from her and down at his feet before his gaze shifted to the hand holding the book. He scanned the shelf as if noting for the first time where they were in the library. "Love poems," he half whispered.

Strella blushed but turned the book over in her hand. "A random pick but a good one, if the one poem I've read so far is any indication."

"Father would approve. He enjoys poetry, especially Queen Nola's verses."

Strella took her hand from Ghel because she was surprised the book was written by a royal. Yet there it was when she opened to the title page. *Love Poems* by Queen Nola Borau. She knew her history well, was aware Queen Nola ruled with King Matten for a few centuries several millennia ago. A very old book then. "I never knew Queen Nola was a poet."

Ghel didn't seemed surprised. "Few did. It was a personal hobby. Her poetry was collected and printed solely for her king." His eyes brightened and he asked, "Would you like to see them?"

"See them?"

Ghel replied. "Yes. See them, and see my favorite room in the palace."

Strella couldn't say no to a glimpse into something Ghel enjoyed, so she agreed before turning to shelve the book again. Ghel stopped her with a gentle tug on her elbow. "No. Please. Keep the book. For now. So you can read more of Queen Nola."

Gripping the slim volume tightly in one hand as Ghel took her other and led them down the stairs, Strella thought she was lucky Ghel found her today and she was now on another, different type of adventure with him. Maybe this was what their life would be, a series of discoveries and adventures, big and small. At least, for the small sliver of life she might have left to her.

S he stood in awe, unable to speak. She'd been in beautiful places before, seen extraordinary pieces of art, but nothing to this scale. "It's magnificent," she whispered as they stepped farther into the Royal Gallery.

It was a vast room, seeming to run the entire length of the western wing of the Winterlands Palace. Benches dotted the middle at intervals, interspersed with huge marble statues of Fae in various poses. Along each wall, spaced a few feet apart, was canvas after canvas, all together a riot of color when she took in the room.

Ghel tugged her hand gently, directing her to a specific section, though she took in all the paintings and statues she could as they walked to a spot more than halfway down the space. She saw landscapes and portraits and paintings without clear subjects, only colors and shapes. Their feet echoed in the otherwise-silent hall. All was quiet, and she didn't mind. She wanted the quiet to try to take in all the pieces around her.

Of course, Hollythorn Manor had a wide collection of art, but their pieces were dispersed throughout the house itself. They had nothing like this gallery, a central location where someone could simply exist among all this beauty. She was so busy taking in all she could, she let Ghel guide her without thinking, until he gently touched her shoulder and she saw they were standing by a sturdy wooden bench with a thick padded seat. "Please. Sit." Ghel guided her down to face the left side of the room and followed her so they sat side by side, admiring the artwork.

She sat and said nothing for a few minutes, too busy looking at all she could around her. Ghel let her, and she might have thought him also engrossed in the art if she didn't turn to see him studying her profile instead. Catching herself before she twisted her hair, she clasped her hands tight together in her lap and said, "I didn't know there was an art gallery."

Ghel shrugged. "It's no secret. Anyone can visit, but it has been a long time since a new piece was added, which may be the last time an official event happened here."

"What was the last piece?"

"A royal portrait of my parents, after their wedding."

Strella hadn't seen it, and she wanted to go look for it—see a young Queen Alene, who likely looked very similar, and a young and healthy King Frit. However, Ghel had brought her here for his own reasons, so she tucked the information away and promised herself she'd come back to explore another day. Possibly with Piris, who also enjoyed art.

"See the painting there?" Ghel pointed directly in front of them at a massive portrait of two beautiful Fae, each wearing a crown of the Winterlands. "That is King Matten and Queen Nola."

Strella studied the picture. The queen sat at what looked to be a writing desk strewn with pages, a bright-blue quill pen in her hand, poised and ready to use. Her smile was slight but present, and her eyebrows pulled enough to make her appear as if in mid-thought. Those thoughtful eyes were a deep brown, a color reflected in the shadows of the painting and her hair. King Matten, a huge Fae man with frost-blond hair and metal-gray eyes, didn't look out of the portrait like his queen. Instead, his head was tilted down, looking toward her, his own slight smile in place.

"I know stories of King Matten, as most in Fae do, I suppose. He remains a favorite among historians and storytellers alike. I know of Queen Nola as it relates to him."

"Do you know their love story?" Ghel asked, leaning slowly toward her.

Strella shook her head and Ghel reached for her, hesitated, then cupped her cheek. "I will tell it to you. When we have more time."

"I'd like that." Like was an understatement for Strella. She loved stories in all forms, but the idea of Ghel telling her a love story, his deep voice soothing and hypnotic, sent a thrill through her body.

Sadly, his hand fell away as he surveyed the room around them before speaking again. "When I was young, I came here often. I didn't like the library, as you know. Wasn't too interested in the various studies either. Much preferred being outside, the stables and the practice rings. But, inside, this was my favorite place in the palace."

He gave her a little piece of himself, and she stored it away in her mind, to turn it over and treasure later. She wanted more if he would give it. "Why?"

He turned away, his jaw tightening, and Strella knew he struggled with his next words. "I felt peace here. The rest of the palace... I never fit comfortably. Here, my fit didn't matter. The art never wanted too much from me. It merely was."

The ache in his voice and the taut pull of their connection made Strella's gut clench. She reached for him, leaning deep into his side as she burrowed her hand under his wild mane of hair to rub the back of his neck. The tension there strained against her fingers as she tried to soothe a pain she also knew. It was hard, a Fae trying to live up to certain expectations even as they feared those expectations could never be met.

Ghel's head turned and leaned over her as his hand grabbed her chin firmly and lifted it to meet his gaze. He searched her face, his own leaking its worry and stress and the weight he likely always bore as the eldest Prince of the Winterlands, before his mouth dropped. He let loose a breath that somehow reminded Strella of prayer to the gods, soft yet earnest and so real. Her own breath stilled as his head descended.

The kiss started sweet, his lips reverent in their caress of her own, but it was a slow burn, turning more and more heated as they nipped and sucked at each other. Strella's hand still gripped the back of his neck, then moved up into his dark hair, gripping the back of his head tightly in a fist before pulling his hair free of its leather confine so it spilled wild and free. A growl moved through Ghel and into Strella, causing her to quiver in the most delicious places.

They hadn't spoken of the night of their fasting, but Strella thought of it often, the taste of him and the look in his eyes as she'd made this powerful Fae come undone. She wanted to feel that again, feel him play her own body so she wound tight before coming loose all over again.

Ghel ripped himself away, turning his head for a few loud breaths before coming back face-to-face and leaning down so their foreheads touched.

"Strella," he croaked out, pausing for a beat before he continued. "Not here. Not now. We must wait."

"Wait?" Strella saw no need to wait. They were joined magically, fasted by his family and clan tradition.

His face turned serious, hard, though not cold or distant. She wondered to herself how she ever thought his face distant and cold before when now she saw it for what it was: assessing, thoughtful, and sparse in what it gave away. She knew what bubbled under the exterior not many seemed inclined to look beyond, the loyalty and care and fierce feeling waiting under the surface, and she was thankful she felt it now, had come to know him enough to see all he was.

"Strella, I am not a gentle Fae, but I would be gentle for you. Treat you as you deserve to be treated: with honor and respect. With care."

She nodded in agreement, not because she agreed in principle but because she sensed he needed this, to perceive himself in a certain way in relation to her. She'd give him this, even if she wanted more in the moment. His view of himself was more important than her unquenched desire.

"As you wish, Ghel."

He pulled her into his arms, the hug a touch shy of crushing, but Strella wanted to be lost in the pressure and heat of him. He kissed the top of her head before setting her right, smoothing his hands down her arms, and taking her hand. Ghel rose, bringing her up with him, and she followed him as they left the beauty of the gallery and their moment together behind.

Chapter Thirteen
Ghel

Ghel adjusted the erection in his leathers before entering his father's private study. He'd escorted Strella back to the library before coming to this meeting, and her taste lingered enough to keep the beast in his pants raging at his gallantry. He swore he'd be no brute with her, he'd wait to bed her at a proper place and time, woo and romance her, instead of doing what his body begged to do: rip their clothes off whenever they were close and rut like an idiot.

He'd never felt such need for someone, such a pull, and it worried him, as most things did. He feared what he'd do to her when he let the reins loose. He wanted to be gentle with her, but he doubted, when the moment came, he'd be able to control himself. He was a hardened warrior not used to the needs or desires of a lady. He knew Strella wanted him, yes. Felt it from her whenever they were together. Still, how she wanted him and if she wanted him for more than his strong, hard body, he didn't know. He wished she did, but there was always doubt at the back of his mind. The nagging voice in his head telling him this body was all he had to give to his kingdom, his family, and his wife.

Those thoughts were what finally calmed his lust enough so he didn't embarrass himself or his family in the meeting. When he stalked into the room, he knew his usual scowl was in place, though he had no reason to scowl at anyone there. His father sat looking small behind his massive oak desk, his mother standing tall and proud at his side. Jarok leaned against one of the high-backed leather chairs facing the desk while Cylian stood at attention, his focus on the king and queen even when Ghel walked into the space and everyone else looked his way.

The door snapped shut behind him as he moved to stand between Jarok and Cylian, his feet planted firmly and his body tight and at attention. He said nothing, seeing no need in unnecessary pleasantries among a group of people who knew him so well.

King Frit lifted a small scroll from the desktop. "Leader Alo broke the archer."

It gave Ghel no satisfaction to know this, though he'd provided his own retribution for what the archer had put Strella through during the attack. Breaking a Fae warrior, especially one from the Monti Clan, would take a great deal of magic, time, and blood, but it was sometimes necessary for the safety of the kingdom. A small piece of him felt relief at least one threat to Strella no longer existed.

"What did he discover?" Ghel asked.

"The attack was planned weeks ago. The Montis knew you would need to travel to the Aurora Outpost before the palace wedding and lay in wait until you arrived at the final turnoff."

"Ghel was the target all along," Cylian said. "Makes sense. He's the heir to the throne and the general of the Winterlands Forces, as well as a fierce warrior in his own right. If Engad Monti was determined to take over the clans and all the Winterlands, he'd have to eventually take on Prince Ghel."

"Coward," Jarok spit out, his face full of stony anger.

"Yes, a cowardly move, but a smart move nonetheless," King Frit said. "Engad Monti is no idiot. He knows Ghel would be a formidable opponent in open battle."

Ghel grunted in agreement. Monti was not a fool, and an opponent felled before a fight even began was the best possible outcome for him.

Queen Alene came into the conversation then. "My brother also says the archer spoke of a spy who fed the Monti Clan information about the royals and events here in the palace."

They knew this already, of course. Had known about the spy for some time. Jarok bit his lip, and Ghel was thankful he didn't voice his concern over Lady Piris. They'd talked of it more since the night of the engagement ball, and although Jarok did not trust the lady, he didn't fully know if she was a spy so wouldn't accuse her. Yet. He held back only at Ghel's request.

Besides, they already knew who had direct communication with Engad Monti and were simply biding their time as they gathered additional evidence.

"Confirmation is a good thing," Cylian muttered, though his brows were creased in serious thought. They'd trusted a great deal of information to Cylian Padalist, who technically was an outsider in their lands. However, Ghel loved the Fae like a brother, had since their time together in the Autumnlands when he witnessed firsthand the harshness of Lord Rylnd Padalist and what Cylian had endured from his father. He trusted him without reservation, something he only gave the people in this room. Strella was quickly becoming someone he could add to this short list, but there were reasons she was not there yet. Reasons having to do with his own secrets and nothing to do with her.

Cylian finally voiced his thoughts aloud. "If Monti suspects the Aurora Clan captured the archer instead of him being lost to the wilderness, he may move up any plans he has."

"True enough," King Frit said. "He's also shown his intentions with his attack on Ghel, even if we didn't have the archer's confessions."

"He'll be bolder now," Queen Alene muttered.

"Let him be bold. It is better for us," Ghel grumbled, bringing his arms up to cross on his chest. "I've called in all the Winterlands legions. The Storm is here with Stone, and Aurora Clan could come in larger numbers as soon as tomorrow. Maybe it is time for us to take a more overt stand."

"What of the wedding?" Cylian asked, and Ghel went rigid at the words.

King Frit paused, then answered. "I still believe the wedding is crucial and should go forward. It is a week away."

Relief washed through Ghel at the news. Strella was his, in his mind and according to Aurora Clan custom, but he was happy to know there were no reasons his family wished to pull back or postpone what they'd planned for months at this point. He wanted to help her, keep her safe and away from this ugly mess and the eventual fallout, and the only way he knew he could do that was to have her as his wife. Firmly establish their relationship in the eyes of all the noble Fae. He also simply wanted her, more and more every day.

His father was weaker in body but not yet weak of mind, and he gave each person their orders before he dismissed them. It was the same plan, solid and safe to ensure everyone who deserved to would come out of the situation unscathed. He worried for Strella still, but everyone in the room would do what they could to shield her. The king and queen had asserted as much from the beginning, but now Ghel echoed their concerns. His focus in this had shifted from duty to his family and kingdom, sweeping her into the fold.

Cylian went off to find out what he could from meetings with various Winterlands lords and ladies. Jarok left shortly after to discuss plans with Stone for future need of the Aurora Clan and to send word to the Windin Clan to be on alert, ready to come when called. Ghel knew his duty, to prep and lead the Winterlands Forces. They all knew a battle loomed; there was no avoiding it after the assault. It was a matter of when and where it would occur, and what they could do to help ensure the outcome fell in their favor.

G hel wanted Strella and knew it was also a part of their plan to proceed with the wedding. However, as the week wore on and the wedding date came closer and closer, he couldn't help but worry about something else. Was Strella ready for their marriage? Did she feel forced into it still? They spent time together here and there, and they talked as well as touched, but they didn't talk of what they actually wanted, which caused doubts to linger. He knew she was holding something back and talked little of herself because of it, but all Ghel wished was that she'd tell him what weighed on her.

He couldn't shake the questions, so he sent Strella a message through Render asking her to meet him alone in one of the smaller, unused palace courtyards. They'd have privacy and time, and maybe she'd feel comfortable enough to tell him what she so obviously wished to tell him. He wouldn't push her to it, but he would give her the opportunity to find the words on her own.

Ghel was staring, unseeing, at the snow-covered stone ground when he heard the melody of her voice calling his name. A fierce desire to hear his name on her lips when she was breathless ripped through him, but he stuffed it down as he moved toward her.

"Strella, thank you for coming," he said as he led her to a covered bench. They were out in the open, but no other Fae was around, just as he'd wanted. He needed space for honesty, or at least a slice of honesty.

He spoke past the lump in his throat and got straight to the point. "I want us to be honest with one another. Are you content with the wedding going forward?"

Strella looked startled, maybe a little guilty for some odd reason. She studied her hands twisting in her lap before looking at him again. "Yes," she whispered.

It wasn't exactly enthusiastic, so Ghel continued. "Are you certain?"

She breathed deep and gave a sharp nod before elaborating. "Yes, Ghel. I am ready to marry you. Before... to be honest as you ask, before I was hesitant but still prepared to do what my father wished. Now, however. Now, I'm happy to be marrying you."

Ghel's muscles relaxed, his heart beating steadier and stronger in his chest. "Good," he said, his voice sounding rough even to his own ears. "As I am happy to marry you."

Strella blushed prettily as her icy eyes shifted around. He knew she had some secret she thought important, and he wanted her to tell him. In her own time.

She opened her mouth to speak but closed it again with a sharp snap before she looked out over the courtyard for the first time. It was a hidden gem. The position in the northern wing blocked it from the sun, which meant night blooms, snow, and ice collected there. The ground was covered in small drifts, icicles clung to the decorative filaments along the wall, and winter jasmine grew in fragrant clumps dotted along the perimeter. "Such a beautiful place," she said and turned toward him with a sad smile. "You've shown me such beautiful places in the short time I've known you, Ghel."

His chest swelled at the thought he'd given her something she found precious. "I would show you all the beautiful things in Fae, Strella." He didn't add he thought none of them could possibly compare to her.

"I know you would. If you could."

Ghel's brows dipped down, but he said nothing, giving Strella silence she could fill if she wished. It wasn't awkward silence. It was the type Ghel knew well because he didn't often say much, especially to people he didn't know. His face smoothed and a small smile danced across his lips as he tipped his head down to hide the direction of his thoughts. Not that they were bad. On the contrary, coming to the realization he was comfortable in silence with Strella made him want to let out a fierce yell of joy. However, he suspected Strella wished to share something with him, so he decided to let her lead, be as unobtrusive as possible so she could take whatever she needed to speak her words. Gods knew he often needed the same time and space when he had hard things to share, even with those he cared for deeply. He hoped Strella did care for him, as he cared for her.

Lost in his own musings and happy realizations, he didn't hear the other Fae coming until they were nearly on top of the pair. He jumped up, hand to his ever-present sword, placing himself between Strella and the huff of breath he heard from their left. He found Lord Hollythorn there, leaning insolently against a stone arch, staring straight at him.

"I was here for some time, Prince."

The judgment of those words rankled him, but not as much as the truth in them. He'd been so lost in thoughts of Strella, he'd let another Fae get incredibly close without him realizing it. No matter it was her father. Ghel didn't reply, however, merely nodded in the Fae's direction as he felt Strella rise beside him.

"Father," she said, and Ghel wondered if her voice held a note of annoyance or exasperation, or if he simply imagined it because of his own.

"Strella, dear. How are you? It is far too cold in the open for you to linger long." Hollythorn stepped toward his daughter. Ghel did not know him well. Didn't know him at all, in fact, and wished to keep his distance as best he could. Although it would be harder and harder in the future, what with him becoming a relative by marriage. He considered it a small price to pay to be with Strella, though mere weeks ago Ghel's thoughts had run in the opposite direction.

"I'm fine, Father, but thank you for your concern." Strella moved around Ghel to step between him and Hollythorn. Ghel couldn't fully gauge the outlines of their relationship, one so outwardly different from the warmth and openness he experienced in his own small family. His father was king, but he never looked upon his sons with anything but love and pride, never acted distant with them in public or private.

He couldn't say the same for the Hollythorn family. For an outsider, their relationship looked far more formal and rigid, but he recognized much of his evaluation was colored by his thoughts on Strella's father. Mikka Hollythorn was a cold and distant man. Ghel could admit he occasionally showed slivers of actual care for Strella. What did it say about him as a father? Or how Strella viewed him as a father? Ghel needed to mull over this, given all he knew would come to pass in the near future.

"Still, Strella. Come. There is no need for you to remain." Lord Hollythorn gave the prince an open sneer. Ghel marked it, of course, but did not lower himself to comment on the rudeness. He wasn't one to feel others owed him anything for being a prince, so he didn't care if the Fae looked down on him. Given all he knew of the man, it was to be expected. However, Strella twisted her hands together, her head turning to look from Ghel to her father, worry and confusion all over her.

"Strella. Come." The bark of command made Ghel growl low in his throat.

"She will do as she wishes," he said, unable to stand by as Strella was yet again controlled by this man. He moved closer to her, caught her eye, and whispered, "Do as you wish, my Star."

She gave a small smile his way and patted his arm, her touch a physical reassurance he didn't know he needed until he felt it ride through his blood.

"I will go with my father, Ghel. We'll talk another day."

She moved toward Lord Mikka, who gave Ghel cold eyes until he turned to lead her out of the open courtyard. The prince stood there for long minutes, the cold an old friend he didn't mind. What he did mind was the new worries piling higher and higher in his mind as his wedding day approached, as the inevitable revelation of the secrets he knew he kept, and the ones he suspected Strella kept. All hovered like an icicle, ready to drop, dangerous and unpredictable in their fallout.

Chapter Fourteen
Strella

Strella waited for Piris to leave her chamber the night before her wedding to Ghel. There was no way her friend would have allowed her to roam the halls of the palace alone at night, especially the night before a big royal event, when any number of guests were now also staying there. She'd tie her down or knock her out to keep her in her bedchamber. Far better for Strella to be a little more like Piris, a little more stealthy, and sneak from her room an hour after Piris went to sleep with admonishments for Strella to rest for the next day.

Her wedding day felt slightly anticlimactic for Strella, as she and Ghel had already completed the fasting ceremony, which was a wedding of a sort. However, the big ceremony, conducted in the throne room and presided over by the king himself, was the type of event Strella thought of when she thought of weddings. She'd never thought of her own wedding, of course, because she'd never imagined she'd marry. Now, she was happy to be tied to Ghel. Still, they'd been interrupted in the courtyard and she'd not been able to tell him of her impending death within the year.

Her mouth dried when she imagined it, telling the prince what she knew would happen. She'd been fretting over it since their return, tossing at night, restless and focused on what could come. Taking stolen moments between official engagements and meetings and soon-to-be-princess duties to worry herself sick over how and when she'd tell him. How he'd react to her prophecy. Whether or not he'd immediately reject her and break the bonds they'd already forged.

Yet she had to do it. It was only fair. He deserved the chance to back out of their arrangement. She wouldn't begrudge him that if he chose to do so, despite what they'd experienced together so far in their short acquaintance. Ghel's small smiles, his heat, seared into her soul and would linger all her days even if he ended their marriage before it officially began. She feared he would not because of the Aurora fasting, but she'd been unable to tell him before. If she was honest with herself, she was possibly unwilling to tell him as she came to care for him more and more.

She held part of herself back to be sure. She stopped herself from thinking too hard and deep about her feelings, all in an effort to keep them locked tightly away. He'd burrowed his way into her, but she would never express it, never hint too fully at it, for fear it would lead Ghel to care too much, expose himself too much when she was destined to die soon. He already cared for her. She felt it with every touch and glance, in the way he showed her all the beauty the Winterlands had to offer. He'd yet to express it in words, so she held out hope his care hadn't grown too deep. Maybe like her, he'd held parts of himself back because of their odd circumstances and relative newness as a couple.

In her walks with Piris, she'd discovered the royals' wing close to her own rooms. Her friend, using her special talents, had outlined where the rooms were situated as they'd walked one evening, so she now knew where to go. Strella's rooms as princess were located right next to Ghel's chambers. Surprisingly, there were no guards stationed there, although she was startled to see Stone Aurora leaning against the wall several doors down from the entrance to the hallway. He'd come up sharp when neared, fighting stance at the ready. His body eased and a lopsided smirk spread across his face as he saw who trespassed.

"A late-night surprise for my cousin?" he asked on a whisper, stepping close while keeping a respectful distance. He was a warrior, big and bold as Ghel and, like his cousin, appeared to be a good man in his care and concern for others.

She nodded, unable to answer, though what he thought was going to happen was not her plan.

He chuckled and moved forward, closer to the mouth of the hallway and farther away from Ghel's rooms. "Lucky Fae," he said before bowing in her direction as he passed.

She turned when she finally found words. "There are no other guards?"

Stone looked behind her, focusing down the hallway before he said, "No need, when so many warriors live here." He nodded and turned back as a voice, low and hushed, caused Strella to spin around.

"Strella? Are you okay?" Ghel was there, standing outside his doorway. Of course he'd heard her and Stone talking. He missed nothing.

She twisted a hand in her hair, not caring in the moment how her fidgeting made her look.

"Come, Strella," he said, beckoning her with a crook of his finger. "Tell me why you've come."

She glided toward him as if compelled, her feet moving although she couldn't find her voice. He stepped sideways into the darkened doorframe, gesturing with an outstretched hand for her to enter, and she followed his lead, stopping steps into the room to take in his space.

Ghel's chambers held a cozy sitting room with a large hearth and a roaring fire nestled deep in a corner casting shadows around the space. A warm leather smell filled the air because of the ring of overstuffed chairs arranged in front of the fire, all looking comfortable and inviting. There were bookcases, not filled with many books, but trinkets and maps and pictures. A large desk, strewn with papers and plans and quills, was positioned along another wall facing a night-dark window.

Strella was so busy taking in the space, focused on soaking up all she could of Ghel and what he surrounded himself with, she jumped when a hand landed lightly on her shoulder. Spinning around, she saw Ghel's eyes lighten as he looked at her, even as a small frown marred his face. "Strella?"

A tug at her hair reminded her she was still twirling it in her hands, and she dropped her locks despite the calm the action always offered. Taking in a deep, loud breath, she focused on her possibly soon-to-be-official husband. "I am well, Ghel, but there is something I must say before it's too late."

Ghel, all serious lines and taut muscle, moved them to the warmed leather chairs. The fire danced across his black hair and flared in his dark eyes, the usual golden glow of his skin even more pronounced in this light. For the first time, Strella noticed he wore a loose undershirt and leather pants, and her mouth dried for a different reason when she spied the soft smattering of dark hair across his broad, hard chest.

The connection between them was tense, vibrating with worry on both their ends, and Ghel leaned back to offer Strella personal space. "Please, Star. You can tell me whatever you wish."

Gods, it gutted her, hearing his voice so soft, her nickname on his lips. She couldn't look at him, didn't want to hear him but couldn't stop her ears. All she could do was go on.

"I've told you—hinted at secrets I have," she said, looking into the fire rather than at the Fae man beside her. She felt him lean forward, closer, his heat as blazing as the flames she faced. After a few deep breaths in and out, she twisted her courage in place before she blurted it in one quick sentence. "When I was eight years old, Seer Willow found me, told me I would die at the same age as my mother, which is the age I am this year."

The thud of muscles hitting leather sounded, Ghel leaning away from her as if struck. She hung her head. Shame, fear for her future, concern for Ghel, and worry over his thoughts all warred in her mind, no one emotion winning their fight. In a rush, she said, "I should have told you earlier, but every time I tried, I couldn't. Some reasons for my delay were outside my control, but I'd be lying if I said I didn't fear telling you, how you would feel when you found out your betrothed would soon die."

"Strella. Look at me." Ghel's command shook her free of her tangled thoughts, so she turned her head away from the flames and looked at him. His dark eyes sparked, his face a stone mask of fury, and she knew he had to hate her in that moment.

"Tell me everything. Now."

So she did. She detailed how Seer Willow had found her playing alone in the holly grove of her home as a child, how she'd told her she would not die like her mother but would die the same age as her mother before the seer disappeared into the trees. What she felt in that moment, and every moment after, knowing she was marked for death by the most famous seer in all the Winterlands.

Ghel looked ready to blow when she finished, and she could understand why.

"I know it is hard to hear, and you have much to think on. I will not blame you if you don't want to proceed with the wedding tomorrow."

The prince jumped from his seat in a flash, almost too fast to track, and he scooped Strella up in his arms, burying his dark head in her light hair and squeezing her close. "Never," he bit back, but his word was unnecessary as the tie binding them twanged hard and strong in her chest. He held her for long minutes before setting her down and stepping away. The prince touched her face, searching her eyes for something he couldn't find, and said, "I've met Seer Willow, have seen her prophecies play out in a few instances before. In my experience, Strella, they do not always come to pass in the way one thinks."

Strella gaped at him. She'd never heard anything of the sort. Seer Willow, the most famous seer in the Winterlands for centuries past, was beyond reproach in all she said. What she predicted came to be, according to everything Strella had ever heard. "What?" She could get out no more, unable to express all she felt, the hope and dread now coursing through her.

Ghel hugged her tight once again. "Strella, my Star. Seer Willow is true, but not always entirely accurate. Her prophesies come to pass in unexpected ways, sometimes because the Fae in question know and work toward the prophecy themselves, live life as if it will be. Sometimes for reasons outside their control. However, nothing is guaranteed."

She shook her head. "Piris also believes it isn't true, but I feel it in my bones, Ghel. I know it will happen."

He gripped her shoulders a touch too hard and growled out, "It will if you will it, Strella. This is what I'm trying to tell you."

She shook her head, turning out of his grasp. "No, Ghel. You must prepare. You must know I am not long for this life."

"I refuse to believe it."

"Refusing to believe it doesn't make it untrue."

With gritted teeth, he asked, "What does your father say of this?"

Strella searched his face, once again struck by the anger she saw there when he spoke of her father. Prince Ghel did not like him at all, and she did not know why. "He doesn't know," she admitted.

Ghel laughed a merciless laugh. "Of course not. Lord Mikka Hollythorn would not tolerate such a wrinkle in his plans."

"Plans for me to marry?" Strella pressed, seeing something flit across Ghel's face, something darker and more fierce than before.

He shook his head, but she needed to know what it was. Something nagged at the back of her mind, had since they'd arrived. "I believe you also have secrets."

"Your father is the one with secrets. Speak to him."

Strella moved to the door, willing to call Ghel's bluff. He scooped her into a hug, stopping her progress. "No, Strella. Do not go to him."

"Why not? He's my father. He would never hurt me."

"Hasn't he already? Offered you up as sacrifice for his own ends?"

"What do you mean?"

Ghel set her back down on the chair and knelt in front of her before clasping her hands in his. "There is much you don't know about your father."

"Like?"

He hesitated, worry floating over his features, but he did tell her. "Your father is working with Engad Monti."

Strella couldn't breathe for a moment, but when she could, she gasped. "No."

Ghel squeezed her hands tight. "Yes, Strella. Their plans, as far as we can tell, is to take over all the Winterlands, including the royal line."

"How?"

Ghel hit her with a stare, and she blinked as her mind raced. "Me?"

A nod from the prince. "Yes. You marry me, the royal family is taken out by Monti in some way, and the princess becomes sole heir and queen. A queen Lord Mikka believes he can control."

She shot up so fast, Ghel stumbled back in her wake. Strella paced and thought before whirling on him. "You knew for a while, long before our marriage was arranged."

He looked away, not able to meet her eyes, as he said, "Yes."

Strella stilled. "You knew and still agreed to marry me."

"You must understand, we needed to have him closer, we needed to know how deep his reach was, who all was involved."

"You suspected me?" she asked, tears beginning to fall.

He moved toward her, to take her again in his arms, but she stumbled backward, nearly tripping herself, so he stopped his advances. "Strella..." Her name was an ache on his tongue, and she felt the pull of him, their magic strong and sure. Yet she couldn't trust it, much like he couldn't trust her.

"No. You thought I planned with my father, wanted to overthrow your family, bring war to our lands."

"Only until I met you. From then on, I—we all—knew you could have no hand in this."

Strella didn't know what to think, what to believe. Who to believe. She couldn't think her father capable of this, but his behavior since his announcement of her betrothal had been questionable, especially his actions toward Ghel and the rest of the royal family. Gods, she wanted to deny it outright, but she couldn't, not with how serious the accusation was. How it meant the death of the king and queen. The death of Ghel. She shook uncontrollably at the thought, tears of worry mixing with the ones caused by the pain of his mistrust.

"I must go," she said, stopping in her frantic pace to careen toward the door.

"Strella, no," Ghel called, blocking her path, but she couldn't think straight, couldn't take any more. She'd come to tell her life's secret and learned another. It was too much for her in the moment.

She sidestepped him, almost making an escape before she once again felt the familiar weight of him at her shoulders. "Please, Star. Don't leave like this. We should—"

She shook her head. "We will marry tomorrow, but I am obviously not your Star. Never have been if you never trusted me."

She thought she heard a choked groan, something like pain coming from Ghel's throat, but she had to ignore it, because she had to run. Needed to leave and give herself time and space to think. Though there was little time left.

So much jumbled up her mind, but she had a purpose here, an original reason for the discussion that had gone so very far afield. She wanted him to have a choice. She'd clearly made hers, despite his lies and mistrust, but her conscience needed a firm answer from him as well. "That is, if you still wish to marry a dead woman?"

Ghel growled. "We will marry tomorrow."

With an answer given and an ache firmly planted in her chest, she didn't look back as she walked out the door. This time the prince didn't try to stop her. Stone attempted a joke but stopped when he saw her clearly in the dark hall. He didn't speak, but he did follow her at a distance, all the way back to her chambers, as she quietly cried every step of the way.

She tried to muster a smile for Piris, but the woman knew her too well, saw through her forced happiness almost immediately. She pressed, but Strella kept her mouth shut tight. She would tell Piris everything that had transpired between her and Ghel, but after the wedding. She also knew her friend well, and if Piris discovered the royal family had lied about her, attempted to use her for political machinations involving her father—even if Ghel claimed the intentions changed after he'd met her—she would shake the foundations of

Fae to keep Strella away from this family, from Ghel. If she waited until after the wedding, Piris would be livid but resigned. Her friend would help her navigate the new course she'd planned as she lay awake all night: keep herself closed off from Ghel as best she could while being the spy he'd once suspected her of being. Of course, she'd be spying on her father, gathering information to help her land and the royals even if they held suspicions of her, now or in the past. She'd prove herself up to the task by either confirming his treason or clearing her father's name.

They stood alone in an alcove, awaiting the musical signal so they could walk arm-in-arm down the long golden aisle placed in the center of the throne room, all eyes on Lady Strella Hollythorn, who would soon become Princess Strella Borau. Piris, the only one standing with her during the ceremony, was already in position, so it was one of the few times she and her father had had to talk that day without anyone else present. He looked her up and down, his face serious, a sad line creasing his forehead as he nodded to himself. Finally, he spoke. "My daughter, about to become princess. If only your mother could see this."

His voice drifted softly, somehow both wistful and cold, his eyes glazed with unshed tears. Gods, she ached for his ache, loved him despite how he treated her and what he might be doing to their lands. Strella swallowed hard before answering. "I would have loved to know her."

He took her hand, firm in his grip, and with a harsh breath, said, "You are all she hoped for. All I hoped for. And you will be so much more, my daughter. I will make it so."

Her heart stuttered. She squeezed his hand back and whispered, "What do you mean?"

Lord Mikka Hollythorn bit his lip, a sure sign of nerves from a man who so very rarely showed any, enough to make his daughter still her breath for his reply. "You will see, daughter. You will see. Soon you will be safe from everyone. Safe to live a long life without any fear or danger or need."

She was about to say she'd led such a life with him long before her marriage, but he dropped her hand, pulling her into a fierce hug, and held her so hard she almost asked him to stop. At the last second, he pushed himself away and straightened his formal tunic as he straightened his face, becoming once again the impeccable lord. The first note hit, and he offered his arm. Strella took it, so much unsaid between them, but there was nothing for it now. She was off to marry a prince—someone she might have called her prince until late last night. The people looking on her as she walked the aisle may have thought she had unshed tears because she was so happy to marry. Strella, however, knew the reason why her eyes glistened, as did Ghel, who looked on her with thoughtful, worried eyes as she stepped closer and closer to him.

Chapter Fifteen
Ghel

Strella was a vision to Ghel, a goddess of old, a regal lady from the age of heroes passed up to him so he could stand in awe of her. She walked down the long aisle toward him in a frilly winter white gown, her pale-blonde hair twisted into intricate braids and forming a nest for the crown. Her posture and steps were perfectly measured and sure, royal diamonds sent by his mother lying across her throat and dripping from her ears. She looked like the Aurora territory—snowy and beautiful and like home.

Her eyes made his breath freeze and his heart ache. They were icy in color, yes, but always active, kind, thoughtful, and full of life. Then, as her father guided her down the aisle, they were shuttered, almost dead. Truly icy in a way he'd never seen on her. The worst part for Ghel was he knew he was the one who'd changed the way her eyes looked. She smiled at familiar faces as she passed them, but the smile never reached those dulled eyes.

He wasn't the only one to notice. Piris was staring daggers at him from her spot across the dais. He wondered if Strella had told her of their conversation but dismissed the idea. Piris was a warrior, fierce and loyal. If she knew for a fact how Ghel had hurt her best friend, he'd have been met with a far more solid and deadly dagger at some point that morning, prince or no. She knew something was off, that Strella was unhappy, but not why or how, so she didn't act. Lucky for him. He doubted Piris could take him in a fair fight, but their fight wouldn't be fair. Not because he didn't fight women—a warrior was a warrior regardless—but because he wouldn't fight Piris. Strella held too much love and affection for the woman for him to ever harm her.

Her father, on the other hand... Lord Hollythorn was smug and cold at the same time, controlling their steps as they moved closer to Ghel, his family, and Piris. He wore a light-blue tunic and breeches, so light someone could confuse it for white when he wasn't standing next to the brilliant white of Strella's gown. Ghel thought he saw care in the way he gripped his daughter's arm, in the slight dip of his chin when they had first started their procession down the aisle, and in the glow of pride in his face as he escorted her. Maybe, just maybe, there was something redeeming, but he was still a traitor who needed to be dealt with in quick order.

Gods knew Strella loved him because he was her father and had raised her, but there were many who raised children who did not deserve love or devotion. Lord Mikka Hollythorn's crimes were far-reaching, deadly, and could never be forgiven. He faced harsh consequences for his actions. Still, because Strella found some reason to love him, Ghel knew he would hesitate to end him despite having plotted it for so long. No, Ghel's mind was now changed. Lord Hollythorn would rot away in the Winterlands Palace dungeons or be condemned to penniless exile, but Ghel could now never land a killing blow—by his own hand or by decree. He could never allow his family to do so either, because of Strella and her love or, maybe more aptly, his love for Strella.

Ghel did love her and admitted it to himself now. He loved her kindness and bravery. He loved her intelligence and strategic mind. He loved her loyalty and concern for others. She was a true lady, compassionate and thoughtful and willing to do whatever it took to care for her family, her friends, and her kingdom. She appreciated beauty in art and the world around them. Her face and figure stirred lust in him, but these were the least affecting of her attributes.

Prior to being promised to Strella as a means to a pressing political end, Ghel had given little thought to who he would marry. Now he could not imagine marrying any other Fae in the entire realm. She was to be his, and it sparked righteous joy in his heart.

The spark was tempered by her own hesitancy, which he knew was based in what he'd confessed to her. He wanted to smack himself for how wonderfully he'd botched the previous evening. Strella had come to him to confess the worry he'd seen lie heavy on her. It was a shock to hear her say she would die, condemned by a prophecy from Seer Willow no less. Ghel had direct dealings with seer prophecies on a few occasions. It wasn't that they didn't come true, and Seer Willow's visions of the future were often even more accurate than others in Fae. As he'd told Strella last night, it was more about in what way they would come true. Besides, he would give his life for hers, protect her with a fierce fire no one else would be able to extinguish, so he refused to see it as she did. He convinced himself she'd missed something in the wording as a child or Seer Willow hadn't revealed the entire truth because she was so young. Regardless, he'd dispatched a messenger that morning to find Seer Willow and bring her to the Winterlands Palace. He needed to ensure he knew all the details, could plan and strategize for whatever threat may be looming for his bride. By the gods, he would not lose her so soon after finding her.

It must have been his whirling mind, running through possibilities and scenarios, that had made him misspeak last night. Once she'd asked him about her father, however, he could not lie. It was one thing to lie by omission, but he loved Strella. He could never lie to her face. Ghel told her because he'd been so out of sorts, he could think of nothing else to do. She also needed to know who and what her father was, prepare herself for his inevitable downfall.

She'd been stricken. The two-part blow of discovering her father was a traitor to their kingdom and that her betrothed engaged himself to her to find out if she, too, was a traitor had taken out his sweet Star. He couldn't blame her for her reaction. She loved her father, and even if she didn't outright say it, Ghel felt in his gut she was at least coming to love him. That was... coming to love him, until he'd confessed he'd suspected her of being a spy at worst and a clueless dupe at best. It didn't help he was so bad with talking, with explanations. Jarok and Cylian may have been able to stop her from leaving with pretty, calming words. He'd only bungled things and forcefully tried to detain her, and he was ashamed of himself, proving once again he was nothing but a brute. She'd fled his chambers, and he couldn't blame her for it. Stone had returned after seeing her to her rooms to berate him for Strella's tears, which he deserved. Seeing her now, her eyes cold as their color, he died a little inside at the pain he'd caused his love.

Lord Hollythorn and Lady Strella reached the stairs of the dais after long minutes and climbed upward with grace and ease. Lord Hollythorn stopped a few steps from Ghel, releasing her arm to face her before bending to kiss his daughter on the cheek. She gave a tight smile to her father and let his hand drop, making the last few steps toward Ghel on her own. He wanted to reach for her even then but waited until the proper time.

As she moved to stand on the same step as Ghel, his father moved from his throne several steps above them, walking with the slow, pained pace of the sick even as he held his crowned head high and proud. He gripped a cane hard to keep himself upright. He raised a hand toward the crowd. They'd been chittering amongst themselves as they sat, but with this gesture, they quieted so all could hear King Frit.

"Today is a joyous day indeed," Ghel's father said, "as we gather to join my son, Prince Ghel, with Lady Strella Hollythorn. Please, all in attendance, rise."

As one, the entire room stood for the recitation of vows, a spell cast to transform their betrothal bond to a marriage bond, forge the string of their betrothal magic into steel, and make their tether stronger and more durable. His mother moved to stand next to his father, a velvet pillow holding the prince and princess crowns sitting in her hands. Ghel had seen the princess crown for the first time that morning. There had been no princesses in his living memory to wear it. It sparkled in the light—a mass of diamonds set against silver so polished it refracted rainbows in the space. His own crown, which he wore so rarely, sat next to it, a larger, less jeweled version, though the silver shined so bright it was almost like a mirror, reflecting the rainbows cast by the diamond crown next to it.

Strella reached for him, and although he knew she did it because it was expected, he gripped her hands in his, trying to pass down his love through their bond and physical connection. Sadly, Strella looked at him for the barest of moments, choosing instead to focus her eyes on a spot over his left shoulder. No one looking from a distance could be able to tell, but it was a punch to the gut for Ghel, who willed her to look at him with all his thoughts.

His father said more words he didn't listen to, letting the formal decrees and titles and pleasantries slip away from him in favor of focusing on his bride. However, he did notice his cue, the point when he was required to actively participate in the ceremony. "Prince Ghel Borau, what say you?"

He didn't look at his father but stayed concentrated on Strella. He sucked in a deep breath and let the vows tumble out, adding force and depth to them because he felt they were so true.

"In the stillness of Winterlands,

Our love shall flourish, hand in hand.

Even as our land lies in wintery repose,

Our love will eternally bloom and grow.

Amidst snow and stars that gleam

We will live, love, and dream.

I vow, on my magic and land,

To never falter or fail. Never drop your hand.

Together we will lead our land true,

I will care for our people as I care for you."

By the end, Strella's eyes had finally wandered to his and she stood frozen, as if surprised by what he said. It should have been no surprise. They were the words every Winterlands royal said during a marriage binding, so surely someone had told her of them. Ghel's heart stilled as he felt the threads connecting them strengthen. He waited, now nervous and sweating, worried she would put a stop to the wedding.

His father boomed, his voice stronger than his frail form, "Lady Strella, what say you?"

Strella's voice shook in a way that made Ghel's gut pinch, but she repeated the words, completing the spell. A sizzle of magic coursed through Ghel as their bond was once again reinforced, becoming as strong as it could get. Marriage bonds could be severed, but they were even more complicated than ending betrothal magic.

Silently, King Frit reached for Ghel's crown, and he stooped low to make the placement easier for his father, who had a much smaller range of motion these days. His father's hand fell heavy on his shoulder where he gave his son a reassuring squeeze, causing the prince's emotions to roll for an entirely different reason. Strella curtsied deep, dipping her head so King Frit could also place her crown, officially marking her as Princess of the Winterlands.

"I now give you Prince and Princess of the Winterlands, Ghel and Strella Borau. Long may they serve our kingdom." His father threw up a hearty yell, and all in attendance followed suit, clamoring almost as loudly as the Aurora Clan had at their fasting ceremony. Ghel's heart was full, his mind racing as he grasped tightly onto Strella's hand and faced the crowd of nobles and dignitaries from other kingdoms. He felt it like the loss of a limb when she twisted her hand ever so gently and moved inches out of his hold.

T hey'd had no time alone since the previous evening. When the ceremony had ended, they had been rushed forward to move through what felt like to Ghel an endless line of people wishing to congratulate the newly married couple. He was frustrated, tired, and sustained only by his concern for Strella's needs. He'd bent down halfway through the line to whisper in her ear, "Do you need rest, Strella?" She'd given a quick shake of her head without looking at him and greeted the next Fae in line, poised and kind as always.

Then they'd been whisked off to the feast, where they sat at an elevated table with the rest of the royal family, Lady Piris, and Lord Hollythorn. The latter acted haughty as always as everyone else surrounding the couple engaged them in conversation. They ate good food—he'd never had issue with the fabulous cooks in the palace—listened to a variety of speeches from his family and several important figures attending, and drank sweet wine provided as a gift from the Summerlands. He didn't drink too much because he didn't want his mind hazy for the evening ahead. Strella drank little too, but she also ate little, as far as he could tell. She remained the perfect picture of a princess, crown glistening and manners impeccable, but the coldness in her eyes didn't melt the entire time.

Finally unable to handle any more formalities or time without proper conversation with his now-wife, Ghel leaned into his father and said, "May we leave?"

King Frit stared hard at his son, eyes furrowed as if he somehow sensed his eldest's unease. His father didn't yet know about the conversation with Strella the night before. That was another confession Ghel would need to make, though it would wait for the next morning. His father knew something was off but didn't press him in front of all these people. The king nodded and rose to give a quick speech, which Ghel mostly ignored. He was instead focused on Strella and the way her arms moved ever so slightly, likely because her hands were twisting together in her lap. She hid her fidgeting well from her guests. Ghel could tell, however, and wanted her away from here, where they could finally talk.

When the crowd cheered and clapped again, Ghel rose, moving to his bride and helping her to her feet. They gave small bows to the king and queen. Strella moved to her father for a quick good-bye kiss. Piris leaped up to hug her tight as Ghel gave his brother a hard clap on the back in farewell. They were off to his chambers—now their chambers—to be alone for the first time as husband and wife.

Strella had been deathly quiet their entire trip from the feast hall to their chambers. The maids had been busy all day, transferring or shuffling both Ghel's and Strella's belongings from their separate chambers to create the joint suite. Here they had two bedrooms, two massive closets with maid access, two bathing chambers, and a shared sitting room between everything. Not as massive as the royal chambers, but Ghel didn't want the space in the royal chambers. Being closer to Strella, even if she barely looked at him, eased him.

From his quick perusal of the sitting room, everything looked to be mostly as it had been before, with a few of Strella's things now peppered here and there. He imagined the same could be said of the closets, bathing chambers, and beds chambers. Thinking of his bedchamber being turned down and strewn with winter roses, as was tradition, made him grind his teeth and internally curse himself for his oafishness.

Strella had wandered by the large fireplace and was trying to secretly twist her hands, bring herself small comfort in her nervousness. He knew he needed to say something, reassure her somehow, but no words came. Silence stretched between them, tight as their magical bond and no longer comfortable.

Clearing his throat, Ghel finally forced himself to speak, deciding on a practical approach to the conversation. "As you can see, this is now our joint sitting room. If you look to your left, you will find the door to your chambers. To the right are mine. Do you have any questions?"

Slowly turning to face him, she closed her eyes before she asked, "Where will we be having intercourse this evening?"

Her face was pinched but set, and Ghel shook his head to attempt to clear the anger that rose in him, anger at himself for ever doing anything to make her think he would demand such a thing. She obviously did not want him, not now. Maybe no longer. He wished to the gods that would not be the case. The memory of her hot, slick skin and the sharp cries she'd made when he'd brought her pleasure in the Aurora territory was nearly enough to have him spilling in his own breeches like an untried Fae teen. However, he'd never take or demand from her what he wanted her to freely give.

He grumbled, "I am a brute, yes, but no monster, Strella."

Her eyes flew open, and a wrinkle creased her forehead. "I did not—"

He couldn't take more just then. The entire day had been worry and pain with aching beauty wrapped up in an emotional jumble, and he was barely holding himself together as it was. To hear accusations from her lips then would rip him in two. He needed a break, as he was certain she did as well. He stalked forward, and the small step back she took tore a hole in his chest, but he kept to his path, straight for her so he could bend close to her face.

"Hear me, Strella. You will never be forced to do something in this palace or anywhere else in the Winterlands. Anywhere else in Fae as long as I have breath in my body. You have been used and forced far too many times. No, my Star. We will share pleasure again only if and when you so choose. Until then, I will wait for you. I will wait for you until the colors blink out of the Aurora sky if I must."

Her lips parted and she sucked in a breath as she stared into his eyes. He saw her hand raise, as if she would touch his face, but she stopped its progress before she skimmed his beard. He straightened himself to give her the space he said he would as she skimmed her raised hand over her head.

He stepped back two giant steps and asked, "Do you want me to call a maid or Lady Piris to help you ready for bed?"

She sharply shook her head but refused to look at him. Muttering a good night, she veered in the direction of her chambers. Before she passed through the door, he thought he heard a whispered "thank you," but he wasn't certain, so he chose to ignore it for his own sanity. To think she thanked him for being a decent Fae man would cause him to rage at the unfairness of her life so far and the way he had added to it. Instead, he lumbered toward his own chamber to spend a sleepless night amongst rose-strewn sheets, alone.

Chapter Sixteen
Strella

"I cannot believe! Of all the conniving, sneaky things... And people think mimics are all automatic liars. Ha! They have nothing on your father or the royals." Piris's rant continued as she paced her new guest room suite, far from the royals and Strella's new chambers. Lady Piris moved to her new rooms after the wedding, no longer the princess's lady-in-waiting, as a chaperone of sorts was no longer required. Princesses and queens had maids and attendants and courtly friends, so Piris was technically free to leave the palace. Her only reason for remaining was her suspicion of her friend's unhappiness, so she deserved the truth.

Strella had told her what she learned regarding the reason behind her betrothal and marriage to the prince, or at least why the royal family had wanted it to happen. Ghel claimed this was no longer the case, that he knew her to be true and loyal, trusted and cared for her. Gods, Strella wanted to believe that, believe the achingly sweet words he'd said to her on their wedding night just a few evenings ago, but she wasn't ready. She needed time to think, to dig deeper into her father, and possibly herself, and find her own truth. Peep was her best friend, so it helped to unburden herself and her mishmash of emotions with someone she trusted without reservation. The umber seemed to shrink daily for Strella, so it was good to keep her friend informed, even if it meant watching her worry and rant.

It also didn't hurt Piris was an experienced fighter and knew a thing or two about hiding serious secrets. Strella had taken days to consider all her options, think about what she knew of her father, and came to her own conclusion: Ghel's assertion of treason could be true. However, she wouldn't condemn him without solid proof of the fact, something she could see for herself as irrefutable evidence. Treason meant death, so she needed to be certain of his transgressions. To have absolute certainty, some lying and sneaking was required.

"I don't disagree with you, Piris," Strella said, interrupting her talk of what she'd do to them all for hurting her. Oddly enough, Piris focused almost exclusively on how she'd take down Prince Jarok. "The royal family was duplicitous to say the least, but they had some reason to be." Piris snorted with derision and Strella ignored it. "My father, on the other hand, would have no justifiable reason to commit treason. If he has."

Piris turned sharp eyes on her friend, but they softened when she caught the expression on the princess's face. She eased over to her friend, taking a seat in one of the sage-colored chairs around her small fireplaces, where Strella sat fidgeting her hands so she could try to calm her with one of her own. "Star. Honey. I hate to say it, but—"

Strella shook off her hand to stop her words. "I know, Peep. I know exactly who and what my father is, which is why I can entertain the idea of him doing what Ghel claims he has done. I still require proof. Hard evidence."

Piris nodded, her shoulders pulling back in the determined set they sometimes had, the set of a warrior on a mission. "I will find proof or clear his name. For you."

Strella melted. There was no love between her friend and her father. They tolerated one another, but neither particularly liked the other. It had always been that way. What had also always been this way was

Piris's drive to help her friend do whatever it was she needed to do. Even if she disliked Lord Hollythorn, most likely because of the cool and judgmental way he had with Strella, Piris would help find answers for her friend, whatever those answers may be. She'd help Strella find any proof she needed to put her mind at rest either way, despite the fact neither option appeared restful to Strella. Either the prince falsely accused, or her father colluded. No good options existed for her because of the course of her life and the affection she still couldn't help but feel for each man.

She wished to rip out those feelings. Toss them aside and think no more of either, come what may. She couldn't. For very different reasons, both were grounded in her heart, and it would take a great deal to dig them out. Which brought her back to what she and Piris needed to do to set her heart free in one way or another.

"We need a plan," Strella said, though she didn't really know where to start. Another reason she had come to Piris, who had a mind for such things.

Piris shrugged her shoulders. "Easy enough. You distract your father while I search his chambers for evidence."

"That will be dangerous for you, Piris. If caught…"

Another snort. "Of course I won't be caught. I'm better than that, Star."

Strella still worried, though she knew her friend well. Knew she'd be mindful while also being focused. "Fair enough. How, exactly, can we make this work?"

Piris sat beside Strella on the bed, hitting her on the shoulder with an affectionate knock as she did. "Leave it to me, Strella. I have spying in my blood, according to some at least."

Strella gave a laugh. It was hollow, but she still laughed, which had to be a good sign for the new princess.

Piris convinced Strella the simplest plan was the best plan; she'd ask her father to lunch, and while he was away from his chambers, Piris would search for any signs of treason. As smart and strategic as Piris was, she couldn't guess what such a sign might be, but her efforts would be focused on his sitting room, where he'd surely made a makeshift office for himself to conduct lordly and merchant business while in the palace, as was his usual habit when traveling away from home.

The following day, they put their plan into action. The princess sent her father a note, asking him to lunch with her, alone, in one of the small but formal royal dining rooms in the north wing of the palace, far from his chambers. She used her new stationary, with her new princess title, to appeal more to him. Lord Mikka Hollythorn had always enjoyed formal elegance, as his daughter well knew.

At the noon hour, Strella fluttered in her seat, nervous over her father's appearance. She did not worry if he would come. He'd sent a quick reply with his own formal lordly stationary stating he'd be delighted to join her for a meal, alone. He stressed the word alone, underlining it with a flourish, which worked well for her plans, meant she didn't have to explain Piris's absence.

She was far more worried about what might transpire during their lunch. She'd discussed it with Piris, and together, they'd formulated a course of questions for her to covertly lead her father to reveal his thoughts on the royals or the kingdom or Engad Monti. Strella was not one for subterfuge, so she worried she would give their plan away by pressing too much or too quickly. It was a delicate balance and an important one, hence the hand twisting at noon.

Before he could be considered late, her father strolled through the open door, his step firm and sure as always. Strella rarely thought of her father's bearing because it was such a constant in her life. Whoever spent time thinking of how someone they loved moved and acted day to day? But now she considered her father from as objective an eye as she could, thinking about how Ghel and the rest of the royals must see him.

Lord Mikka Hollythorn had been Lord Hollythorn for over one hundred and fifty years, having taken the mantle from his own father when he was a young Fae of only thirty. His noble rank passed to him because of birth, as did the crumbling manor house where he was raised by his father and mother, but the wealth he commanded had come about through his own intelligence. Mikka Hollythorn proved cunning in social situations and business both. He'd caused quite a stir when he started to entertain merchants and talk business, which was often seen as beneath noble Fae, but no one could argue with the wealth he'd generated for himself and others in his circle. Within fifty years, he'd rebuilt the wealth of his line as he'd rebuilt his ancestral home, giving both Hollythorn Manor and the Hollythorn name a respectable, monied cast neither had enjoyed in centuries.

He was ruthless but unfailingly polite, cunning but willing to spread his knowledge and wealth when he thought it could ultimately benefit him. He'd even loved fiercely, according to whispered stories of her mother, although Strella had never experienced that depth of love from him. Not to say he didn't love her—in word and action—as his daughter. He simply kept her at a distance, something she came to understand as a result of losing her mother, the love of his life, tragically in childbirth. She understood it, forgave him for it long ago, and because of her own certainty of death, was thankful for it in some ways.

When he stepped into the formal dining space, the dusky blue-gray walls trimmed with darker gray trim and molding framed his pale face and hair, as did his dark-gray formal attire. She'd known he'd enjoy this room in particular. He liked darker decor in rooms, which was reflected throughout Hollythorn Manor. Maybe he even already knew this room, because he almost matched it.

Strella rose to greet him out of habit. Technically she should not. Strella was his daughter, but she was now Princess Strella and outranked him within the noble Fae social and political hierarchy. Still, children's reactions to their parents were so very hard to break, and Lord Hollythorn did not insist she break this one, as maybe he should. Instead, he gave her a slight nod before leaning in to place a quick kiss on her cheek in greeting. "Daughter. So good to see you this afternoon."

"You as well, Father."

They both sat across from one another, and for a few minutes, conversation drifted toward pleasantries—weather and the room decor and, when the food was spread before them, how wonderfully the chefs of the palace prepared their meals. When a lull lingered as they enjoyed warm root vegetable soup with fluffy rolls, the smell of smoky spices filling the air between them, Strella gathered her courage and forged ahead with her predetermined line of questioning.

"How fares business, Father?" A simple enough question to start and one she'd asked many times before.

"As well as always, Strella," he answered absently as he placed a pat of soft butter on a hot piece of roll and took a delicate bite, always impeccable in his manners even when he was alone with his daughter.

"Lady Piris tells me her own father's shipping interests have been disrupted somewhat," she said, staring down at her soup bowl to hide any nervous strain on her face. This was not true, as far as Strella and Piris knew. It was, however, something to pique her father's interest. Hollythorn had invested heavily in sheep and wool at first, but the real money was made in supporting the trade and inventions of others for a fee, including a few investments in past shipping ventures with Lord Volesion, which was how Strella and Piris had met as children so long ago.

"How so?" he asked, putting down his butter knife and spoon to give his daughter his full, icy attention. His interest was definitely piqued.

"I don't know to what extent, as Lady Piris did not share. However, she did say it was on account of the recent troubles here. With the Monti Clan."

Strella let her words hang and waited, her father giving nothing away as he thought in silence. Then, a little of the hard ice in his eyes dampened, and he unexpectedly reached across the table to her, placed his hand over hers, and patted it gently. "My dear Strella, I still have nightmares about what you endured because of the Monti Clan. I do hope mention of it doesn't hurt you."

He thought her weak, this Strella knew. Part of this was because like all parents, he had a hard time thinking his child fully grown and capable at any age. Part of it also stemmed from his particular views on social position and her place within their household. She was his daughter, was to be a perfect lady, and as a perfect Fae noblewoman, was to be soft in all ways not strong. She wished he thought differently of her and other women, tried to show him she herself was more, but he wouldn't see it. Now, however, such a view helped with her own ends.

"I am afraid, Father. Afraid what the Monti Clan might do to me if I ever again encounter them." She disliked doing it, but she put a little extra husky croak in her voice, made herself sound shaky to drive home the point.

Her father gripped her hand tighter to reassure her. "You have no need to worry."

"Because Ghel will protect me?" A goad for her father, but also true, even if she wasn't exactly happy with Prince Ghel at the moment. Regardless of her feelings, she never doubted for a moment his protective nature. Whether she deserved such protection, or wanted to feel such protective care from him, was another issue for another day.

Lord Hollythorn's back shot impossibly straight, his hand leaving hers to once again pick up his spoon as he scowled down at his soup. "The prince is of no concern in this matter."

"He is the one who saved me before."

"You wouldn't have been in danger if it weren't for him," he spit out, thumping his fist, clenched around his spoon against the table in an uncharacteristic show of emotion.

He took a few seconds to breathe deep before he screwed a bland, practiced smile onto his once-hard face. "Strella, I swear to you, you have nothing to fear from Monti and will soon have no reason to think more on the prince."

"What do you mean?" Strella couldn't help herself. She wanted clear, unambiguous words. What he'd just said was damning but not solid proof of anything. It seemed Lord Hollythorn also realized this for himself, as he waved his empty hand in the air as if nothing of importance had occurred.

"It's nothing, Strella dear. Forgive my emotions. Let's talk of other, more pleasant things. Are you now preparing your royal wardrobe?

Would you like guidance? I can call on the silk merchants I know to bring you their finest selections."

She knew she'd lost her chance. Strella gave an internal sigh but let her father direct the rest of the conversation. She'd gotten nothing of true importance. All she could do was hope Piris had found more. Something told her either way, her father stood on shaky, possibly criminal grounds in this rebellious mess. After his misspoken words, she was dreading more and more the side she suspected he landed in the coming confrontation between the Boraus and the ever-encroaching Monti Clan.

Chapter Seventeen
Ghel

S trella had left a note for Ghel on a side table in their common sitting room. She'd been kind enough to mark it with an ink well and large quill so it caught his eye, but she'd written in flourishing script, which for Ghel wasn't too kind. Strella didn't know this—yet another thing Ghel had lied about by never saying a word. After finally deciphering she was in the library and wished to speak with him regarding something, he crumpled the crisp white official Princess of the Winterlands stationary in his hands. He'd noticed the way it matched his, the color and positioning of words and embellishments similar if different in small details. He so rarely used his own official princely stationary, but the way they matched somehow eased a bit of the anxiety caused by the note.

It did not calm his resolve. When he thought about it, he knew Strella needed to hear the whole truth of him, should have heard the whole truth of him and his failings long before she'd agreed to marry him. Gods, she'd been so brave, coming to him the night before the wedding and revealing the prophecy. Whether Ghel believed the word of the prophecy didn't matter. Strella believed, and she'd revealed a vulnerable part of herself to him in offering up her secret. Instead of offering his own personal secret, he'd let slip the royal plans and suspicions. Strella deserved to know those as well, but as he stalked to the library, Ghel realized she needed more of him, personally. It was one way he still had to show her not only who and what he was but that he truly trusted her, despite the beginnings of their betrothal.

Strella was seated at a study table when Ghel entered, head bent over a large book, one yellowed page pinched between the pale, delicate fingers of her right hand as if she were mid-turn. She'd heard him enter, so while her head stayed bent for a few beats, her ice-blue eyes looked straight into him.

"Hello, Prince," she said, pulling into a straight, stiff-backed position against her wooden chair. "You found my note."

Ghel didn't say anything. He tossed the paper he clutched in his fist on the table, the crumpled ball skidding across the slick, aged wood until it landed against the top of Strella's book. She focused on the note, her brow furrowed and a frown on her face, and Ghel cursed himself for not thinking how it might look from her perspective, seeing him toss her words aside as if they did not matter. As if she didn't matter.

"Damnit, Strella. Apologies." He ran a rough hand through the mass of dark hair he forgot to pull back that morning, holding it for several beats before he began again. "Please, what did you wish to discuss?"

Strella gave him a look of confusion but picked up the note, studying the ball in her hand, then studying him for a few seconds before she whispered, "I have an appointment in a few days, one I request you attend. I said this here." Holding up the ball in her palm, delicately perched like a bird about to take flight, she asked, "Was my script too messy to read? I wrote the note quickly, and my father has accused me of being sloppy in the past."

He couldn't stand her giving excuses, as if she were the issue in this situation. "No, Strella. No. I... I cannot read."

"What?" she asked, shock clear across her face. "That's not true. I've seen you read myself. I'm sure I have." Her brows wrinkled, her eyes went distant, and Ghel knew she was running memories in her mind, trying to reconcile what she'd assumed about him with what she'd seen in their time together.

Ghel felt the tension in the muscles of his torso. His knees wanted to lock, but he forced himself to ease into the chair in front of him, across the table from a confused Strella. "No, I apologize. You're right. It's... more complicated. I know how to read. I just..." He trailed off, thinking of how he would explain it. His family knew, had known since he was little. A few of his old tutors knew, but he'd learned early not to reveal such a secret to anyone else. His family had no issue with it, did not act shamed by his failings. Ghel himself was, however, and wanted no one else to ever know. Until this moment.

He looked around the room, one he'd hated as a child for all it represented to him, and started his confession over again. "Here, in the library, I spent hours trying. Desperate to read more fully, as easily as Jarok and my father and mother and tutors seemed to read. But I couldn't. When I looked at lines of writing, they moved and curved, like the snow hills of the Aurora territory. They..." Here he mimicked how he viewed writing with his hand in a wave pattern, demonstrating to Strella as best he could how he saw words. "It's not simply this. I also see individual letters differently, in reverse or out of order, or sometimes as if parts are missing, gaps in the ink no one else can see. So, yes, I can technically read. I know the process of reading. It is simply something I cannot do efficiently, which is why I avoid writing and reading."

Strella's head was cocked in thought as she considered him before asking, "You've been like this since you were a child?"

"Stupid? Yes."

She snapped her icy eyes toward him and frowned at his words. "Not stupid. I've never known you to be stupid, Ghel."

"Now you know I cannot read."

"You just said yourself you can read, but it is a different process for you for some reason."

He nodded. "Yes, as I said, stupid."

"Difficulty based in the way your mind works differently and stupidity are two separate things." Strella scoffed, as if upset by his words. Ghel stared at her. He'd expressed worry over his abilities as a child and had heard similar things from his family and tutors, so he'd stopped saying the words out loud. He'd been determined to see himself as lesser, as inferior, as nothing more than a sword to wield for his kingdom because his mind was different from those he knew. Ghel had accepted this fate long ago. With his father's waning health, he was more and more stressed about what would happen when he was forced to become king. Ghel had always thought an idiot on the throne could cripple the kingdom he loved, but part of the belief shook loose in the face of Strella's quick dismissal.

His wife fluttered her hands nervously in the air, as if she'd only just stopped herself from doing something else she wished to do with those hands. "I have seen your mind at work, Ghel. You are sharp, thoughtful, strategic. You would not be general if you were not."

"I'm a warrior, Strella, not a scholar."

"You're a warrior in charge of legions," she said, her voice rising with each argument she made. "In charge of the army of the Winterlands, in fact. You also know art, appreciate beauty. You can discuss a wide array of topics with intelligence and feeling. You are a sharp political and military strategist. No, Prince. You are no idiot. You are simply different."

Strella's breathing was heavy, her eyes shining in a way they had not in days, and Ghel couldn't argue with her. Not because he believed her but because he was mesmerized by the passion pouring from her eyes and the kind words spilling from her pink lips. He wished nothing more than to throw the book from the table, drag her across it, and cover her mouth with his.

She wasn't done, however, and showing once again how very astute she was, she reached a calm hand toward Ghel's, placed hers on top, and squeezed fiercely. "I... I have my issues and concerns with how our relationship began on your end, Ghel. I cannot lie about this. However, I have no qualms about your abilities as a prince, a husband, or as future king of the Winterlands. You will lead well, strong and true, with both heart and intelligence."

Her words wounded and calmed in equal measure, taming an old pain inside him he'd had for ages while igniting a new, fierce flame. He couldn't help himself then. He dragged her hand to his face, nuzzled it like one of his dogs, and placed a kiss in the center of her palm. The gentle kiss was filled with more reverence than a worshipper at prayer. Fitting, as he bore her down with a dark, hot stare and made his own vows to her.

"Strella, I know you need time. I will give you all you need. Now and always. But I cannot hold back any longer. You must know. I love you. Have loved you for some time."

She started at the words, as if surprised. How could she be surprised? Ghel's life was now hers, had been hers since she walked into the tearoom and saw his vision in blue. She opened her mouth to reply, but no words came out, so she snapped it shut, turning her head to stare at the bookshelf instead.

He whispered to her, "There is no need for you to say more. I know I've hurt you, and you have every right to remain angry with me. I still needed to show you all of me. Now you have all my truths."

Not giving her time to respond, he rose and left the library. He ached to do more but knew the best gift he could give her in the moment was peace. He needed it also after all of those words he'd spilled. Yet the glimpse of her warming eyes as he left gave him reason to hope his words did not exactly fail him this one time.

I nstead of leaving a note, Strella sent Piris to find him. After a few jabs at Jarok, who was sitting with him discussing the current movements of the Monti Clan according to Winterlands scouts Ghel had sent to track the growing group, she turned her full attention to Ghel. Not for the first time, he measured her stance, her stare, and the way she held herself even when apparently at ease. He knew Jarok had yet to uncover any sordid secret about the Fae noblewoman, and he truly hoped Jarok never would. Mostly because of the love Strella held for her but also, in part, because of his respect for her as a loyal friend and obvious protector of his wife. Plus, it didn't hurt that the verbal sparring she constantly engaged in with his brother flustered Jarok in a way he'd never seen, which was amusing as long as Jarok did not take it too far.

Now, however, he suspected she had no use for him, given the derisive look when she turned his way, a cold sneer marring her face. He understood then Strella had finally told her best friend what had occurred, which was to be expected.

"The princess wishes you to meet her in your chambers." After the last syllable left her mouth, she turned her back on the princes and left. He deserved far worse from someone who loved his wife, so he said nothing to stop her.

Jarok snorted. "That woman."

"Lady," Ghel stated. She could snub him in her own way, but he would not let another disrespect his wife's friend.

"Lady. Of course, brother. My apologies," Jarok said, his voice dripping with sarcasm as he gave a mocking bow.

Ghel sighed. "Don't we have enough to deal with, brother, without your petty snipes with a noblewoman?"

Jarok looked chastised. "I'm sorry."

Ghel moved to leave but turned toward his brother, saying, "Your apologies should not be for me, Jarok," before leaving him to think about his behavior on his own. He was a smart, capable, and politically minded Fae prince. He should have been able to control himself better around the woman, at least in Ghel's estimation.

Piris and Jarok's bickering left his head as he moved to the chamber he shared with his wife. It'd been three days since the incident in the library, when he'd exposed his most shameful secret to Strella. Somehow, the shame of it had lessened with their talk and the small comforts she'd given him. It didn't hurt Strella had warmed to him more and more since then, as if giving this last hidden piece of him to her had mended their connection. He'd even felt it in his magic, the metal binds gaining more weight. With each look his way, each small smile, and each passing word, his hope renewed. One day she would trust him again, come to love him as he loved her.

When he arrived at their sitting room, all thoughts of Strella and his hope vanished. He was left unsure. Speechless, as usual. For there, right next to the large hearth and a roaring fire, Strella stood in a sparkling sapphire-blue gown, chatting with Tevan Catspur, the most renowned painter in all of Fae.

Ghel had met him on one of his trips to the Summerlands many years before, when both were younger Fae just starting their work. Even then, Ghel had recognized the genius in Catspur's work, which consisted primarily of Summerlands landscapes. He'd been commissioned for a Springlands Castle Garden landscape before, which was an extraordinary piece of art he'd only seen once, but beyond this he only knew the Fae to work in his own land.

"Oh, Ghel. Please. Allow me to introduce you to Tevan Catspur, a truly extraordinary artist and a distant relation to the Lord and Lady Volesion."

The familial connection surprised the prince, as most Fae families didn't cross territories. Yet another mystery connected to Lady Piris.

"Of course. Tevan Catspur. I am honored to speak with you again."

"Again?" Strella asked, looking from the prince to Tevan.

The painter gave a bow to the princess and said, "I was about to tell you as much, Your Highness. Please forgive me I did not inform you sooner. The prince and I met several decades ago in the Summerlands, when I was but a young and humble new artist. He gave me much praise and, even more importantly, a comment or two on the piece I displayed. Before he knew I was the artist, of course."

Ghel felt flustered. It was one of the many, many socially awkward moments in his long life, but one that had stuck with him over the years because he did truly respect Catspur's talent. "Again, I apologize."

"Oh, no, Prince Ghel. Don't apologize. You have quite the eye, and your comments helped me improve my work then and in the future."

Ghel left it at that because he didn't know what else to say and wanted to end the direction of the conversation. Turning toward his wife, he cocked his head in question.

"Yes. Right. Um, before our wedding, after you showed me the portrait gallery, I had an idea for a wedding present. For you." Her hand rose to gently twirl a strand of hair as she explained herself. "Piris helped, of course. There was a bit of a delay, because of the distance and all, but now he is here, and we can discuss."

"Discuss what, Strella?"

"I thought Tevan Catspur could do a portrait. Of you. For the gallery."

The idea shocked him. It would be a great honor to sit for a portrait with this brilliant artist, but Catspur didn't do portraits, which he muttered out loud to himself.

"Yes, well, as to that. The princess thought I could place you in a Winterlands landscape, as a portion of the whole. To be honest, I've always wished to explore the snow with my oils. I'd be thankful for the opportunity."

Overcome with a swell of emotions, Ghel stood stone-still and silent for long beats before, in a gruff whisper, he asked, "Will you stand with me?"

"Pardon, Your Highness?" Tevan asked, but Ghel had been speaking to Strella.

He faced her fully, determination etched in every hard line of his body. "Will you stand with me, in the portrait?"

Strella swallowed hard, her hand absently tugging her hair before she corrected herself, and simply nodded her agreement.

Spinning toward Tevan, he asked the artist, "Can you paint us both?"

Tevan's feline-like yellow eyes blinked, but he didn't miss a beat. "Yes, Prince Ghel. The original plan was to sketch you here, then add you to a landscape I would complete after visiting a few locations I've heard of in the Winterlands, to choose the right spot based on the sketch. It will not be hard to add two figures instead of one."

"What places are you considering?" Ghel asked, curious what description had grabbed the artist's interests.

"I've seen the Ice Plains already, of course, and the palace. I'd also wished to see my family's original home at Volesion Peak and, if possible, some of the Aurora territory."

"At night?"

A smile stretched wide across the painter's face. "Precisely."

"I will send you with a group of Aurora Clan soldiers tomorrow. Feel free to explore safely with them, but the ridges around the outpost have the best vistas, in my opinion."

"I'll trust your opinion, Prince," Tevan said, dipping his head slightly. The words made Ghel's chest fill with something like pride.

"Excellent," Strella said. "Now what should we do, Tevan?"

They stood side by side for about an hour as Catspur sketched them from a seat by the fire. It was hard being still for so long, but Ghel knew it would be worth it. He'd be in a Catspur with his love, a dream he'd never known was possible. She had, however. She knew he'd want this, not stopping the process even after he'd shattered her trust.

When he saw Catspur out of their room, with promises of a proper Aurora tour once again, he shut the door softly. His hand shook on the knob, and he took a moment to steady himself before he turned back to his wife. "Can I touch you?"

She stood by the fire, firm and beautiful, and gave his question thought. "Yes," she whispered.

He stalked toward her, his steps heavy and hard, but when he took her in his arms, he was all gentleness. He brushed a strand of blonde hair from her face and said, "You've given me a great gift."

"The painting will be a good addition to your gallery," she answered on a sigh, her skin prickling.

He bent to scent her on the neck, causing her to shiver in his arms. Moving up to her ear, he barely gave his words sound, but he knew she heard them nonetheless. "No. The Catspur will be great, I'm sure. The true gift is to touch you again." He held her close for several seconds before stepping back.

She stumbled a bit, and he shot a hand out to steady her stance.

Her eyes were winter frost and fresh starlight. Her light pulsed between them, and it was a beautiful thing to behold. To feel. But far less beautiful than the soft kiss she gave him, stretching up on her toes to place her mouth on his.

Ghel stayed motionless, letting her lead. The kiss didn't go far. She moved back within breaths, but he felt the sear of it down to his feet. Strella didn't comment, only spun around and headed for her rooms, leaving Ghel transfixed, rerunning the memory of the last minute through his mind for a long, long time.

Chapter Eighteen
Strella

Two days after the session with Tevan Catspur, Strella's emotions were more jumbled than ever. She was certain her father had strayed from his oaths to the royals, something all lords must take when they came into their titles in the Winterlands, from his continued behavior. He was a Fae who curried favor when he could, and his blatant disregard for the royals in their presence, combined with the cryptic comments he'd made to her when they were alone, was enough to make her more than suspicious. However, she and Piris had both failed to find any definite proof.

Part of the reason being she'd pulled Piris back, afraid of what might happen to her friend. She herself had been busy with formal duties and correspondences as princess. Nothing she wasn't used to on some level as the lady of a large manor, except there was more of it now. The real reason, she knew, was her tangle of emotions involving both her father and Ghel.

She didn't really wish to condemn her father. What daughter would? As for Ghel, she found day by day her hurt and anger lessening, her love and care returning. Strella looked deep within herself and recognized she had been hurt, remained hurt, over the royal secret Ghel had revealed the night before the wedding because of wounded affection and pride. She had pushed her growing feelings for the prince down as she'd grappled with her own secret. When he'd revealed the true reason they were matched, she'd felt as if their every interaction might have had an ulterior motive for the prince. Could she have stupidly thought he cared for her—and she had come to care for him—when he only remained close to her because of something her father had done? She had known from the beginning it was an arranged marriage, something neither especially wanted, but she thought all that had changed early on in their interactions. Was that the real lie?

These questions reared up constantly since his reveal, but every time she really thought about it, she became more certain the answer to each was no. Even if he hadn't told her the whole truth, he'd proven his care for her in his every action, especially since their first encounter in the library, which had only been days after they'd met.

He continued to prove it still, which was why her resolve to keep her distance was wavering.

Piris, of course, held her grudge—might always hold it, because, as she herself had admitted, "I can't forgive easily because I love you." She didn't hesitate to add "maybe you can, however, because you also love." Strella wasn't ready to admit it or think too hard on it, so she brushed off Piris's words and didn't bring up the prince with her again.

Alone, however, where she wasn't forced to admit anything to anyone else, she sat with her emotions and had a long, hard look at them. She couldn't fault the royal family for their course of action. It was all in service of the kingdom, at a dangerous time for everyone. At the same time, she had held back a serious secret from Ghel, and although they had yet to discuss it again, he'd taken her words seriously as he'd talked through the meaning of the prophecy, until his own secret had come pouring out. She could hardly fault him for doing something she herself had done on some level.

No, Strella was no hypocrite. Add to this her latest discovery about Ghel and his more emotional exposure to her, and the reasons not to trust him decreased daily. He'd given a real part of himself to her, a sad and painful part, as she had done when exposing Seer Willow's prophecy. More than anything else, this had endeared him to her, allowed her hurt feelings to thaw. His willingness to give her whatever she needed to be comfortable and allow her choice in their lives had also confirmed her growing realization; Prince Ghel cared for her, would always care for her, as she cared for him.

Her kiss after the Catspur sitting had been an impulse, but one she did not wish to take back. She'd ignored him for the days following the incident, but only to make sure her emotions were solid and her mind settled. In the end, it all fell in favor of the prince. He was hers, she was his, and it was time to let the pain go so they could reconnect, physically and emotionally.

S trella knocked on the door to Ghel's chamber later that evening. They'd sat with the royal family at dinner, making polite conversation as she went over and over again what she'd need to say later when she went to the prince's rooms. Jarok pulled Ghel away to talk about the Monti's plans with Cylian, so she'd waited for him in their joint sitting room with a book unopened in her lap as she stared into the fire, twisting her hair practically in knots. She only knew he'd returned to his rooms when she heard his outer doors open and close.

The fact he chose not to disturb her in their joint space made her more nervous, but she pulled on her courage and moved toward the inner door to his dressing chamber. The knock sounded loud in the space, and she wasn't sure if it was because she was a little too ready to get the words out of her.

Ghel swung the door open so hard, it thudded against the wall, worry creasing his forehead as his deep, gruff voice asked, "Strella, are you well?" His keen eyes took in the entire sitting room in a sweep, searching out any potential issue or danger.

"Um, yes, Ghel. I need to speak with you about something."

Her hesitancy, her twining hands, and her shaky voice seemed enough to put Ghel on edge. He reached for her upper arms with a warm, soft touch while pushing her backward so he could step into the sitting room. The door clicked shut behind him. His serious, dark eyes scanned her face as they'd scanned the room. "Yes?" He didn't push, didn't demand. He was intent and focused on whatever she might need, but he was willing to give her the lead automatically and without hesitation. Yet another sign Strella was making the right decision.

"Ghel, I've been thinking. About us."

The prince's grip tightened, but not to the point of pain, and the magic between them thudded like a deep bass. It echoed in Strella's body, answering some hope she'd buried deep inside herself, a stirring of their magic she'd tried to ignore for so long now.

"I want—I need for us to go on as we should."

"You'll have to explain what you mean, Strella."

Strella swallowed and looked away a moment but quickly came back to his warm, deep-brown eyes. He deserved an upfront approach.

"The more I've thought about it, the more I've regretted my initial reaction to the royal stance on my father and your suspicions of me."

"Oh, love, I didn't suspect—"

Strella put her hand up. "Yes, you did, for a time. Maybe only a brief time, before we met and connected, but for a time. As you rightfully should. It's your duty to this kingdom. I understand, as I do my own duty now as princess. I think—no, I know, my initial reaction was based far more in surprise and hurt feelings than anything else. With more time, I've come to understand and to forgive."

Ghel's voice was low, a growl but not something menacing. Not for Strella. She could detect the longing there, something she'd heard a good deal from him in the past. "Strella, do you truly mean this? You forgive me for my lies?"

"Some lies are necessary in our position, Ghel. It would be naive to think otherwise." In fact, Strella was keeping her own lie of omission still, as she'd discussed with Piris, both thinking it more their duty than the duty of the royals to uncover the extent of Lord Hollythorn's duplicity to their homeland. "You've never outright lied to me." She stepped closer, pulling a deep breath so she could smell the earthy mix of him, the scent of fresh ground buried under snow and ice, the musk and pine that was all Ghel in her mind. "You never lied in this," she whispered as she skimmed his chest with her hands, traveling the deep, hard planes of his body. "Never with this either." She reached up to hover over his eyes. "Or this." She patted his chest again, this time over his heart, the place where she felt their bond the most, where she knew he also felt their magic.

"My Star..." he whispered, cupping her face in his massive hands, always so gentle with her. The soft scrape of callouses caused a shiver to race up Strella's spine.

"Yes, as you are my prince. I think it's more than time enough for us to make our bond stronger."

She pushed up on her tiptoes, knowing he'd never bridge the distance between them without a clear sign from her. As their lips met, the spark and sizzle connecting them instantly coursed through her blood, running wild with each beat of her heart. It pulsed from chest to gut to limbs, finally making her head spin after long seconds as Ghel took over the kiss and bent her deep, plundering her mouth in the most delicious way.

He tasted of the same earth and pine and magic, and Strella wanted to drink every drop of him down deep. Ghel moved his arms to her bottom, gripped it tight, and kneaded as he pulled her against him hard enough for her to feel the evidence of his arousal. She gasped into his mouth at the contact, which seemed to be all Ghel needed to continue. He pulled her up with ease, her legs going around his thick, muscled waist on instinct and gripping him. She was now elevated a few inches above him, and she used the leverage to take over the kiss and do her own plundering, savoring every taste and feel of him from above.

As she did this, she barely registered they were moving, but they had gone quite far. She felt herself falling back. Ghel snaked an arm up her spine to grip her neck and ease her to a soft surface. Strella broke away enough to register they were in a bed. A bed she'd not seen before, which meant he'd moved them from the sitting room into his own room.

"Is this fine?" he whispered an inch from her face, one hand still gripping the back of her neck as the other reached up to sweep a few stray hairs from her face. Strella gave a quick nod before she reached up to the back of his head, to pull the thick leather band out and let his mass of dark hair tumble down around them, creating a cocoon of sorts where only they were allowed.

The magic twanged hard between them, and Ghel moved the hand at her back to slowly, methodically, to unlatch her buttons. As he did, the top of her creamy-pink dress loosened, and he used his other hand to nudge the shoulders down farther, enough for his hot mouth to trace fire down her bare skin. He undressed her inch by inch with heated purpose, trailing licks and kisses along the skin he exposed.

When he pulled her dress and chemise aside at her breast, a deep rumble ripped up his chest, so hard and full she felt the tremors of it as he latched onto one of her bright-pink, achingly hard nipples. She made her own rumble at the jolt of feeling it caused, gripping the back of his head and pushing him harder against her skin, an invitation he took as he pulled her nipple deeper into his mouth, sucking with abandon.

He paid equal attention to each breast before he moved down, trailing more kisses along her stomach, then lower, before he lifted her ass from the bed to free her from her dress and underthings. He looked down at her exposed sex, licked his lips, and dove between her legs, giving her a long, slow lick from bottom to top.

Strella squirmed as Ghel grunted, enjoying the feast before him. Mewls of pleasure ripped up her throat. Ghel gripped her thighs tight and focused his tongue on the bud at the top of her slick, aching sex, flicking back and forth with increasing speed before sucking deep then easing back, then starting the process all over again. It was a maddening pace, winding Strella higher and higher. She called to him, grabbed at his long hair, and pulled hard, but he only grunted his own pleasure as he ate her with gluttonous fury.

Her body writhed and twisted, wanting more and less at the same time, until the dam inside her broke and she screamed Ghel's name, closing her convulsing thighs hard around his head as his face remained buried in her pulsing center.

She felt weightless and grounded. The thing grounding her was Ghel, who after a few sweet, soft kisses to her sex, rose to look down at her face, his own shining with her juices as his eyes glowed with love and the reflection of her starlight. She had been glowing for a time, but she'd been so lost to passion, she hadn't noticed. Ghel stroked her starry chest with a reverence that made her stomach twist.

"Ghel, please," she said, not knowing what else to say.

"Are you sure?" he asked, his hands still gripping her thighs. He'd stop if she asked, would never push her, but she needed to feel more of him then.

"Yes. Please. I want you inside me."

Ghel bent to kiss her, and she experienced the joint taste of them, together. It made her core flutter. He moved to center her on the bed and lay down gently beside her. He began by petting her body in long strokes, stoking the fire that had calmed with her release but hadn't fully disappeared. He moved down to enter her first with a finger, kissing her neck and shoulders as he did, only pushing in with a second when she moved her hips along with his rhythm. When he added a third, she gasped.

He paused.

"No, no. Don't stop," she said, twisting her hips so his long, strong fingers hit a delicious spot inside her.

"More. I need more." She panted as he drove her higher and higher.

Ghel moved away, but only to position his body above her. She registered the weight and hardness of him everywhere and wanted nothing more than for him to plunge deep. Instead, he paused once again, looking deep into her icy-blue eyes, his dark-brown ones illuminated by her pulsing light. He propped himself up on and elbow to take more of his weight as he used his other hand to guide his hard length to her center.

"Are you certain?" he asked once again, and instead of answering with words, Strella reached around to grip his ass.

She guided him down and pushed her hips up, stopping only for the initial shock of the stretch of him. He took over, slowly, diving inch by inch until somehow his long, wide arousal fit snugly inside her. She felt fuller and more connected than ever.

"Okay?"

She nodded and moved slightly, testing her limits. When the head of him hit a new spot inside her, she sucked in a sharp breath and moved harder against him. He knew what she wanted and obliged, slowly at first.

Strella reveled in the push and pull of his flesh, in the delicious scrape of him in and out of her, as her lust spiraled in her blood, beating a new song in her veins. Ghel growled and grunted, his hips snapping harder and harder against her as his own pleasure began to take over. The only sound in the room were the sounds of flesh hitting flesh, harder and faster, and the ragged breaths of two Fae lost in sensation.

Strella took in a deep inhale, and she let out a cry of pure joy when she came hard around him. Ghel buried his face in her neck, nipping her as he pumped in and out a handful of times before grunting as he found his own release inside her.

They lay there, breath ragged and hearts jumping, content in each other's arms. Strella knew, beyond doubt, her decision to let go of her pain had been the right one. The only way forward. The only way she'd be happy in the life she had left. The stray idea of her life being short caused her arms to convulse around Ghel, who scooped her up and twisted so she lay flat on top of him. Her light sputtered as she stared off into the room, and his warm, strong hand pulled a strand of damp, stray blonde hairs from his chest and twisted it around one of his thick, calloused fingers.

Chapter Nineteen
Ghel

G hel walked into his father's official Royal Meeting Room at the end of a conversation between King Frit and Cylian. "Tell your liege lord we can discuss such matters at another time, when the Winterlands do not have our own internal struggles."

"The Autumnlands thanks you for your time and continued friendship." Cylian stood from his chair and bowed deep as he spoke, unfailingly polite even in the face of a rejection. Knowing Lord Rylnd, Cylian wasn't likely to be happy about whatever request he'd been forced to put before Ghel's father.

The king nodded his acknowledgment before looking toward his son, a soft crinkle of his eye forming at the sight of his eldest. "Ah, Ghel. We have much to discuss."

He bowed his head to his father seated at the massive oak chair carved with winter roses at the head of the rectangular meeting table. As Cylian passed to leave, Ghel grabbed his forearm to hold him. "Is all well?"

"As well as it can be, where my father is concerned," Cylian mumbled, the words meant only for Ghel's ears because they were friends. Because Ghel himself, when in the Autumnlands as a young Fae, had witnessed the ministrations of the Autumnlands' lord and understood exactly why Cylian disliked his service so much.

The prince gripped his arm tight in reassurance, placing a hand on his shoulder. "We've had little time to talk since the fasting, friend. If you need—"

Cylian cut him off with a raised hand. "You've had far more important worries, Ghel, and far prettier ones." His smile was a touch sharp, but Ghel knew his friend meant his words and did not begrudge him the time and attention he'd paid to his lands and his new bride in recent weeks.

"Still, Cylian. Know I remember our previous discussions and we, Jarok and I, are at your call. Whenever." Not at his father's call. Never that, but at Cylian Padalist's call anytime.

Cylian's mismatched eyes swept over Ghel's face, lighting with a different type of hope than what Ghel had for his union with Strella: a hope for change. His fire-red hair shimmered as he nodded, solemn and sure, before exiting the room without another word.

King Frit didn't interrupt the friends or contradict Ghel's words. By right he could. He was King of the Winterlands and held full command of his son's sword by right and bond. However, he was no Rylnd Padalist. He'd honor his son's relationships and vows, trusting they served his kingdom as they served his son. Not for the first time, Ghel considered the differences between the Fae noble rulers he knew in the Springlands and Autumnlands and his father.

King Frit was beloved. Mostly, given the current upheaval and betrayals in his lands. He ruled with both head and heart, as Strella claimed Ghel would one day, something he couldn't rightly say of the those in any other Faelands. The Springlands boasted absolute rule from their king and queen, being tempered or indulged depending on who sat at their side as royal adviser. The lord of the Autumnlands was intended to keep the peace, ensure all in the borders prospered and share a congenial relationship with the Goodfellow of the Glen, the real power in the Autumnlands. However, for centuries, Lord Rylnd Padalist has been acquiring more and more power as he whittled away at his lands, using terror and his sons to do so. The Summerlands, of course, were ruled by the Council of Five and not a noble Fae necessarily, as each member was chosen by a trial when one member died or relinquished their duties, meaning nobility or royal blood wasn't a mandate to rule.

Each ruled their section of Fae in their own ways, some more egalitarian than others. Ghel may have been biased, but he truly believed his father, with his wit and care and familial love for all his people, was the greatest of these rulers. Yet another reason he dreaded the day when King Frit would succumb to his illness.

His father brought him back to immediate concerns when he said, "Ghel, son, come sit. We have much to discuss." The deeper crease in his wrinkled brow told Ghel whatever he had to say was serious.

Ghel sat close. "What is it, Father?"

A bone-deep sigh fell from the king, as if the very thought of whatever words were to come made him too tired to continue. Still, he said what needed to be said. "We must speak as king and general, Ghel. Your mother's birds have come with news. The Kelper Clan has fallen. Now, the only clans left to stand against Engad Monti are the two most powerful: the Auroras and the Windin. It would take much to topple these two, but they are divided, whereas Engad Monti is controlling a whole—those conscripted after defeat as well as those who voluntarily follow him."

"Has word gone out to the Aurora and Windin Clan leaders?"

King Frit nodded. "Yes. Your mother sent a bird to her brother with a small scroll. Render has been dispatched to inform Gova Windin so she might prepare for an attack."

Ghel thought a moment. "Engad Monti has three options. Attack the Auroras on the outpost, the Windins in the Winding Forests, or come here."

His father stared hard at him. "Yes." He gave nothing more, which was his usual sign he wished to have Ghel's unbiased opinion on the matter.

"The Montis will come here."

"Are you certain?"

"He's already implemented a direct attack on me, which has shown he considers us fair game. It was a risky move, one a man like Monti wouldn't have made without certain assurances. He knows we know his intentions: to overthrow all established rule. He also knows both we and the Aurora Clan are united and on alert. The best course of action, for a Fae like him, would be to storm the Winterlands Palace with his combined forces, hoping the Auroras and the Windins couldn't both make it in time for aid."

"Why not go to Windin or Aurora first?"

"Windin and Aurora Clans are the two largest and most formidable because of their isolated and easily defendable locations. Having the Winterlands army and arsenal at his back would help ensure victory against one, then the other. He needs our forces, combined with his own, to take down both clans in their own lands." Ghel paused a moment. "If he can also strike at the Aurora Clan as he fights us on the open Ice Plains, he has a better chance than marching on the Aurora Outpost."

"Very well," he said. "As general, it is time for you to muster your troops. Call all back to the Ice Plains and pray to the gods they arrive in time."

True fear hit Ghel at the thought of an attack on the palace. He feared for his family, but maybe more so, he feared for Strella being once again caught in the middle of an attack on him and his land.

"I know this look," King Frit said with a small smile in his voice. "A sad look, but familiar. It is worry for love."

Ghel nodded, following the switch from political to personal as quickly as his father had made it. "How do you handle it? Especially with Mother?"

The king barked out a dry laugh. "Your mother would expect nothing less, as a hardened Aurora warrior. She always has been and will always be a fighter. So is your princess, although they fight in different ways."

Ghel knew it to be true. Strella would understand his worry but would counter it with her own determination and strategy, just as she'd done when they were attacked on their way to the Aurora Outpost. She'd proven herself then. He needed to trust her to continually prove herself. She gave him no reason to doubt her, even if her strength didn't lie in battle. He could battle enough for the both of them.

"She is a special noblewoman, our princess," the king said in the silence that had descended around them.

"Yes."

He reached out a wrinkled, frail hand toward his son, who met him halfway, gripping his father with gentle love. "Someone worthy of you, as I hoped from all I heard of her and knew of her mother."

"Did you truly know somehow?"

A shrug from the king. "I suspected. Wished for my lonely son to find in her someone who would help ease an ache his family never could."

Tears rimmed Ghel's eyes. "Father..." he called in a harsh whisper but was unable to continue.

"You are a great general and strategist. A great warrior. But above all, you are a great man, and your mother and I suspected you yourself wouldn't see this, or allow someone else to see it, if you were not forced to do so for a reason outside yourself."

Ghel was shocked. Had his parents really planned all this for him and not just to catch Lord Mikka Hollythorn in his treachery? His father continued, patting his son's broad, bearded face. "You need something outside yourself at times to trust in who and what you are. Have since you were a child. It makes me sad for you, as your father, but happy as your failing king, because I know it will make you a truly great ruler in your own right."

Ghel sniffed to keep his tears at bay as he reached out to pull his father in a deep, strong hug. He felt the other Fae's bones, the slight coldness leaking from him, and shuddered at what it meant for everyone in the land—but most immediately for him, his father's son. A few tears fell despite his attempts, but he wiped them away and straightened in his close seat. "Any goodness I have as a ruler will have been learned at your side."

King Frit's eyes sparkled with pride and sadness. He didn't answer but patted his son's cheek again before looking around the room and saying, "Your mother will be angry we had this conversation without her."

Ghel laughed because it was true. "I'll speak with her."

"Good. She will need you in the future. In many ways."

Ghel's throat tightened as he swallowed, nodded, and took his leave. He felt both lighter and heavier walking away from his father. The weight of the future hovered above him, ready to descend, but he had his mother and brother and clan to help. He also had his wife by his side, which gave him far more strength and determination than he'd ever had to make his corner of the world a just and lovely place. For his kingdom, himself, and for her.

He'd sent a messenger to Strella, informing her she was needed in the formal tearoom. Ghel was nervous—sweaty-hands and tapping-foot nervous. More nervous than he could remember being since his time with tutors or his early years in the practice rings. He fidgeted like she did, an endearing quality for Strella but one he thought made him look more like an oaf than he normally did. Large warrior men appeared odd when they fidgeted, while gorgeous Fae noblewoman looked endearing.

Ghel clenched and unclenched his fists, cursing his nerves, and absent-mindedly wiped his giant paws down his satin-clad legs. Which, of course, caused a large sweat stain to bloom right on his thigh, a beacon for all to see. He gritted a curse through his teeth and scanned for something to help the situation, but it was too late, as his wife was walking into the tearoom. The smile on her face froze as she took in the scene around them. The room was set up just as it had been the day they'd met, down to the same formal tea service and tray of food. Ghel had worn the same blue-and-gold tunic and breeches he'd worn on the day, though admittedly they were now sweat stained. The only real difference immediately noticeable was he and Strella were completely alone.

She'd stopped to take in the room, so Ghel encouraged her. "Please, Strella, come in."

He waited as patiently as possible, internally cursing himself for thinking this was a sweet idea for his wife, or even something she would like, while she took in every detail. When he thought he might burst with embarrassment and nerves both, she turned a glowing, wide smile, her eyes sparking with magic and something else, and said, "Like the day we met."

He nodded, mesmerized by her face and the soft glow peeking through the gauzy edges of her lavender day dress. Lost in her a moment, he eventually shook his thoughts free and moved, walking to his wife so he could take her hands in his. "The first day, I was not my best, and we started with too many secrets between us. I thought, maybe, we could do it over."

Strella swallowed hard, her eyes sparkling for a different reason, and Ghel cursed again at himself. "Oh, my love. No. Don't cry. I'm sorry." He pulled her to his chest, a touch too rough because he was too busy castigating himself, but he managed to hear her mumble something in his tunic. She squeezed him twice in quick succession and he pushed her back, giving her air to actually breathe when she wasn't buried in his bulk.

"Happy tears, my sweet husband." She patted his chest to reassure him and returned to where she had been, resting her cheek there. "No one has ever been so sweet to me," she whispered on a sigh.

"A gross oversight from every Fae you've ever met," Ghel grumbled, offended on her behalf. "You deserve so much more than I... I can give you."

"Impossible." She pulled back to stare into his close face, her words a fierce vow on her lips, a balm continually easing something buried inside the prince.

He'd planned more, and he didn't wish to let her go, so he moved them both, pushing her back toward the food-and-tea-laden table with every step forward he took, maneuvering them quickly and efficiently as he ignored the flush blooming across her chest and the sweet gasp she let out at his movement. His grip may have tightened a touch on her hip, but only because he couldn't help himself. He did, however, refocus and force one hand off his wife, so he could reach for the wrapped gift nestled among the things on the tabletop.

"I, uh, thought you might also like this. It was a part of my father's private collection. Now you can start your own private collection if you like. A library all your own."

Strella took the offered package, her wavy blonde hair covering her face from Ghel's view as she turned it over in her hands. She delicately unwrapped it, placing the silver ribbon and paper on the table as she unraveled each, until she studied the book in her hand—another slim volume of Queen Nola's poetry, different from the one in the library. It was a special edition, bound and presented to her husband, the king, as a gift on their wedding day. Strella said nothing but opened it to a few random pages to read.

When she finally looked back at him, she held the book to her chest and said, "Thank you, Ghel. I will treasure it."

He wanted to say it wasn't the treasure she was, but he wasn't able to get the words out just then. Instead, he gestured with his free hand toward the food and tea beside them. "Hungry?"

She shook her head, one arm reaching up around his shoulders, her hand burrowing into his hair and taking it out of its leather thong as the other held the poetry collection firm against his back. She liked to do that, free his hair, and the memory of her doing it last night made a jolt of lust and magic rip through his body.

"Do you want something else, my Star?"

Again, she said nothing. Only nodded and pulled herself closer, staring up at him with those icy-blue eyes full of warmth and happiness and something else he didn't dare name because she'd never said it. The warmth of her, the look of her, and the feel of her against his chest combined with the smell of her—fresh air and snow and home—made his control snap. He pulled her body up as his head came down, and he crashed into her lips so he could take long, hard pulls on her mouth, devour her as best he could.

She circled his hips with her legs as he somehow registered the muted thud of a book hitting a rug, and he turned them, sweeping a hand across the table to send the tea and food crashing to the ground as well, thankfully on the side opposite from where the one-of-a-kind book landed. Ghel wasn't thinking of this though. He was thinking of how she tasted. Of how the magic and lust roared between them. Of how she ground back against him, arching her hips into his cock with her delicious pussy. Gods, all he could think about was her, had been this way for many weeks now, and tasting her, feeling her sweet warmth wrapped around his cock, had made it even more maddening, and they'd just had sex the night before. He had a fleeting thought, wondering if he would forever be this distracted around her, then immediately realized he didn't care. He'd die a happy Fae man if this was his lot in life, to be continually in love and lust with his wife.

He thumped her onto the table, a little too hard, and managed to rein himself in then. His lips left her sweet mouth and he laid his forehead on hers to catch his breath. "Apologies. I need—I must be gentler."

Strella, panting, said, "I do not want gentle. Not now. Not from you."

A roaring pounded in his ears, but he shook himself clear. "Are you certain, my Star? I would always be gentle with you."

She moved her head, nipping at his ear to whisper there, "You would never hurt me, and right now, I want to feel my warrior."

Ghel growled deep in his throat and pushed her flat to the table as he hoisted her skirts up with his free hand. After ripping through her underthings with ease, he made short work of his breeches, pulling them down past his ass so he could free his cock. He lined himself up, hissing out at the feel of her hot, wet core against him. Gripping her hips and tilting them up slightly for a better angle, he slammed home, driving deep in one forceful thrust.

He didn't hold back, pounding into her stroke after stroke, and she met him the entire way, her pants becoming groans, then beautiful, inarticulate cries mixed with the occasional, raspy "Ghel," which only spurred him on. He might have called himself mindless, brutish, but not quite. He held her tight, so she didn't slam her back and hips too hard against the table, and listened to every sound, making sure it was all pleasure on her end.

"Oh gods, Ghel. I'm... I... I can't."

"Yes you can," he gritted out as he stopped his stroke, ground against her, and planted himself deep, moving one hand to tweak her clit at the same time. Three quick flicks and she exploded around him, her scream of pleasure echoing off the tearoom walls. He reared back and started to rut again, lasting only a few more moments before he roared his own release.

It was hard and rough and not at all what Ghel had planned, so worry supplanted his afterglow. "My Star, are you okay?"

"Yes. More than, Ghel." She pushed herself up on her elbows and blew loose hair off her face, her sweaty, flushed look a little hazy but happy. "A lovely surprise on many levels, husband."

That word: husband. From her lips. After having her and seeing her appreciate something he'd done? It may have felt better than what they'd just finished. May have, but he felt pretty damn good right then for many reasons, so it was hard for him to tell. Instead, he focused on sweeping his wife up into his arms and giving her another searing kiss.

Chapter Twenty
Strella

S trella was happy. Perhaps happier than she'd ever been in her life, thanks to Ghel. When she'd decided to set her hurt pride aside, to trust in what he showed her day after day in their interactions rather than ideas he might have had of her prior to them even meeting, their relationship blossomed. She'd been falling for him from the day she laid eyes on her warrior prince, but every touch, every kiss, and every laugh made their magical bond stronger and her feelings more real. He was hard and cold on the outside, always had been, but he held a fire only she touched, and it made her feel more powerful than ever before. It added an extra spring to her step and a knowing smile to her face that she'd never experienced.

This did not mean there were not still worries. Piris held a grudge and stayed distant from the royals, even after Strella had talked with her about how she now saw the entire situation as necessary and, ultimately, a positive for her life. Her father's machinations remained hidden in the shadows. Most pressing, however, was the worries Ghel confessed to her. He continued to be open and honest with her, even when the words were frightening. Her prince told her his fears that the Monti Clan would soon march on the Ice Plains to force a final confrontation at the Winterlands Palace gates. Ghel made strategic moves to prevent this, of course, but also to prepare for it. Strella shuddered to think of her prince out in battle against Engad Monti.

Not that she thought him inferior or incapable, but any accident or stroke of luck could occur. She'd long ago resigned herself to an early death, but she would rather die a hundred times over than see Ghel cut down.

Which is why her own machinations and strategies were still important. She was determined to find proof of her father's misdeeds, now in the hope it would reveal crucial information for the battle Ghel assured her was coming soon. Hence her not-so-secret meeting with Piris in one of the lesser-used guest sitting rooms. Piris was no longer her lady-in-waiting, a role required only when a Fae noblewoman is betrothed, so she had officially become a guest of the palace and Princess Strella. However, as lady and princess, their maids were constantly underfoot. Piris suspected hers were purposefully sent by Prince Jarok, and Strella hoped it wasn't true. Strella's chambers were also open to Ghel, and given his current need for her at all times, he could barge into her sitting rooms when she and Piris were discussing things she'd rather wait to tell him. He didn't know what she and her best friend had planned, not because she didn't trust him still but because she knew him to be a tad protective and he might attempt to stop them. She felt they could be close, so she decided to keep the secret just long enough for Piris and her to find something useful.

For these secret chats, they'd taken to meeting in a little-used sitting room in the guest wing of the palace. It was small, situated in the corner of two intersecting hallways, the door off to a slant and not easily seen from one direction. The room itself was triangular in shape, the narrow entrance gradually widening until it was large enough to set a two-person chaise and two small, tufted tea chairs, all covered in cream silk fabric. The walls were cream-paint accented with wooden trim around the seams and the singular, untouched window. The room was clean, of course. A maid must have been dusting it regularly. Otherwise, it appeared untouched to Strella's eye.

When she entered a little late for their meeting—thanks to Ghel's hands and tongue over lunch and a need to readjust herself in some key areas—Piris was already lounging on the chaise. To say her friend lounged was a bit of a lie. Piris rarely relaxed, her warrior body and mind always on alert. It was more accurate to say she appeared to lounge, leaning against the side of the chaise on an elbow as her auburn head was tipped down, studying the sharp nails on one of her hands. Her eyes snapped down a second after Strella entered, a second after she'd assessed who was walking into the space. The tension in her shoulders also eased as she said, "Your hair is a bit of a mess," with a chuckle, guessing correctly why her friend was late.

Strella breezed farther in, unconcerned. "Hello to you too, Peep." Taking a seat close to her friend on the chaise, she leaned in and kissed her on the cheek.

"Oh so happy now, Strella. Good sex will do that to a Fae woman." Piris straightened and turned to face her friend eye-to-eye, studying her with the same assessing tendency she saw in the princes and the queen, in any of the warriors she now knew. Whatever her friend found there made her face relax into a grin, and she moved to stroke through Strella's hair, straightening the stray strands. "I may still be angry with your prince, Star, but I am happy you're happy."

"Oh, Peep!" Strella exclaimed as she hugged her close, unable to say more because of the love welling inside for her fiercely loyal friend. The princess was happy, she wanted Piris to also be happy, and to maybe relax in life. Sadly, it might be some time before it could happen, given the reason they were there to chat.

"Enough of that," Piris said, squirming out of Strella's grip. "We have things to discuss."

Strella nodded. "Any new discoveries?" Piris had searched her father's chambers at least three times. She'd had to move around maids and butlers, but she'd tossed the room from top to bottom according to her reports. Still, nothing.

"Okay. Seems we may be going about this the wrong way." Strella twirled a stray strand of hair with her index finger, deep in thought. There had to be something, anything. It was impossible her father had completed a plan of this magnitude and left no trace of it anywhere. Admittedly, Lord Mikka Hollythorn was both intelligent and ruthless, but Strella knew he kept meticulous records.

"You've searched every drawer, tabletop, writing desk? Looked through his account ledgers and correspondence?"

"More than once at this point."

"It must be hidden in something else then, where no one would think to look. Or have reason to look." Strella realized almost instantaneously what it meant. "You'll never find it. I have to do a search."

Piris huffed out a no, but Strella continued.

"You know a great deal about my father, but not everything. I obviously also don't know everything, but of all the Fae alive today, I know the most about him and his habits. I might be the only one who could find something he purposefully kept hidden."

Piris stared hard at her but said nothing, which told Strella she was on the right track. "Now on to how I get into his rooms..." They'd been using the standard ploy of time alone with Strella for all of Piris's searches, which wouldn't work for Strella.

"I will summon him," the queen said from behind the pair of friends as the beat of a bird's wings signaled the flight of a small brown hawk over their heads. Both shot up, Strella startled and surprised while Piris's muscles tightened, and she maneuvered herself in front of the princess. The queen stood in a doorway neither knew was there before, positioned in the right corner of the room, hidden by the seams and cream paint to look like a normal, solid wall.

"My queen, Your Grace, I..." Strella had no idea what to say as the queen moved toward the duo, her feet sure and her back straight even as the circling hawk swooped down to land with a ruffle of feathers on her broad shoulder. Piris dipped her head and let it remain lower, even as she eyed the queen and her bird of prey warily from under tendrils of long, deep-red hair.

When the queen reached them, she said, "Sit," with firm command, gesturing back at the chaise as she stepped around them to take one of the two small wooden chairs. The women listened and hastily sat, waiting for whatever it was the queen wished to say.

"Surprised your clandestine meetings have been noted?" she asked, her hard slash of dark eyebrow quirking up at the question.

"Your Grace, I do apologize. Lady Piris and I—"

"Are obviously trying to find evidence of your father's treason. Good." Queen Alene settled back into the chair, rolling her shoulder as the hawk hopped down to perch on the arm of the seat. "You've been unsuccessful so far."

Heat hit Strella's face at the words, and Piris clenched a fist before the queen said, "Not a judgment, dears, simply fact. If you had found something, you'd have brought it to us by now."

It was true, but it still cut to have Ghel's mother know she'd tried and failed.

"No matter. I believe Strella is right. She should be the one to search, as she'd have the best chance at success."

"It's dangerous," Piris said, her fist still clenched.

A smirk danced across the queen's lips as she looked Lady Piris up and down. "You have fight and loyalty, both good qualities I admire, but sometimes they must be put aside for the greater good. Something our princess here knows from her own experience." Queen Alene's eyes warmed a touch as they looked at her daughter-in-law. "We had to be certain, you know, but if you were ever truly suspected, I would have been far more present in your early days here."

Strella caught the jump in topic and swallowed hard. She'd only discussed the royal family's early suspicions of her with Ghel and, since forgiving him, had been busy with other, more enjoyable things with her husband. To have it in her face, now, was something else entirely. It was not only Ghel who'd been uncertain of her. Still, the princess had forgiven her husband of this; she needed to forgive the rest of her new royal family as well.

"Of course, Your Grace. I understand." A look passed between them, something sweet and fierce Strella had never known, before the queen rose without saying more.

As she passed the side of the chaise where Strella sat, she laid a firm grip on her shoulder, and Strella thought for a fleeting moment it must be what the queen felt when one of her birds landed on her. Softly, almost at a whisper, the queen said, "Mother." Tears sprung to Strella's eyes as Ghel's mother stalked back toward the secret door, her bird gliding after her.

She hit the frame and spun, looking fully at Piris with her hawkish gaze. "You and I need to have a chat, Lady Volesion."

"Anytime, Your Grace." Piris dipped into a curtsy. Strella noticed the slight shake of her hand, which she quickly gripped in her own. Piris calmed herself and asked, "How long have you known about our plan?"

Strella was curious of this as well. The queen looked from one young Fae woman to the other before she shrugged and admitted, "I didn't, fully, until today, but there is much I know about this palace that others don't. My birds know even more." With that, she turned her heels and left, the door closing tightly behind her.

"Gods," Piris said, slumping onto the chaise. "She is one seriously intimidating woman."

"True," Strella said, still standing and looking at the space her mother-in-law had just occupied. "She's also smart and loyal and strong. All good things to have on our side, and I think, Peep, she is on our side."

They were again in Ghel's bed, and he was again moving inside of her. So deep. So slow. He'd built her up with soft touches and gentle kisses, a vastly different experience than what they'd done in the tearoom. She enjoyed both in all honesty, but this felt more raw and real somehow.

As he moved, gliding back and forth over a delicious spot inside her, he looked down at her face. He steadily stared, his dark eyes boring into her soul almost. With the feel of him moving in her, his earthy smell all around her, and his steady gaze taking up all her vision, she couldn't imagine her world without him. He loomed so large, not just then but in every way, she would never escape. She broke eye contact, turning her face away and letting a tear roll free without his intense stare witnessing it.

He changed the angle of his slow, steady thrust, grunting as he lifted her left leg an inch to hit even deeper, impossibly deep, so deep they seemed joined. All she held back tumbled out of her: tears and emotion and her orgasm. A big, messy ball of feeling she couldn't quite manage.

Ghel noticed right away. His hawkish warrior's focus never missed anything. He stopped mid-stroke, pulling out of her as he rolled them to their sides and hugged her tight.

"Did you finish?" she asked, her voice breaking on the tears that for some absurd reason wouldn't stop. He grunted but gave no real reply, letting her cry on him for long minutes as he rocked her and completely ignored his own wilting erection.

"It's not fair—"

A deep rumble cut her off. "Enough. No more of that. Why are you crying, love?"

Gods, the word made her cry harder, but she finally managed to calm enough to talk after a few more minutes in his arms. He wiped tears from her face with a rough thumb and she shook out a breath, steeling herself for what she knew she had to say. "I love you," she whispered, before burying her face in his chest.

His hold loosened slightly at her words and worry flooded her. Then, he asked, "This is reason to cry?"

Strella realized what it must look like for him and suddenly felt horrible. "No. Oh, no, Ghel. It is not a bad thing I love you because it is you."

"But it is a bad thing you love me?"

"Only because of what will happen."

"You know for certain what will happen in our future?"

"Beyond the immediate issue of my father, there is also the prophecy."

To Ghel's credit, he didn't mock or dismiss her worry. He held her tighter, rubbing a strong hand up and down her back in a manner so soothing, she thought she'd fall asleep if her emotions weren't running amok.

She filled the void herself. "I know my father is up to something, as do you. As do a lot of people, I suspect. We'll have to deal with him at some point."

"He is your father, Strella. I would never ask..."

"I know you wouldn't, which makes you noble and me feel guilty, because any other traitor would be dealt with swiftly and, likely, with a quick death."

Ghel didn't confirm or deny it, but she knew it to be true. If her father wasn't taken immediately to the executioner once his crimes were made public, it was because Ghel loved her, which meant their love was already causing royal problems.

"You also may not believe the prophesy, but I do, and to have you love me as I love you causes a great deal of guilt and worry."

"It's my choice, Strella, to love you, knowing all it means."

"True," she said. "Yet knowing I love you too, makes it more... real in a way."

Ghel huffed out a laugh. "It was already very real, my Star, whether you said the words or not. I do, however, hate you have this conflict in you."

"I hate I'll bring you headache and pain, because I love you."

His eyes closed tight, his arms doing the same, and she heard the ghost of a sigh leave his lips before he said, "Those words, from you, it feels I waited a lifetime to hear them. I'm pained it causes you distress, but I'll never be sorry I love you and you love me."

Strella nodded, unable to argue because she felt the same. There was guilt and worry and stress, but it didn't overpower the joy loving and being loved brought to her short life. She should be sorry for what she'd do to him, but she couldn't quite be sorry enough, which made her a horrible Fae.

"Look at me," he commanded in a rough voice. When she gazed at his face, she saw the truth and reverence playing there, and his words were a brand, a searing from his soul to hers. "We will deal with your father and this prophecy and any other problem in our lives, but no matter what, I promise you I will stand with you to the end: my end, your end, the end of Fae as we know it. Nothing will break my love for you, not even death."

Strella cried again, the twang of their magic a deep bass she felt in her gut, the truth of his words resonating. He loved her and she loved him, and for a warrior like Ghel, it meant they would fight anything that might threaten that, including death itself. It made her heart heavy and buoyant at once, an odd sensation she couldn't reconcile, but she decided she didn't need to do so. Not tonight. What would come, would come, and they would face it together, at least until they could not face anything together any longer.

Chapter Twenty-One
Ghel

G hel was listening to Lord Hollythorn drone at his daughter, barely containing the urge to snap at every other word he said. His own father had organized a family luncheon, and for the life of him, he didn't know who'd invited the traitor along. Yet there Lord Hollythorn sat, yapping at Ghel's patient and kind wife and completely ignoring everyone else seated around the table.

Ghel's father and mother sat together at the head, watching everything and occasionally sending sly smiles to one another. Ghel flanked his father on the left while Jarok flanked his mother on the right. Next to Ghel was Strella, whose father prattled on at her left. She hummed every now and then in a noncommittal way whenever her father pressed for a response. Ghel was surprised to see the fork in his hand wasn't bent in half given how hard he was squeezing it to help himself find the patience to deal with this Fae man. He was equally surprised to see how much Strella openly disregarded her father as well, as he'd noticed them having several solo lunches together over the past weeks. He'd soon be tried and punished, and a small pit formed in his gut thinking about how it would surely hurt his love.

A clatter of silverware on a plate drew his eye across the table, where he saw Jarok scowling openly at Lady Piris, who sat straight and, for all appearances, unbothered as his brother also gripped his fork roughly, holding it hard and upright against his plate piled with winter greens and grilled fish straight from the Great River. Ghel would chuckle to himself if he also wasn't annoyed with his brother's continued behavior toward his wife's best friend. The rustle of feathers brought his eye to his mother, where she and her snowy owl watched the Fae pair at her side with a narrowed gaze. Looked like Jarok would get an earful from their mother at some point. Served him right for his hostility toward a woman his princess considered family, which meant Ghel now considered her family as well. Jarok needed to fall in line.

As Ghel opened his mouth to direct his brother's attention to anything but whatever was annoying him about the lady at his side, a red streak flashed at his right, causing him to instinctively drop his fork and move to the short sword strapped to his thigh beneath the pristine white tablecloth. He was familiar enough with the streak to realize it was Render a few seconds later, but not soon enough to stop his instinct to protect the people at this table—which included all he loved. And his father-in-law.

Render bent to the king's ear and whispered softly enough Ghel couldn't make out the words. His father started and struggled to rise on his once-strong legs. Without a word, his mother moved to help him, gripping his forearm so he could lean into her steady frame and push himself up to standing.

"It appears our luncheon will be cut short. The Montis march across the Ice Plains."

Strella gasped, her hand moving to her mouth as her eyes darted around the table. Piris cursed—under her breath but still clear enough for all to hear. Jarok and Ghel both rose instantly, bodies tense and ready for whatever was to descend on their home, their family.

His years as general took over, and Ghel started making commands. "Render, go inform Cylian of the events. He is welcome to stay at the palace or ride with me; it's his choice. Father, you should go to your rooms, with Princess Strella and Lady Piris, as they are the most fortified in the palace. A contingent of guards will group there, outside your doors, for as long as they are needed. Jarok, you will also stay behind. We need you here as another line of defense. Just in case."

Jarok's dark, upturned eyes were narrowed but he nodded with a snap, understanding why he'd be the defensive lead at the palace gates. Ghel didn't say anything to his mother, but she filled the breach by herself. "I will stand with Jarok." In the distance, he heard the piercing cry of one of her red hawks and knew she was already giving her own silent orders to her birds of prey.

King Frit may have wanted to argue—Ghel wanted to argue as well—but their wife and mother was an Aurora Clan warrior trained and true. There would be no keeping her from this fight. He was at least thankful she didn't demand to ride to battle with him. He saw her grip on her husband and knew she was staying behind because of his father.

King Frit didn't begrudge his son these commands. He knew his current limitations, even if he didn't like them. He also trusted his son without reservation, especially when it came to protection and battle.

A noise at the door marked Cylian's entrance, his stride hard and long. Ghel saw he wore his battle weapons of choice: a rapier at one hip and a long dagger at the other. He wielded both with deadly precision, something Ghel knew from many hours of practice and a few battles with his friend. Looking right at the prince, Cylian said, "I stand with you."

Not wasting time, he gathered Strella in his arms and hugged her tight. Gods, the idea of her hurt or harmed made rage roll in his veins. He calmed himself by holding her, reaching a shaking hand to cup her cheek and bring her icy-blue eyes to his. He saw unshed tears there, which made his own stick in his throat. "Love. All will be well. I will make it so."

"I love you, Ghel," she whispered, reaching her head up to plant a sweet, soft kiss to his lips. He couldn't leave with that, his heated blood moving him to deepen it, bend her back across his hold and dive deep into her mouth, taste as much of her as he could in a room full of others. He ripped his mouth away to growl, "I love you, my Star."

"Come back to me," she said, her voice soft but steady.

He nodded, unable to say the words. He could never be fully certain he'd return from any battle, and he would never lie to his love again. He'd try his damnedest, however.

Looking at Piris, he said, "Stay with her. Always. Get whatever you need from each of your chambers and get to the royal chambers as quickly as possible."

"Of course," Piris said sharply, as if partially insulted he felt the need to command her to do something she'd already be doing. Her hand stayed shoved deep in her right pocket, tightened in such a way he knew she gripped some type of weapon there.

He looked at his other family, his father and mother and brother and hoped they also knew how much he loved them. Then he decided to say it. He didn't know what would happen, and he'd learned omission was never a good thing. "I love you all. Be careful and stay safe."

He received loving replies and looks all around. He took one more precious second to bend toward Strella's head, to kiss her soft hair and breathe deep so her smell lingered in his memory, before turning to Cylian and, with a nod toward his friend, stalked from the room without another glance back, making his mind focus on the hard fight ahead.

G hel arrived on the outskirts of the Ice Plains, his sled dogs swift as always. A makeshift camp had already been erected next to the road to the palace, blocking immediate entrance as he'd requested via messenger hawk before he'd prepped and left the palace. Cylian came up from behind, with a different but no less swift sled team. Cylian was partial to horses, but the horses left in the palace stables had yet to receive magical prep for travel in the ice and snow, the knowledgeable Fae having been called to the cavalry.

Ghel took the time to unhook his own dogs, knowing they would want to be by his side but needing them for another duty. "Stay," he commanded Beaut.

She whined, wanting to be with him, and the other four followed suit.

"No," he commanded. "Stay. Hold the line."

She understood and resigned herself to guard duty, snapping at the others until they formed a strong line across the road. No one they did not know or recognize as a Winterlands soldier would get past the pack without a great deal of pain and suffering. He gestured for a stray soldier to take Cylian's dogs so they could make their way to the lead tent several hundred yards in the distance.

The Ice Plains were vast, spotted with thinly covered shallows of ice-cold water that were treacherous if one wasn't used to them, which was one benefit for having a battle on his grounds. He'd talked with his assistants and military leaders long before this day and established a plan for the attack he knew would come. The tents would act as both a defensive line and a way to form boundaries where Ghel wished them to be. His men practiced regularly on the Ice Plains. He doubted the Monti Clan soldiers, those volunteering and conscripted, knew half as much about where they would be fighting. It was an advantage Ghel would press, hoping to gain the upper hand from the start by positioning the Monti Clan to run right into the northeast section of the field, where there were more icy water traps than other areas of the Ice Plains. There was risk, but risk was the one constant in battle.

"Look," Cylian said, his voice rough and hard as he pointed in the distance. Ahead, a barely perceptible line of Fae marched forward, a horsed man dead center in the lead.

"He does have guts and leads his men. I'll give him that," Ghel growled. There were things to admire about Engad Monti. Ghel had interacted with him a few times in his life. He was a villain, that was sure, given all he'd destroyed and attempted to destroy in Ghel's homeland, but he was no coward. He was a warrior of the Winterlands, like Ghel, and the prince had some level of respect for that. If he hadn't attempted this rebellion, hadn't attacked and killed so many already, and hadn't threatened all he loved, Ghel would have never had an issue with the leader. He'd overstepped, and would soon learn he was overreaching. Ghel hoped it was him and his sword that would strike the man down for all he'd done.

"The rebel will fall today," Ghel vowed under his breath. His friend stiffened at his side, and he patted his back hard, knowing where his mind wandered but having no time for that particular conversation at the moment.

As the two Fae friends entered the lead tent, seeing a group of military leaders hunched over a makeshift map of the field before them, their focus became battle. Mostly. For the prince, a small part of him remained back at the palace, in fear for his family and his love, but he'd used the fear to push him forward. It would not paralyze him but fuel him to do whatever needed to be done to ensure he returned to them, and ensure they were there, safe and sound, for his return.

Chapter Twenty-Two
Strella

No one marked Lord Hollythorn's swift exit from the lunch after Render's arrival, except for Strella. She watched, wary, as he gave her an odd smile before stepping farther and farther from the table as everyone talked about the coming battle. When she finished her good-byes to Ghel and finally lifted her head out of the fog of worry over his immediate departure and imminent fight, she noticed he'd exited the room.

Piris whispered something about hurrying to her as they walked from the room, each in attendance focused on what they were to do. Strella allowed her friend to lead her away, much like the queen led the king away to the royal chambers. She knew she and Piris were to meet him there, to stay under guard as the battle raged outside. Prince Jarok and Queen Alene would stand at the palace gates, another line of defense in case... Gods, she couldn't think of the in case, and not because of fear for herself. If Monti's men reached the gates of the Winterlands Palace, it meant Ghel had no more fight in him. He would die before he allowed such a thing to happen; she knew this without a doubt.

As her friend hurried them along the corridor to her rooms with Ghel, Strella also thought of the smile from her father. His eyes had sparked with something like hope when she'd looked at him. Or, more rightly, when he looked at her before disappearing in the emotional discussion they'd had at the royal table. He knew what was to come; she was certain. She was even more certain if she could get to his chambers, or him, she could uncover it, possibly find something to help Ghel win the battle. She didn't doubt his prowess or his determination to protect the people and place he loved, but anything could happen in battle, and the more information he had, the better it would be for him.

However, her immediate issue was Piris. Her friend would never let her openly rummage through her father's room when she'd given her word to Ghel to squirrel her away with the king. To keep her safe. Looking at her now, her heavy brow more down-turned, her broad face set in a hard mask, and her jaw as tight as the muscles across her body, Strella knew she'd have a hard time of it, unless she did something drastic.

When they reached her chambers, they didn't pause, Piris half dragging her friend by the hand into her own suite, where her things were still stored, despite her nights spent in Ghel's bed. She moved to the smaller closet reserved for lesser-used items like bags, which Strella had once noticed opened out into the room, as Piris said, "We will grab only what you might need for an extra day or night. If the battle lasts longer than that—" Piris stopped, turned, and gave Strella a devastated stare.

Strella knew what she couldn't say: if the battle lasted longer than a day, hope dwindled.

"I will also pack a bag, just in case," Piris muttered, moving to grab a small travel case with a long strap and dump the contents on the floor without concern. She was in the far corner, rummaging through the case to get it completely empty, as Strella hovered at the threshold, knowing what she needed to do even as she hated doing it.

Without a word, she stepped back quickly, slammed the door shut, and managed to grab the small chair from her vanity table and wedge it under the handle of the door just as her friend's body slammed into the other side. The wood groaned and shook but held firm. For now. Strella needed to go, because Piris would find whatever she needed to find to get out of there, and she'd be livid with her friend when she did.

"I'm sorry, Peep. I love you. So much. Take care of yourself and the king. I'll return when I have answers."

Piris screamed from behind the door, her voice harsh and guttural. Strella didn't let herself hear the words. She blocked out the sound as best she could as she ran out of the room, heading straight for her father's chambers.

She spent at least ten minutes ripping every single piece of paper out of her father's traveling desk, upending all the books scattered across his sitting room, and pawing through every drawer in every side table around the space. Nothing. She found nothing.

Admittedly, she realized it had been a frantic, ineffective search. She forced herself to stop, think. Consider where her father might keep something secret. She eventually moved from the sitting rooms to the bedroom. Lord Mikka Hollythorn would keep record, for assurances, but he would keep it close and not where a random person might walk in and find it amongst his other things. She eyed his space, stopping on the largest piece in the room and thinking about how her father had an odd tendency to make his own bed every morning. He'd demanded she fire more than one maid after they touched his bed for one reason or another. He never let any woman touch his bed. Strella suspected it had to do with lingering trauma over her mother's death, but it was a fact few people knew about him.

She herself had never touched his bed, learning at a young age how upset he became when she even came close to it. It was a weird sensation for her, to walk over and disregard years of conditioning to sit on the soft mattress and bedding. She smoothed her hands over the bronze and gold coverlet, feeling the lush fabric and thinking about what her father may have done and why he may have done it. She fluffed the pillow, her hand sinking into the fluffy down until it hit something hard, small, and square in the underside.

Flipping it out of the way, she found a gilded box, something like a book with hinges on one side. When she opened it, a beautiful Fae woman's face stared back at her. It was a miniature portrait of her mother. There was one large portrait of her mother and father together in his chambers at Hollythorn Manor, the one picture she'd ever seen of her mother. In that painting, her parents both stood with their backs straight, postures formal, and faces serious. Here, however, was something different. Her mother was in profile, a profile that looked somewhat like her own, thanks to the same petite, upturned nose, but her cheeks were fuller, her one visible blue eye was more stormy than icy, and her hair was more golden wheat than pale ice. There was a smile on her lips, her face filled with amusement as if she'd been caught seconds after a laugh. It was loving and free and joyful in a way Strella had never thought of her mother, because grief was what she associated most with her.

As she stroked the image pressed behind a thin sheen of glass, she noticed it was uneven, with one corner raised a fraction of an inch. Turning over the enclosed frame, she found a small divot on one side, enough to poke a fingernail into so she could lift up and separate the glass frame and portrait from the golden back of the structure. There was where she found the letter.

It was a fragment, a final section. Just enough to prove her suspicions and her fears. The message started on some forgotten or discarded page, because the page saved here began mid-sentence.

"—the wooded curve for your signal. As you do this, we will spring our trap for the prince under cover of snow. He will fall, and his forces soon after. You and the Benders will take the palace with stealth. If all goes according to plan, your daughter will be queen by the morning of the next full moon."

The signature was sloppy and skewed, as if rushed off without much thought, but it was still clear: Engad Monti. There it was in ink and paper, undeniable proof of her father's duplicity as well as what they planned to do, attacking on two fronts, both using surprise to gain an advantage. All to make her queen for some ungodly reason.

She smoothed her mother's joyful portrait back into place and laid it gently on her father's bed, taking the extra seconds to be careful even if she had no seconds to spare. Stuffing the letter into her corseted top to keep it secure, she rushed out of her father's room, knowing she didn't have time to sound alarms yet. She needed to stop her father from giving whatever signal he was to give. Then she needed to warn Ghel, as quickly as possible. She sent words to the gods, a fervent hope she'd reach him in time.

She didn't have to rush far, however, because her father rushed into his sitting room as she attempted to exit.

Anger and confusion mixed on his stern face. "Strella, what—"

"How could you? Why would you?" Strella cried, unable to stop herself, the weight of her fear and disappointment and love bearing down on her, almost knocking her to the ground.

"What are you even saying, Strella?" he asked, coming to take her by the shoulders. He looked around, eyes a touch too wide and wild. "Never mind. We have little time. Run to the king's chambers and wait for my return. Let me enter when I call for you."

"Is that how you'll kill the king, having your unsuspecting daughter let you into what she believes to be safety?" The words were choked, a cry and accusation at once, as she dipped into her corset and brought the folded letter between them, waving it in his face until she registered his recognition. For long seconds, Mikka Hollythorn stood frozen in the face of her accusation.

"You don't understand," he began, but she ripped herself away and turned her back toward him.

"You're right. I don't understand treason."

"Listen," he hissed, stomping around to lean into her face. "Listen to me. All this, all was for you."

"What do you even mean?" she yelled, not wanting the blame for his actions. He pulled her into a hug but she twisted free, finding Piris standing in the doorway, panting with a murderous look on her face. Jarok and the queen both hovered behind her, so Strella twisted again, trying to distract her father as the three trained warriors stepped with silent feet into the room. "None of this could be for me."

"No, no," he pleaded. "Can't you see? This is the only way to keep you safe."

"Safe from what?"

"Everything," he cried, his eyes blazing with love and worry and a spark of something slightly wrong, grief and love turned into an ugly, twisted thing. "You must be kept safe from all, from everything and everyone, at all costs."

He pulled her in for a tight, almost-punishing hug, and she didn't struggle. She even shook off Jarok's advances, gesturing for him to wait with a free hand. "Father. Father. I'm safe here and now."

He pulled away, his tone pleading. "Strella, I had to protect you. Make sure you were never harmed. Never in a position to be harmed by anyone. The only way to do so was to make you queen."

"I'm already a princess," she said, shock and sadness warring in the waver of her voice as Jarok finally moved up to wrap his arms around her father's back. He struggled and crackled with light, but Jarok nodded toward Piris, who, with a quick sweep of her legs, took Hollythorn down so hard on his front, the air rushed out of his body. A tangle of guards ran into the room, but it was already done. Strella's father was down and fully subdued by Jarok and Piris.

He yelled and struggled when he gained his breath again, but the worst of it was his pleading look and voice when he was restrained, on his feet, and looking toward his daughter. "You don't understand," he gritted out. "Your mother... Your mother was protected and still died. You need something more. A position no one else could touch. You need to be queen... on your own."

"And, what? Have you by my side, helping me along the way?" she bit back. She knew he cared for her, had used protection as cover for the way he'd hidden her away most of her life, so his explanation was not completely outside the logic of his life. However, it also served him in very clear ways, whether he wanted to openly admit it or not.

"Strella, my girl," he croaked, his voice like shards of glass making his throat bob.

"Enough," the queen said, joining the fray from her perch at the edge of the room. "As a mother, I can sympathize over your worry, but as queen, I cannot abide your betrayal." She commanded the guards to take him, but Strella stopped them.

"Wait." Rushing to her father, it was her turn to plead. "If you love me, truly care for me and my safety, tell me this: how will Monti ambush Ghel on the field?"

The queen and Piris gasped at the news, and Jarok cursed loudly. Strella ignored them all, boring into Hollythorn's eyes with a silent plea. One final ask, from daughter to father. He recognized something there, the hints of what grief could do to her soon, and maybe the love she still had for him, so he relented. "Along the eastern edges of the Ice Plains, where pockets of icy water and piled snow will give them cover. They'll lure him there with Engad Monti as bait, into a triangular trap, then rush him from all directions."

"Thank you," she whispered, tears trickling from her icy eyes as more fell from his. He sighed and slumped, letting the guards drag him away to his new place in the palace dungeons.

"Strella?" Piris suddenly appeared in her face, holding her head up, giving her strength to stand, to go on, and to remember what she had to do.

"I have to save him, Peep."

"We'll send word," Jarok assured her.

"Render is already on the Ice Plains, fighting," the queen muttered almost to herself, as if working out the various obstacles alone instead of in a room filled with other people. "Most of the sled dogs are dispatched. I can send a bird, but..."

"I have to save him, Peep," she pleaded again, pain bleeding into her voice.

Her best friend swallowed, eyes watering at the edges, but nodded and somehow stood taller. In a low voice, she said, "When you hear it, move. Go to the stables, to your father's stallion. He's swift and strong. He'll get you to the field in time."

"Hear what, Peep?" Strella asked, a new worry leaking through.

"If you can go off to battle to save your prince, I can use my magic to help you," she said as she stepped around her friend. Piris gave a small shove into her back, urging Strella on, before she sat firmly on one of the cushioned chairs in the space.

Jarok and Queen Alene were frantically planning in the center of the room, too worried to notice any of this. Too worried to notice anything until the king's voice filled the room as a slight chill hit the air.

"Stop this at once."

Queen Alene and Jarok whipped around, looking for their husband and father, a man whose illness should have made it impossible for him to be there, let alone use his icy tendrils of magic.

Strella closed her eyes and cursed under her breath, but she trusted her friend to know what she was doing. Piris had sacrificed her secret for her, using her magic in front of others, revealing she was not a null but a mimic, one of the rarest and most-often-exploited forms of Fae magic in the land.

"Go, Star," her friend said, her voice morphing from the king's to her familiar deep feminine lilt halfway through her command, causing the prince and queen to stare at the lady with dawning understanding of what had occurred. She gritted her teeth, also having to trust all she knew of Ghel's family and believe they would do nothing to Piris while she was gone. Everyone had far more immediate concerns.

Strella took the chance Piris had given her, running from the room as everyone was distracted with worry and the discovery of a mimic. She didn't stop until she reached the stables, not even long enough to saddle Whip, her father's stallion. She had no time and chose instead to hop on his back and hold on to his mane. Strella dug in her heels, and Whip jumped forward, gaining speed as he dashed from the stables and out, toward the battle raging below them. Toward her prince, whom she had to save.

Chapter Twenty-Three
Ghel

I t had been many years since he'd fought side by side with the son of the Autumnlands. Cylian was a master at the rapier and dagger, gripping each tight as he stabbed and slashed his way across the field. Ghel took a moment to consider his friend, not in worry but in admiration. He thought it a shame the lord of the Autumnlands did not value his middle son more or give him much choice in what he did. Because when Cylian had a choice, like today, he fought fiercely for good.

Ghel couldn't muse about the sad position of his friend for too long, however, as the beating of Fae feet behind him gave him a second's warning before a large member of the Monti Clan moved to strike him across the back of his neck with a short sword. The prince managed to duck and pivot in one swift movement, gaining a small nick across his shoulder from the encounter. He hissed out a breath, but the pain passed in an instant, his magic rearing up to heal the small cut almost as soon as he'd received it. His own heavy broadsword, too bright with Fae blood, slashed across his attacker's belly, digging in deep enough to make the man double over, gripping what should remain on his insides with a dirty, clenched hand.

There was no time to watch him fall, signal for a healer, or do much else except pivot back and focus once again on his main objective. Across the field, stationed along the eastern edge of the Ice Plains,

Engad Monti fought off all comers. He did not move or falter, simply standing in wait as he watched Ghel's progress across the field. The prince had known it would likely come down to this, a fight between the two of them. It appeared he had been right. Now, he was a few dozen yards away, close enough to see the determined set of Monti's face and the blood dripping down his own heavy blade.

He stepped forward and cracked a Monti warrior fighting one of his men on the forehead with the pommel of his sword, causing the Fae to drop to the slushy mess of ice and water and blood marring the grounds outside the palace. Ghel shoved the man aside with a kick, unconcerned with anything except the leader fighting several yards in front of him, when he heard the sharp cry of a hawk to his left.

Fear gripped him then, more than it had any other time in the battle, because it was the familiar call of one of his mother's hawks. She had a message, and it would be something dire. His mother wouldn't interrupt him in battle with anything less, as she knew from her own warrior training how important focus was in any fight.

Ghel's eyes searched the sky for a moment before he found his mother's red hawk circling high above the fray, off farther to his left, at the edges of the battle along the road leading from the palace to the Ice Plains. Cylian noted what the hawk circled before Ghel, cursing and immediately changing directions moments before Ghel, who'd frozen in true horror at what he saw.

His wife, Strella, sat saddle-less on top a galloping stallion, a huge beast of a horse, with her hands twisted in the black hair of the creature, her body low across its neck and back, and her hair whipping around her in the wind. Ghel's body, mind, and heart stopped for several beats, far too long, given what was in front of his eyes. Anger and worry and confusion raged in him when his body and mind started working again, and he gripped his sword tight as he took off at a full run to intercept his wife.

"What's happening?" Cylian yelled at his friend, having gained on him quickly.

Ghel didn't reply, his sole focus on getting to Strella before she was caught by a stray swing of a sword or dragged down from her horse by a fighter smart enough to use her as a shield or pawn.

The hooves of her horse pounded in the ice and muck, clopping through both as Ghel's feet brought him closer and closer to her. She finally looked up, spotting the prince in the chaos somehow, and her brows pulled together as she veered her horse right into the battle, right toward her husband. Ghel pushed himself harder, and he overtook his friend, fear and determination giving him an extra push. Still, it was a battle. He had to occasionally shove soldiers aside, strike a few who attempted to try him when they should have seen the look of fury and need on his face. Strella's horse slowed as she wove through bodies upright and on the ground, occasionally knocking a few aside who stood in the way.

Ghel cursed and sent fervent prayers up to the gods as he made his way to Strella. When she noticed they were within shouting distance, she screamed, "It's a trap," and loosened her grip on the horse's mane to point toward the eastern edges of the Ice Plains where Engad Monti waited.

Render, out of nowhere, streaked toward his wife in a brilliant glow of red, and Ghel breathed a sigh of relief to have someone he trusted holding on to the stallion and stopping her progress.

She waved her hands frantically at the messenger, pointing and talking, but her voice was low, and he was still far enough away that he didn't catch all she said besides few stray words here and there: trap, snow, waiting, Monti, Hollythorn. Enough for him to guess what this was about. Strella had somehow uncovered a trap set by the Monti leader and her father, one likely meant for him, and he'd apparently been falling right into it as he'd moved closer and closer to the man on the battlefield.

Shockingly, Render left his wife alone, vulnerable, and bolted toward the eastern edges, a red streak ripping through snow drifts and coming out with unconscious soldiers, who he could now obviously see had been lying in wait for him to move closer so they could surround and attack him in a larger number.

She may have saved his life, but Ghel did not find her risking her own life to do so an acceptable option in this scenario. Any number of soldiers or messengers could have been dispatched to let him know the details, and he'd make sure she knew exactly how impractical and reckless her choice to come alone, on an unsaddled horse, into the middle of a raging battle, was. As soon as he got his hands on her and kissed her hard.

It was then, as his anger and happiness and respect mingled, he finally noticed the icy gleam of her horse's hooves. He knew all the horse trainers, the Fae with horse affinity magic who ensured their horses could safely travel over ice and snow, were all here, on the frontlines of battle. They'd likely left any horse in the stables unattended, because who would ride a horse from the palace into the mucky, icy, bloody battlefield?

Her massive horse slipped again, this time causing Strella to lose the grip she had with her legs as her hands tightened in the stallion's hair. It wasn't enough, however, and the stallion reared up, struggling with the battle and its discomfort and its own uncertainty, and lost its footing. It hit the ground hard, with Princess Strella taking the brunt of its fall, the horse landing squarely on top of her with a crash.

Ghel screamed, a guttural sound so deep and pitiful, the Fae around him froze in astonishment, as the horse struggled to right itself, somehow kicking the crumpled Strella free in the process before it gained slippery feet and thundered off into the distance. His wife slid across the icy slush of the edges of the battle, thumping hard against a stray outcropping of compacted snow before finally landing with a loud cracking sound. He hoped it was not the sound of her body breaking, but he was still too far to tell. She stirred, attempting to suck in air, obviously pained and winded from the horse landing on top of her, but he saw at least she was alive and could move her limbs, back, and neck. Another crack came, louder and deeper, a grumble of ice he knew all too well. His feet pounded as he tried to reach her, but the ice beneath her still-gasping body, the ice covering one of the treacherous water holes of the Ice Plains, gave way. Ghel had a second to see her face register what was happening, her hand shoot toward him, and her mouth open in a scream before she disappeared beneath the ground, into the icy depths below.

He yelled and ran faster, watching for the longest minute of his life as she bobbed up and down in the water, flailing, until she went under for a final time, swallowed by the cold depths. He moved as fast as he could, but he was not Render, who'd run off to save him. He did run faster than he had in his life, as did his friend. Cylian caught up with him steps away from the edges of the jagged ice, before Ghel plunged in himself.

"Ghel, no! You need to help her, not disappear as well."

Ghel screamed inarticulate nonsense and shoved his friend so hard, the lord skidded on his backside a few feet away, but he knew what he said was true. He did what he'd learned to do all those years ago, when he'd first started warrior training along the Ice Plains. He got on his belly, eased to the edges, and shoved his hands down, blindly looking for his love. He kept at it, though his hands numbed from the cold, seconds turning into another agonizing minute before he felt familiar strands of hair, enough for him to grip tight. He cried out in a mix of triumph and worry as he pulled her up by the hair and eased her out of the black hole of water she'd been in for far too long.

His arms tingled from exposure to the cold water, but his magic washed through him, dispelling any consequences. Not for the first time, he cursed his power for not being useful to anyone outside himself. Ghel swept wet strands of hair aside to look at his wife and marked the blue of her lips, a blue so icy, it matched the eyes he knew so well even if they were closed tight. Her face and hands were cold to the touch. More distressing was the fact she seemed to not be breathing.

"Star, my Star," Ghel cried, frantic and unsure what to do.

Cylian kneeled beside them, recovered from his blow and apparently holding no grudge. "Prince. Ghel. Look at me!" When he raised his eyes so full of pain to his friend, Cylian gave instruction. "She isn't breathing on her own, Ghel. You must breathe for her." Then, his friend moved her head, opened her mouth and pinched her nose, and gestured Ghel toward her. It made sense while being wholly new to Ghel, so he trusted his friend and did as he asked. Taking large gulps of air, his lips met hers and he pushed his breath into her, willing it and his love in at the same time. Seconds became eternity as Ghel repeated the process. Cylian even smacked his wife on the chest between breaths.

After one long breath and particularly hard smack, Strella's upper body shook and lurched. She coughed, and it was the best sound Ghel had ever heard in his life. He felt the tears freezing on his face as he turned Strella to her side, noticing water coming up as she coughed more, coughed harder, a sure sign she was alive and breathing at the very least. When her coughing calmed, he scooped her into his arms, feeling her icy limbs and trying to warm them as best he could. He spared a moment to look toward his friend, wet and bloody on the ground with them but relief etched in his face, and whispered, "Thank you." Paltry words for what he now owed a man he'd already loved as a friend for most of his life.

Cylian gave a sad smile and a nod, then stood, reaching down to help Ghel and his wife stand as best they could.

Strella slumped into Ghel, finally looking up into his face with those icy eyes he loved so much. She tried to speak, a croak coming out instead of words, and he shushed her. "No, love. You need rest now."

She shook her head and pressed on, pausing Ghel with a soft, cold hand to his chest. "I—I died," she said, her voice a harsh, shaky whisper. "Like she said, I died. But you brought me back."

Tears hit Ghel's eyes again, tracked down his face, and he scooped her into his arms, holding her gently off the ground. He buried his head in her cold, damp hair and breathed her in deep. Breathed his first free breath in the long minutes since he'd spotted her riding toward him in the middle of the battle.

Chapter Twenty-Four
Strella

S trella stood on shaky legs, thanks to the strong arms of Ghel wrapped around her torso. He held tight, maneuvering awkwardly. He was usually far more sure and graceful in his warrior body, but his intent eyes bore into her as if she might vanish at any moment, and his hands gripped with a fierce need she recognized.

She'd died. Been literally dead. Her heart had stopped, and she'd no longer been breathing. She remembered nothing after the initial panic and realization of it, but she knew death in her bones, as if her body recalled a trauma her mind couldn't fully process yet. It was okay, because Ghel had been there, saving her and giving her what she'd needed to come back to him. As she now knew, also deep in her very bones, he always would. Just as she would always ride into any battle, face death down, to save him.

"My Star." He cried into her hair, which was quickly turning into icicles from the remains of the cold water and the chilly winds along the Ice Plains. "Reckless. Unthinking."

"I-I kn-know… b-b-b-but I—" She couldn't get the words out because her body was shaking violently, and her teeth clattered together in her head hard enough to cause her to viciously nip her cheek. She felt the sharp bite of pain for a moment before the cold suffusing her took hold again. She still tasted the blood, iron sparking her tongue as she tried to get her words out.

"Hush," Ghel said, not in admonishment but in concern. He engulfed her in his big arms, surrounding her with his musky scent and warmth. It almost hurt, the heat seeping from him to her, but she welcomed it, happy to have it. Happy to be there, with him, neither dead nor gone.

She felt stark relief as she shivered uncontrollably, like an invisible jar had been lifted off her. She'd died at the same age as her mother, just as Seer Willow had predicted when Strella had been a child. Ghel had pulled her back from death, somehow, and she was here, free of the weight of doom for the first time in decades. Just as Ghel had predicted, the events foretold had come to pass, but in a way she'd not expected. She had a life ahead of her, a life with Ghel, and she clung to him harder at the idea of being done with at least one of the worries of her life, thanks to him.

They were, however, still in the middle of a battle, and slowly the din of warriors clashing all around her seeped back into her consciousness. Several Winterlands soldiers had surrounded her, Ghel, and Cylian, shielding their prince and princess as they recovered from her death. Ghel made no move to return to fighting, keeping a tight hold, stroking the top of her head, and muttering words of love and thanks she barely registered. Cylian watched with a pained look on his face, something usually hidden, some old hurt rising to the surface. She didn't know what it was, but it was stark enough to make her ache for him.

All thoughts rushed away when she heard the vicious yell from down the field. "Prince Ghel!" someone bellowed in a deep, scratchy voice she didn't recognize.

Ghel immediately tensed. He seemed to recognize the call. Strella forced her head up, despite his big hand trying to keep her shielded, and looked beyond them. Several yards away, close enough to chuck a rock at, Winterlands soldiers outfitted in recognizable royal uniforms stood against a line of soldiers with a Monti Clan banner waving over their heads. On top a small rise above them stood the man she assumed was Engad Monti.

Strella'd never actually met the Fae. She'd heard stories, impressed talk at first that had become progressively worse until it had turned fully into whispers. Then, once at the palace and betrothed to Ghel, she'd experienced and learned so much more. An odd thought flitted across her mind as she saw him there; he was not as tall as she'd imagined. He was fit, with a broad, muscled chest and powerful arms, now leaning against a broadsword as he stared down at her husband with the same assessing look she recognized from Ghel, Piris, Jarok, and the queen at times—the calculating and strategic look of a good fighter. Still, he was noticeably shorter than the average Fae warrior, who tended to be well over six feet tall. He was short enough for his height to be noticeable, especially for a clan leader.

The Fae was covered in ice, ground slush, and redder things slowly turning brown on his clothes and skin. He hadn't slinked back from battle and had done as much as he'd asked of his clan, which was commendable in a way. He'd proven he was no hypocrite, even if he was a tyrannical rebel bent on killing her prince and wresting power from the Winterlands royals.

"Enough for the day, don't you agree?" he called down to Ghel.

"Yes," Ghel gritted out, hate in his gaze.

"How about we end this like true leaders?"

"One-on-one?"

"Aye."

Ghel gave a curt nod and turned swiftly to bend down close to Strella. "Stay with Cylian, no matter what happens. Do not leave his arms."

"But—"

"No, Strella. You must swear it. If I see you, hear you, it may distract me. Monti is a good warrior, a solid fighter. Good enough I cannot afford a distraction."

Strella swallowed hard, her throat scraping painfully as she did so, but she agreed, understanding what he needed.

Ghel asked Cylian, "Will you hold her, warm her as I fight, keep her safe if..."

"Of course. I will guard her with my life."

Before he handed her into Cylian's arms, he broke his hold on her long enough to also take up his friend. "I cannot thank you enough for what you've given me this day. You gave me back my life, and I will never forget it."

Cylian didn't reply, only waited to take her. Ghel then encircled her in a fierce embrace, bending down to lay a chaste kiss on her cold lips. "Cylian will warm you."

"Return to me," she croaked out as he passed her to Cylian, who took Strella in a loose hold from behind.

"I love you, my Star" was his reply. He didn't promise to return, to be right back. Nothing. Because Ghel never made promises he couldn't keep. He walked with the confidence of a warrior prince toward the rebellion leader, but he walked forward knowing he might well be struck down in the fight.

Tears streaked down Strella's face, but she didn't cry out. She wouldn't distract her husband in any way. She would watch and wait, whispering to the gods all the while to ensure Ghel survived the fight. Slowly, she felt a soft heat tingling across her shivering back. Cylian with his fire. He was warming her as he'd said he would. "Thank you," she whispered, for both the warmth and for whatever he'd done to help her and Ghel when she'd been dead.

She felt a friendly squeeze across her midriff and heard the sharp catch in his voice as he said, "Happy to help my friends. Happy to help love find a way around fate."

The bite she heard there told her something about his past, a pain brought up because of the day's events, but she did not press. Cylian was a friend, now more than ever, and she hoped he'd tell her in the future so she could help with whatever hurt lingered in him. Right then, however, she kept her focus on Ghel, who moved with sure strides toward an advancing Engad Monti.

They met in the middle, close enough Strella could see the dirt and sweat smearing Monti's creased face. He wasn't wrinkled with age, as most Fae did not wrinkle until close to a natural death. There were lines of worry though, concern on him. The Monti leader was a man who frowned and fretted, and his body marked it for all to see.

He wore fighting leathers in a dingy gray, but the muck of battle could well have dulled the chest and legs of his covering easily. His sword looked equally dull in color, its steel nearly covered by the events of battle, not dripping but not far from it. Strella recognized the sharp edge of the weapon, knew it might be dull in color but would slice through leather and flesh and possibly bone if wielded correctly. She suspected he was more than capable of wielding it, so she focused on Ghel, willing him with all her might to be faster, stronger, and smarter than his opponent.

The soldiers had lined up in a wide circle, creating a clearing for the one-on-one confrontation. The fighting was slow to stop on the outer edges of the battle, but the noises slowly dropped away bit by bit, until it felt as if the hundreds upon hundreds of Fae all along the Ice Plains were turned simultaneously to look at the two men about to face each other for the fate of the land.

"Rules?" Ghel grumbled, his voice low and clear to Strella. Always clear to her.

"Standard," Monti answered, laying his sword against his right leg for a brief moment as he adjusted the wrist on his fingerless leather gloves before gripping the hilt once again. He knew Ghel wouldn't strike him down now because in one way they were the same. They were warriors who held at least a few rules of honor in common. Neither would offer a hit until fighting officially commenced.

Strella knew little of the rules of battle or duels, so the words meant nothing to her.

Ghel nodded firmly, squared his shoulders, and planted his feet before his enemy. "For the Winterlands and to the death?"

Monti studied her husband with an up-and-down look before replying. "Single combat for the fate of this battle, which may well mean the fate of the Winterlands, yes. Death may not be necessary, but know this, Prince: I will not hesitate to kill you if you do not yield."

"I expect nothing less from you." His words were not a snide comment or jab at his opponent, rather a statement of fact, an acknowledgment of the stakes of their fight.

Monti called a man forward. Ghel did not object as a Monti soldier entered the field, stepping between the two Fae, causing them to each push back several feet before entering their fighting stances. The soldier looked from Monti to Ghel, raised a hand high in the air, and held it as Strella held her breath. He swept it down with a cry and exited the fray. The fight had commenced.

They didn't immediately clash swords. The two circled a few times, right then left, studying the Fae across from them and thinking through what would come. Finally, Monti stalked across the space between them, coming at Ghel with a backhand sweep of his massive broadsword. The clang of metal on metal made Strella's body jolt, and she gritted her teeth, forcing herself to bear witness to whatever happened.

Ghel stepped up to attack after the initial blow, which Monti also countered. Then it was a flurry of swords and grunts and clangs for Strella, who wasn't accustomed to watching combat. She was able to register certain actions or attacks when there were clear breaks, or when she noticed the heightened noises from the crowd. She grew more and more nervous as the fight went on because it became apparent Ghel and Monti were even in skill, except Ghel had his magic on his side.

At one point, Monti made a quick jab with his sword, causing a gasp to rise up Strella's throat as her husband grunted, but she stifled the noise as best she could. He shook it off, blood dripping down his leathers. Before Strella's eyes, the blood flow eased, just as it had with the arrow wound, and Ghel was at full fighting strength in a matter of moments. When Ghel made a slice into Monti's thigh, a hiss leaked from the leader's lips, and his blood continued to flow. Seemed to Strella all Ghel had to do was wait, defend, and get his strikes in where he could, and he would be the clear winner in the fight. Monti was no match for his healing magic.

Monti must have realized it as well and pushed forward harder, starting to take more risks in his blows to force Ghel off balance, to gain some advantage. Ghel could heal quickly, but if his heart stopped or he lost too much blood at once, his magic likely wouldn't help him. Monti had to have known he needed more devastating hits to have a chance at winning.

He also talked to Ghel. Ghel remained mostly silent, as was his way, but Monti grunted out jabs—at the royals and Ghel mostly—hoping to get a rise from the prince and gain an advantage. Her husband knew what he was about and didn't respond. Not until Monti took the time to look at her and smile wickedly. "Do not fear, Prince. We have special plans for your bride."

Ghel didn't say anything, simply stepped into Monti with his shoulder, getting sliced across the belly as he did and not gaining a hit himself except to push the other Fae man slightly off-kilter.

Monti laughed, seeing his opening. "It may have been better she died on the way to the Aurora Outpost. She's a distraction to you, you poor besotted fool."

Ghel gritted out, "She is no distraction. She is a reason," and Strella saw him take deep, purposeful breaths, move with more focus in his step, and take in more with his assessing eyes. He'd pushed past the words and was again taking the lead in the fight.

He seemed to learn something from the Fae he fought and made his own claims. "What is it you fight for, Monti?"

"Freedom for the Winterlands." He grunted as he twisted and tried to slice Ghel down. Ghel met his sword and pushed him back several steps.

"Your freedom looks an awful lot like chains binding everyone to the Monti Clan."

He countered in blow and words. "I break the chains of the royals and their favorite clans, give other warriors a fair chance."

"A chance to die by your sword or serve it?"

Monti didn't respond but sidestepped with a little too much haste. Ghel took the opening, sweeping his sword down in a punishing blow. Monti was able to recover enough to catch Ghel's sword in time, but it shook the clan leader, and he scrambled away. Squinting, looking hate filled and exhausted all at once, he gritted out, "I fight for those who have no voice in the Winterlands, those like me, who've been held under the Borau boot for far too long."

Ghel gave a harsh laugh. "You may think you fight for the Winter-lands, envision yourself a hero of the people, but you offer them duty or death, without any sacrifice on your part. You're no real leader, to your clan or the Winterlands."

Monti had had enough of the banter. He skidded back, far enough to take a moment to transfer his sword to his left hand, stoop to the ground, and come up with an icy pebble in his right hand. It grew in a flash, honed with the Monti stone magic into a wicked sharp blade in the blink of an eye. He flipped the stone dagger and ran for Ghel, using his sword to counter Ghel's defensive blow as he reared up and came down, lodging the stone blade right beneath Ghel's left shoulder, close to his heart—possibly in his heart. Strella was uncertain. However, his move left him open, and despite the injury, Ghel swept up his battered sword, moving it at impossible speed and strength so it caught the wrist holding Monti's own broadsword.

Ghel grunted in pain after the move, the sound drowned out to everyone but Strella as the clan leader screamed in agony, surprise, and loss. His wrist poured blood, and at their feet was Monti's sword, his left hand still gripping the hilt. With the stone dagger buried in Ghel's chest, the other Fae warrior was without a hand or weapon, on his knees before the raised sword of the prince.

Ghel held his blade tip at Monti's throat. To his credit, the warrior stopped screaming, steadied his breathing, and looked into the eyes of her husband. "Do it. 'To the death,' you said."

"Do you yield?"

"Never to a Borau."

Ghel shook his head, disgust clear on his face as he lowered his sword. He kicked the Fae in the chest, forcing him to his back as he cradled his wounded arm, his foot firmly planting him. "You can choose to yield or not; you are clearly defeated. I've won the duel and the battle, as per the terms."

"Kill me on the field, like a true warrior," Monti gasped out.

"No, Engad Monti. Like the traitor you are, you will be tried for all the land to see. You will find the justice you deserve, the justice the Winterlands and all the clans you decimated deserve."

Turning his head around the circle, he yelled, "Will the Monti Clan keep honor and abide by the terms set by their clan leader?"

Monti soldiers shifted uneasily, but cries of "yes" and "aye" and downcast nods moved around the field. It appeared no one would challenge Ghel's win or what it meant.

"As you should." He grunted. Turning to a contingent of Winterland soldiers to his right, he called, "Lieutenant Yanni."

"Aye, Prince," answered a tall, battle-muddied Fae who stepped forward.

"Pick nine men to help you accompany Engad Monti to the dungeons of the Winterlands Palace."

"Aye, Prince," he said with a brief bow, swiftly moving to do as he was commanded by his royal general.

In minutes, Engad Monti was chained, bound at his arms and feet, and dragged away by a group of ten Winterlands soldiers. Headed to the dungeons where his accomplice, Strella's father, was likely already waiting. Both would be tried, as was just. As each deserved.

Strella couldn't hold herself back any longer once Engad Monti was dragged away. She broke away from Cylian, who let her go, her body now warmed from his heat and ready to jump into Ghel's arms. Her husband was bloody from the fight but whole, alive. It was all she could think of. They were both alive, and she needed to feel him close to make sure it was real.

When she reached him, he'd already dropped his sword, so he caught her easily, bringing her up as she pushed forward and gave her husband a deep, searing kiss in front of an entire battlefield of Fae, who politely acted as if they saw none of it and went about the business of gathering together to wait for the prince's commands for the remainder of the Monti Clan. They also had to be dealt with in some way, but Strella couldn't let him go yet. She had to take a moment for herself and him. Until he grunted in pain.

"Oh, no," she cried, pulling back and seeing the stone blade still buried in his flesh. "Are you okay?"

Ghel ripped the thing from his chest, and it healed before her eyes. "All is well, Strella. Finally, all is well." He bent forward, gave her a quick kiss on the mouth, then pulled her to his side. He wanted her close. They did have duties to perform, important business to attend for their land and their families, so their desires would have to wait.

Chapter Twenty-Five
Ghel

The issue of the remaining members of the Monti Clan was a mess, which could take years to unravel. Some of the men were born Montis who'd followed without question, and some came from other clans, choosing to pick up a sword for Monti rather than be run through with a blade, which for the royals seemed no real choice at all. To say what was just or true in any given case would take time. Time they did not have in the moment.

Ghel decided his best course of action in the immediate was to command the Montis to stay on the Ice Plains. They were given healers, provisions, and tents. Winterlands soldiers, backed by Aurora and Windin Clan members who'd joined the battle later in the day after receiving the call for aid, guarded all so they could not leave. They were not exactly punished, but consideration for what had occurred was necessary, and there would be many talks in the future about what to do with the followers Monti had gathered in his time as clan leader. The complex problem already gave Ghel a headache, but it was his duty to consider it from all sides as justly as possible, do what was right by the individual and the land as best as he could.

This day, after a long battle and the death and life of his love and a grueling duel, he knew what he had to immediately do was return Strella to Winterlands Palace. She'd had a trying day also, one they would have many talks about in the future. He appreciated her love for him and her sacrifice to save him, but she should be far more careful in the future. He wouldn't bring up his concerns then, maybe not for several days, as she deserved rest. He would, however, bring them up, because there would be no hidden feelings between them. No more omissions.

After an hour of doing all he could to secure the field, he went to gather Strella and Cylian from the command tent. Not only did his love need rest, he needed to discuss a great deal with his mother, father, and brother. He'd sent word with Render after the duel, but he knew they'd want to hear all from him, and soon. "Come, we must return."

Strella's icy eyes were drooping, but she hugged him tight and let him lead her to his sled team, already prepped and ready to take them back. Cylian followed without many words. Ghel held his wife tight to him, shielding her with warm furs as they raced up the road toward home. His mind remained occupied with his wife and his family as well as his duty, so he was wholly unprepared for what he found halfway up the slope.

A group of Winterlands soldiers lay dead or near dying in the middle of a curve nestled against a small grove of evergreens. He slowed his dogs before they hit the carnage, but he and Strella were close enough to take everything in, including the fact it was the group of soldiers he'd sent off to escort Engad Monti to the dungeons. He cursed under his breath as he moved Strella to the front of the sled, unhooking Beaut quickly and commanding "guard!" before he stalked toward the mass of bodies, which he immediately noticed didn't include the Monti Clan leader.

"Arrows, Ghel," Cylian cried, moving forward to again stand with Strella, acting as a shield of sorts as they surveyed the scene around them. Spotting no archers yet seeing the evidence of them in every body before him, Ghel walked slowly to his soldiers, his eyes and head moving constantly to keep an eye on the scene around them, while sadness and rage fought in his blood at the scene lying at his feet.

A rasped "prince" caught his attention, and he saw Lieutenant Yanni raise a feeble hand in the air. He ran forward then and skidded to his knees at his soldier's side, noting the arrows sticking from his thigh, his stomach, and his upper chest. Blood soaked his Winterlands uniform, so much the colors were indistinguishable.

Ghel gripped his hand tight. "Shush, Yanni. We will send for a healer."

"The Monti... Your Highness, he—"

"I see, Yanni. Don't fret. Save your energy."

"No. No. Archers. In the trees. Set up on us as we rounded the curve. Came and went so quickly, I..." He trailed off, his breathing too ragged to speak more.

Ghel didn't need him to. He saw the outline of what had occurred there—the blind spot in the bend usually guarded but abandoned to man the battle below, the archers Monti seemed to favor rearing up again as an ambush tactic, the brief bit of letter Strella had told him of, which outlined a group waiting for a signal from Hollythorn or the Monti, and the likelihood of a secondary plan to ensure their leader wasn't taken to the palace. It all made perfect sense, after the fact.

Ghel held his tongue, but he wanted to curse himself for his lack of foresight. He felt he should have seen, known, and prepared for something such as this. Engad Monti had, and it had maimed and killed his men.

The man beside him, a trusted lieutenant he'd had at his side for many years, struggled to stand.

"Yanni. Still yourself."

The soldier swallowed and nodded, a tear dripping down his pained and dirty face. Ghel sat with him. It was all he could do for the moment. He needed more guards but couldn't leave his fallen men alone.

Finally, Strella called, "Ghel, Rowan and Yew. Send them ahead."

Shaking himself, he saw the logic and agreed, letting Strella and Cylian unhook the rest of his pack so he could call the pair over, send them ahead as a sign of distress. He tied a piece of Yanni's uniform to Yew's collar and told them to bring back others. With quick jumps and yips of understanding, the duo ran up the road to the Winterlands Palace at full speed, taking Ghel's command and message to those who could bring help.

A few seconds later, he felt Strella's gentle, light hand on his back as he watched his lieutenant's chest move up and down in jerky motions. "Lieutenant Yanni?" she asked, and he didn't know if she was clarifying his name or calling to the man, so he nodded in response.

The Winterlands princess knelt by her husband and took a strip ripped from her own dress to wipe the soldier's clammy brow. Yanni tried to speak to her, but no sound came out. "Shh, Lieutenant Yanni. We are here with you. Others are coming. Be at peace."

Something in the words eased the man and he stopped trying to speak, stopped moving restlessly. He hung on, breath by aching breath, Ghel and Strella at his side, until a group of healers and soldiers were suddenly there, taking over care from the prince and princess.

"Ghel?"

He heard Strella's call as she rose, felt her hands tug on his arm. He came up and hugged her to his side, his eyes not leaving the soldiers at his feet—those who the healers had tried to save and those already lost.

"I should have known," he said, heat and pain in his words.

"This is on Engad Monti, not you," Strella said, her words a bite of heat in the cold.

"He will pay for this. For all he has done," Ghel said, a promise the prince made then and there—to himself, his wife, his soldiers, and the gods themselves.

"He surely will, but we must go now. Tell the others of all that's happened today. Plan and not merely react."

Ghel turned to look into the set face of his love, this woman who was so smart and loyal and fierce. Who faced death and blood. Who tried to ease the mind of a dying soldier at his side. "Gods, I love you," he said, tears pricking his eyes at all he felt and all he'd experienced this day.

"I love you too," she said simply. Truly. A matter of fact.

He breathed deep, cleared his head as best he could, and turned his mind toward the next steps. "You are right, as always. We need to speak with the family, form a plan. The Monti is loose and must be recaptured. You also need rest."

"I'm fin—"

"You died today, love," he said, his voice maybe a touch too harsh, the memory of her cold, blue body still fresh in his mind. "You will rest. For yourself and for me."

She didn't argue and followed him back to the sled, letting him drape her in furs before they headed back to the palace, Cylian and a group of soldiers leading and following in case of another attack. Nothing was certain for Ghel now—nothing except his love for his wife and his land and that he would do all he could to ensure each remained safe from this day until his last.

"She's a mimic, Ghel," Jarok muttered as he paced. They'd had a long discussion with a larger group about what they'd found on the road to Winterlands Palace and the possible locations of the missing Monti. In a smaller group, they discussed all that had occurred at the palace and on the battlefield, which was when his family had learned of Strella's death and return and when he'd learned his wife's best friend was a mimic. He'd never have guessed this was her secret. Not only because she was supposedly a null but because there were so few mimics born these days. A true mimic shapeshifter hadn't been discovered in many centuries. A vocal mimic, which was what Piris seemed to be, hadn't been seen in at least a hundred years. Then again, mimics tended to stay hidden as long as possible, because of the Fae's distrust of them and the reality of what had historically happened to mimics when they were discovered.

He wouldn't let the woman his wife loved as a sister be used or abused. Never. However, an idea was forming in his mind. He was no expert on covert strategy; that was his brother's specialty. Yet someone like Piris, someone possessing brains, formidable magic, and fighting abilities, who also happened to be a Fae noblewoman and have access to certain arenas in society, could help them a great deal. He saw potential there if she chose to help.

"It does not make her evil," Ghel said, causing Jarok to pause mid-step.

"Of course she's not evil." He scoffed before he continued his pacing. "She's secretive, though now the reasoning appears far more justified. She's maddening, most definitely. But Lady Piris is not evil."

"Then you agree she can be trusted."

"I wouldn't go that far, brother," he bit out with a scowl. Seemed Jarok was more than a little conflicted about the lady, which wasn't surprising given their constant sniping at one another.

Ghel walked over to his brother, blocking his path and bringing his hands up to grip his shoulders. "Jarok, you know we need all the help we can get right now."

"Yes, but—"

"Do you trust Strella?"

Another snort from Jarok. "Yes. She's my sister."

Ghel's heart squeezed at the sincerity in his brother's voice, in the way he knew, without doubt, his family also loved his wife now, without reservation. "Very well. My wife trusts Lady Piris with her life. I will as well."

Jarok grumbled something under his breath but offered no more outright arguments. Instead, he sighed deep and asked, "What are you thinking?"

"I'm thinking an escort to Volesion Peak may be necessary, given these uncertain times." Ghel elaborated, and Jarok added his own thoughts, the brothers bouncing ideas off one another until a solid, workable plan took shape. Ghel was happy for it. They needed to bring Engad Monti to justice for their land to heal. Possibly more important to him in the immediate moment, however, was the fact he needed to get back to his bed, which held his resting and healing wife, so he could feel her in his arms and again, reassure himself she was alive and well.

Chapter Twenty-Six
Strella

Strella woke sprawled across a warm, hard, bronze chest gently moving her up and down with its deep breaths. She took a moment, closing her eyes to breathe deep herself. Yesterday had been a whirlwind. She'd caught her father and sent him to the dungeons. After uncovering his plot, she'd ridden off to the battlefield without any thought of herself or, more importantly, her stallion's readiness. She would do it again, daily if need be, if it meant saving her prince. He'd been right where she knew he would be: on the front line and headed for the trap. She and Render had helped stop it, but only avoided deadly consequences through the quick thinking of their friend. She'd never again take these breaths—his or hers—for granted. Maybe she imagined it, but they seemed to match now, their chests rising and falling in perfect rhythm.

With her eyes closed, her breath focused on Ghel's, she didn't notice him wake until she felt his strong hand stroking the hair at the back of her head. She lifted and blinked at Ghel. His hair was wilder than usual, swirling around his head in a cloud of thick black against the snowy white of the pillow. His eyes were melted chocolate, all on her.

"My Star."

"My Prince." Strella burrowed her face back into his chest, trailing soft kisses along the expanse. Last night was the first night they hadn't been intimate since she'd forgiven him. While she understood why—they'd both been tired mentally and physically for many reasons—she didn't want to go too much longer without feeling her husband once again.

She felt the rumble of his growl under her kisses before his arms wrapped tight around her and shoved her up his body so she was face-to-face rather than face-to-chest. When her hands were beneath her, holding her up above him, Ghel moved his fingers to her face and stroked downward, studying her for long beats before he said, "None of that now, Strella."

"And why not?" she asked, adding what she hoped was a saucy smile.

"You know why, love. You need more rest."

"I say I'm fine."

Ghel's eyes darkened into pools of deep worry, and he shuddered, a ghost of something passing over his face. "Please, Strella. Perhaps you do not need time, but I need you to take it."

She couldn't argue with his need, so she simply rolled to the side, draping her arm across him as she did so she stayed connected to him in some way. "Very well."

He rolled also, facing her and taking her face by the chin. "I will always want you. You know this, right?"

Strella nodded, and she wasn't lying. However, it never hurt to hear it said out loud. He'd proven the fact over and over with his actions, but the words still mattered. At least every so often.

"Good," he said, serious, giving a small tug on her chin so they each grinned. Ghel's grin fell, however. "We have several things to discuss."

It was true, despite the fact Strella wished to engage in far more pleasurable activities. The cocoon of their bed and Ghel's arms was warm and comfortable and invited her to stay there forever, but they were Prince and Princess of the Winterlands and had experienced an onslaught of various life-and-death things the day before, so talking was more necessary at the moment. She wished she could hide away with her husband, but she knew it was a wish they couldn't fulfill, so all she did was nod in agreement.

"First, your father."

"I would much rather not discuss him here and now."

"Understandable, love, but I need you to know—"

She moved a hand up to rub her forehead, causing Ghel to pause. She entered the silence. "He will come to justice for his crimes. It is what must happen. It is what deserves to happen."

"Yet he is still your father."

"No one is above justice," she said, firm and sure.

"Of course not, but I'm less concerned with the justice I know will come and more concerned with how you will feel about it when it happens."

Gods, he was a good man. They both knew what had to happen: a trial and whatever appropriate punishment was doled out, up to and including death. Her father would stand before other lords and take their sentence. She would have to watch as it unfolded, both unwilling and unable to stop what would come. It caused complex emotions, and in all honesty, she was unsure how she would react when the day came. Yet she was sure of one thing.

"Regardless, you will be there, by my side, to help me through it."

"Yes, my love. Always."

"For now, that is all I can say. He will be brought before a panel of lords and judged because you and the rest of the royal family were kind enough to give him that option. Whatever his sentence is, I trust it to be just and carried out with a degree of mercy. What it will be and how I will feel about it afterward is a problem for another day."

"Wise as always, Strella."

She snorted. She'd proven yesterday she was brave and loyal and true, but not always the wisest when it came to protecting those she loved.

He stroked her cheek with a finger and changed topics yet again. "Lady Piris?"

Ah. The other big secret she'd kept and, sadly, the love she'd let sacrifice itself for her. Her stomach churned at the idea, but she trusted Ghel and his family to do right by her best friend, just as she'd had to trust her friend to know when and where her secret should be revealed. "Yes. How many people now know she's a mimic?"

"My mother and brother, as they were there. And my father, of course. Cylian was told because he is also a necessary part of the plan I have. The few guards, who are all loyal to my family without fault. No one else has been told, and everyone sworn to secrecy."

Good things, all, but Strella still worried her lip. "Are you angry?"

"Because you didn't tell me your best friend, a woman you love, is a mimic and therefore must constantly protect her secret in case anyone attacked her for it or wished to use her magic for nefarious purposes? No. It was not your secret to tell, and even if it was, it was in service of a loyal and true friend. I cannot hold this against you."

"Okay then. Why must we discuss this now?"

"Jarok and I talked yesterday as you rested, mostly about the missing Monti and how to proceed. I may have a plan, and Piris could be very helpful."

Damn, Piris would love this. At least if it didn't involve Prince Jarok. If it did, she'd do it but be grumpy the whole time, whatever the plan was. "She's a warrior, trained from a young age to protect herself and her secret. She'd be useful, more than capable, and would be willing, I think. Would it be dangerous?"

Ghel didn't answer, but the crease in his brow and the way his left arm snaked under them to pull her closer told her it would be. She sighed, knowing she couldn't make it an issue. Piris had sacrificed herself in a real way to help Strella do something dangerous just the day before. She had to at least give Piris the option, but it needed to be an option.

"You will discuss the entire plan with her, allow her to consider it in full before you ask for an answer? She will not be forced if she doesn't want to do what you ask?"

"Of course."

"Are you asking my permission then?"

"Well..." He hesitated but said, "I don't want you to be angry with me."

"If you tell her the truth and let her choose, it is then her choice, and I have no reason to object as long as the plan is necessary and sound."

Ghel pushed his head forward, connecting them forehead to forehead, and said, "My wise and loyal wife."

"My wise and loyal husband." She mimicked him in her own non-magical way, causing the serious mood to break as Ghel's breath huffed out in her face with his chuckle. She closed her eyes, savored the feel of his breath, and her thoughts quickly turned once again.

"My prince, if I may?" She wiggled closer. "I will not push for more, but can we kiss? At least a little?"

Ghel's smile turned into something hotter as he nodded. Strella took the lead. She loved it when he commanded her body, but sometimes she needed to take over, and this was one of those times. She met his lips, gently but with passion, trying her hardest to express her emotions with the press of her body against his... the movement of her lips on his. He sighed into her mouth, hugging her closer and giving back all she gave him. As she knew he always would. As she always would. There would be happiness and sorrow, battles and peace, and arguments and laughter, without doubt. Life was filled with each. The magical part of it, however, was no matter the season, it would be this: her and him—Princess Strella and Prince Ghel—from that moment until whatever end they each found. Together.

Please take a moment to rate/review *Land of Snow and Secrets* on Goodreads or your favorite reading platform.

Keep reading for a hint at the next book, *Land of Ice and Intrigue*.

Epilogue
Lady Piris Volesion

P iris slid her second-smallest blade into its travel sheath and buried it at the bottom of her trunk. Her smallest and sharpest stayed strapped to her right thigh as always, within easy reach of the slitted dress pocket so she could grab the dagger without issue if, or when, it was needed. After piling more dresses and undergarments on top of the hidden weapon, she was moving to close the lid when a soft sound forced her to drop her task and whip around. No one else should have been there as she packed to leave the palace. Everyone was busy with royal duties after the battle ended just two days before. Although she was sad to leave Star, she knew they'd see each other again soon. For the time being, she needed to return to her family and Volesion Peak. She needed a break from Winterlands Palace and the damnable Fae who was leaning against her door frame with his ever-present insolent air.

"Lady," the prince said, a smirk on his face like he didn't believe the word. In many ways it was a lie, but she'd been born Lady Volesion, like it or not.

He gave her a slight bow of his head, managing to look cool and mocking and ready for battle all at once, an irritating trait from the prince. He had a way about him, as if nothing fazed him, at least most of the time. He came off as a Fae who'd be cool and collected in a ballroom or a battlefield, easy and graceful and cunning in each. Even now, shoulder to her doorjamb, he was royal and warrior in one. His warm skin contrasted with the pearl-white fabric so it almost looked like he shone. His eyes, dark and hooded with a slight uptilt at the edges, crinkled in amusement while also taking in every inch of her room in the second he surveyed her space. He took a moment to push the artful yet messy strands of his thick, straight black hair off his forehead before letting his hand fall loose at his side, where it hovered close to the short sword strapped there.

He was a pretty, deadly package. She could admit as much. If he hadn't hated her on sight, and her him, things may have been different, but they seemed to live to antagonize one another—hence her needing to get away for a time. "Why are you here? Shouldn't you be in the throne room discussing royal business, or off doing your better brother's bidding?"

Jarok flinched, as he often did when she brought up his inferiority to his brother. It wasn't true, of course, but was a verbal jab she could always count on to inflict a stab of pain to the infuriating Fae warrior. He recovered and gave her a searing up-and-down look before he said, "We are both required in the Royal Meeting Room."

"Both?" Piris scoffed, crossing her arms over her chest. The royals had no need for her now, none she knew of at least. She'd revealed her secret, which would cause a different type of battle with her parents when she returned home to Volesion Peak, but no one had mentioned it since. No one had even acted different toward her in the past few days, knowing she was a mimic and not a null. Not even the Fae in front of her, who'd she would've bet would use such information against her at the first opportunity.

Jarok stood straight, picked an imaginary piece of lint off the pristine white tunic pulled tight over the chest she could just tell was disgustingly honed and muscled, and looked away as if bored of the entire conversation. It irritated her beyond measure when he did this, dismissed her as if she were nothing, but she tried her best to never let it show. "Come," he commanded, walking off without looking back as if he knew she would follow. She would, by the gods, because even though he was annoying and hateful and pompous, he was also a prince of Winterlands, and she respected his family. She didn't have to like it though, or follow. In fact, she quickened her step, using her long legs to catch up with and overtake the prince, leading the way to whatever they had in store for her in the meeting room.

She trusted Princess Strella with her life, which was why she'd had no issues revealing her secret when it had become necessary. Her best friend would always help her. However, she didn't trust the prince at her back, and if his hint at both of them being required, together, was anything to go by, she knew whatever came next would not be good—for her sanity or her life.

Preorder *Land of Ice and Intrigue* today to get more of Piris and Jarok in July 2024!

Want More?

Want a bit more of Ghel and Strella? Sign up for Sonya Lawson's Substack newsletter via BookFunnel and get a free bonus epilogue featuring the Prince and Princess of the Winterlands.

Be sure to preorder *Land of Ice and Intrigue* so you get Piris and Jarok's story as soon as it releases.

Follow Sonya Lawson on social media. She's @sonyalawson on TikTok, Instagram, Facebook, and Threads. Get all new book notifications by following her author profiles on Goodreads and BookBub, too.

You can find all things Sonya Lawson on her website and her Books page lists all her current publications.

And, once again, please take a moment to rate/review *Land of Snow and Secrets* on Goodreads and/or wherever you purchased this book. All honest reviews are greatly appreciated.

About the Author

Sonya Lawson is a recovering academic who now writes fantasy (in a wide variety of sub-genres). Her work offers a glimpse into different yet familiar worlds that are sometimes dark, sometimes dramatic, sometimes a bit funny, and always steamy.

While she remains a rural Kentuckian at heart, she currently lives in the Pacific Northwest. Her days are often filled with writing, editing, reading, and walking old forests.

You can keep up to date with all her happenings by following her on social media (TikTok, Instagram, Facebook, or Threads). If you join her Substack newsletter, you'll also get early access to news and hot deals.

Acknowledgements

As always, many (many) thanks go to my editors at Novel Nurse Editing, Janna and Angie. Their attention to detail and grammatical focus are top notch. This book wouldn't be what it is without them.

I again went through 100 Covers for my cover design and they nailed it. It's a beautiful cover that matches the vibe well. Thanks to the project managers and artists over there for creating such great products.

I reformed my ARC team for this book because I was starting a new genre. So much thanks and appreciation go to those ARC readers (old and brand new), for taking a chance on an indie writer and giving me a little boost before publishing. All of you are fabulous!

This book wouldn't be what it is without the specific input and help of two beta readers: Kenzie Kelly and Karri Kadin. Not only did they help catch issues, holes, and all the odd little bits that can take a reader out of a book, they offered encouragement along the way. These two are rock stars who deserve all the praise and credit for being excellent beta readers, writers, and friends.

On a related note, I can't thank A.R., B.Z., Karri, Kassie, Kenzie, and Nicole enough for being the loveliest writing group around. Their care, concern, writer minds, business savvy, and encouragement boost all my writing days. I couldn't do this with quite so much focus and confidence if not for them.

My Wednesday Mastermind - Danielle, Jamie, Kat, Olivia, & Scott - are exceptionally good writers, sounding boards, and business people. They've helped me mold my brand (author and book) in so many ways. All the thanks to them for being there, every Wednesday, to push me and help me think through issues and ideas.

More thanks go to all my family and friends (and my husband Ario needs a particular name drop here). They're the most supportive bunch around. They let me be my weird writer self and that's priceless. Every single one of them have all my love, always.

Finally, and most importantly, thanks go to you, my readers. I literally wouldn't be here, doing this, without you, so thank you.

Made in the USA
Columbia, SC
27 October 2024

45171542R00174